INHERITANCE OF THE UNBURDENED

THE UNBURDENED SERIES
BOOK THREE

J.R. GRAY-HEIM

JOSADAH PUBLISHING CO

BEFORE YOU BEGIN

FROM THE AUTHOR

While this story may echo parts of our own journeys, I want to remind you—

your story cannot be confined to the covers of a book.

The pages here may close, but your chapters are still being written, every single day.

Burdens Beneath the Hymns was born from a deep place of reflection—of faith and fear, of belonging and breaking free. For so many within the LGBTQIA+ community, our stories are threaded with both beauty and ache. They hold the weight of silence, of discovery, of learning to love ourselves in a world that sometimes asks us not to.

If these pages resonated with you—if they stirred something heavy, familiar, or even healing—please know this:

You are not alone.

The path to acceptance, to peace, and to joy is ongoing, and you are worthy of every word yet to be written.

When our stories meet trauma, heartbreak, or isolation, they don't end there.

They evolve.

They bloom through resilience, through love, through chosen family and community.

Below are a few places that exist to listen, to help, and to remind you that your story still matters—

and it always will.

Wherever you are, however your story unfolds—

you are seen.

You are valued.

You are loved.

Thank you for walking through these pages with me.

I am deeply honored to share this journey with you.

— **JR Gray-Heim**

LGBTQIA+ Support & Crisis Resources

The Trevor Project — 24/7 crisis and chat support for
LGBTQIA+ youth
thetrevorproject.org
1-866-488-7386 | Text **START** to 678-678

Trans Lifeline — Peer support and resources by and for trans
people
translifeline.org
1-877-565-8860

GLAAD — Advocacy, awareness, and visibility for LGBTQIA+
lives
glaad.org

The National Alliance on Mental Illness (NAMI) — Mental
health and identity-based support
nami.org/LGBTQ

PFLAG — For LGBTQIA+ individuals, their families, and allies
pflag.org

Dedication
To my husband, my best friend—
you are the "better" I always prayed for.
You are my Jeremiah, my steady light through every shadow.

To Adam J. & Tiffany J.—
for loving without condition,
for dreaming out loud beside me,
and for reminding me that the truest faith is found
in how fiercely we hold one another up.
You are proof that grace often arrives wearing friendship's face.

PRELUDE

Unburdened Series: Book 3

By the time summer ended, the house had stopped holding its breath.

The cicadas fell quiet first, their endless hymn giving way to the slow murmur of crickets and porch fans. The air lost its sharp edge, and the world seemed to exhale—soft, spent, forgiven. Out past the garden, the light slanted in longer ribbons, catching the tops of the oaks that bent easy in the wind.

Aunt Shelia said seasons change the same way people do—quietly, until they don't. Van believed her now. He could feel the shift in the bones of the house itself—the way the floors no longer creaked under tension but memory, the way the walls held laughter instead of fear.

He sat on the back steps most evenings, barefoot, one leg drawn up, a glass of sweet tea sweating on the rail beside him. From here he could see the coop where Emmalee chased the chickens when she visited, the patch of mint that refused to die, and the faint track marks Jeremiah's truck had left the night he moved his last box in.

"Feels different," Jeremiah had said that day, standing in the doorway with the same duffel he'd brought when he'd first left his parents' house.

"It is different," Van had answered.

Neither had needed to say why.

The town was still Briar Hollow—still slow, still small, still quick to whisper—but it no longer decided what was holy. That belonged to them now. To the kitchen table where Aunt Shelia left the Bible open beside the ashtray. To the porch where Jeremiah read his school essays aloud while Van tuned his guitar. To the nights they fell asleep with the windows open, wind stirring the curtains like breath.

Faith hadn't left them; it had only changed shape.

Van had stopped asking for signs. He didn't need them anymore. The proof was in the ordinary—the steady hum of peace, the feel of Jeremiah's hand finding his under the table without fear, the sound of Aunt Shelia humming gospel and Patsy Cline in the same breath.

Some nights, when the world went completely still, Van could almost hear his grandmother's voice carried on the cicadas' song, soft and amused:

"See, baby? You made it through the dark. Now learn to live in the light."

He would close his eyes then and whisper back, "I'm trying."

And he was.

Jeremiah's laughter came easy now. It filled the hallways, bright and unashamed. He'd gotten a job at the feed store three days a week, came home covered in sawdust and the smell of hay. Aunt Shelia said he smelled like a good day.

Van still worked shifts at the diner, sometimes with Marlene, who pretended not to see Jeremiah waiting in the booth with a milkshake and a book. The town pretended too—some with grace, some with gritted teeth—but pretending peace was still better than preaching hate.

Dana and Avery came by often, their friendship a patchwork of humor and stubborn loyalty. Avery brought iced coffee and new gossip. Dana brought notebooks full of plans—college applications, essays, what they'd do when the world got wider.

Sometimes, late into those humid evenings, they'd all sit on the porch steps—five hearts that had already lived too many lives for seventeen—and dream aloud about where they'd go next.

"Imagine us," Avery would say, arms wide to the stars. "New York, or anywhere with more than one coffee shop and a gay bar that doesn't double as a laundromat."

"Dream smaller," Dana teased. "We haven't even graduated."

Van just smiled. "Dream anyway."

The air between them would go still then, full of the kind of silence that wasn't empty but waiting. They'd talk about leaving Briar Hollow not like running away, but like carrying something forward—the proof that love had lived here once and didn't die.

On Sunday mornings, the sun still hit the church steeple just right, casting the cross's shadow long and thin across the road. Van passed it on his way to work, windows rolled down, radio humming a song about mercy.

Sometimes he'd catch sight of Pastor Rich in the doorway—head bowed, hands folded—and feel no bitterness at all. Pity, maybe. Understanding, even. Because for all the sermons about salvation, Van had found his not in confession, but in continuation.

The church bells still rang on the hour. He didn't flinch when they did.

In late August, Jeremiah found Van on the porch, sketchbook open, a half-finished drawing of the house taking shape in graphite.

"You're gonna run out of paper before you run out of this place," Jeremiah said, setting a soda beside him.

"Maybe that's the point," Van said, shading the windowpanes. "It deserves to be remembered."

Jeremiah leaned against the post. "You ever think about what's next? After all this?"

Van looked up, pencil paused midline. "Every day."

"And?"

"I think about what we're leaving behind," he said softly. "And what we get to carry."

Jeremiah smiled. "That sounds like your Aunt."

"She's rubbing off on me."

"Good. She's the best of us."

Van laughed under his breath. "She's the reason we made it."

Jeremiah reached for his hand then—slow, deliberate—and for a moment, the whole world stilled. The trees, the sky, even the air itself seemed to wait.

"What's that line you always say?" Jeremiah asked. "From that hymnbook of your grandma's?"

Van smiled faintly. "Be still, my soul."

Jeremiah nodded, eyes soft. "Yeah. That one."

They sat like that until the sun dipped and the crickets began again.

That night, Van wrote in the back of the hymnbook—his grandmother's handwriting still curling through the margins. His words were smaller, newer, but carried the same tremor of faith:

Inheritance isn't just what's left to you—it's what you refuse to let die. We inherited fear, but we'll leave behind love. We inherited silence, but we'll leave behind a song.

He closed the book and set it on the windowsill, where the last light of the day made the worn leather glow.

Outside, the wind picked up, carrying the scent of honeysuckle and earth. A storm brewed somewhere far off—not close enough to threaten, just enough to remind. The kind that came to wash the air clean.

Aunt Shelia's voice called from the kitchen, "Y'all better come in before the rain catches you."

"We're comin'," Van called back.

He took one last look at the porch, at the fields rolling into twilight, at the home rebuilt from grace and second chances.

He smiled—not the kind that hides, but the kind that knows.

Whatever waited ahead—college, distance, a world that hadn't learned their names yet—he would walk toward it without fear. Because the truth wasn't a burden anymore. It was a birthright.

And for the first time, he didn't just believe it.

He *inherited* it.

WHEN THE WORDS FINALLY CAME

PART I – THE CAR

Morning came slow to Briar Hollow, the kind of place where fog didn't just roll in — it lingered, like it had rent to pay. The town sat cradled between two low ridges, roofs silvered with dew, streets soft with quiet. Briar Hollow was the sort of place that remembered everything. Its church bells still rang on Sundays even if half the pews were empty. Its porches still sagged under old stories. Even the wind seemed to move slower, heavy with the weight of things people didn't say out loud.

Folks claimed the town got its name from the wild rose brambles that once tangled down by the river, but most figured it was because the place held on tight — to history, to faith, to what used to be. It held you, too, if you weren't careful. Some said Briar Hollow raised saints and ghosts in equal measure.

The night outside wasn't quiet so much as *listening*. The kind of hush that carried the faintest sound — a train from miles off, a porch light clicking on, a dog shaking its collar — like the world itself had slowed to bear witness.

Van sat in the driver's seat with the engine off, the key turned halfway so the dashboard clock glowed a soft amber 9:42. His hands gripped the steering wheel hard enough that his knuckles looked carved from bone. Every breath fogged the windshield and vanished again, small ghosts of courage that didn't last long enough to hold.

The house sat thirty feet away — small, square, and patient. Christmas lights still dangled from the eaves, their bulbs blinking weakly against the cold. One red one had burned out, a gap in the cheer. The kind of imperfection his father would've noticed but never fixed. Van stared at that dead bulb for a long time, as if the whole night hinged on whether it flickered back to life.

The TV glowed through the living-room window, blue light pulsing across the faded curtains. The shadow of his father's recliner moved occasionally like a pendulum, steady and predictable. His mother's silhouette bent forward slightly — hands folded, still, maybe asleep. It looked peaceful from here, but distance had a way of dressing up discomfort. From the safety of the car, it all looked like a memory he hadn't left yet.

He hadn't expected the world to feel so still after doing something brave.

He hadn't even done it yet.

Van exhaled through his teeth, a sound more sigh than prayer. The air smelled faintly of pine-scented air freshener, old coffee, and the hint of gasoline that clung to his jacket from filling up earlier. His pulse pressed against his throat like it wanted out.

He'd rehearsed on the drive from Jeremiah's — every possible version of how this could go. How to start softly. How to sound respectful but unshakable. How to stay standing when the floor tilted.

Now, every version blurred together. He mouthed the words again, testing how they felt in air.

"Mom, Dad… I've prayed about this."

Too formal.

"Something I need to tell you."

Too soft.

"I'm gay."

Too final.

The word thudded inside the car like a dropped stone — small, but it echoed forever.

His chest ached. He ran a hand through his hair, pushing it back and gripping it at the root until it hurt. He needed the sting to remind him he was still here. He looked at his own reflection in the glass — pale, anxious, older than seventeen. His jaw looked tighter tonight, his mouth too serious. He looked like someone on trial.

He'd almost gone inside Jeremiah's when he'd dropped him off earlier. Jeremiah had leaned against the porch rail, watching the taillights fade, the porch light haloing him like a confession unspoken. Van could still hear his voice: *Whatever happens, you already told the truth. That's the hardest part.*

He wanted to believe that. Wanted to believe truth had armor.

The hymnbook on the passenger seat slid when he moved. The green one — his grandmother's — its spine cracked and soft from years of use. He rested a hand on it, not to open it, just to feel the indentation of her life in the leather. The gold lettering had long since faded to brown. In the corner of the front page, her slanted handwriting curved gently: *Listen between the sounds. That's where He lives.*

"Grandma," he whispered, voice trembling, "I could use you right now."

For a moment — one breath — he could almost see her. The kitchen light low, the smell of chicory coffee and lavender soap. Her hands wrapped around a mug. Her voice, soft but unshaken:

"God don't need perfect notes, just honest ones."

It had been years since that morning, but the memory hit

fresh — the sound of her humming *Come Thou Fount,* her thumb tracing the edge of his jaw, the dust motes in the sunlight between them like gold. The thought made his throat burn.

He blinked hard. The vision faded. Just the car again. The ticking of cooling metal. The fog breathing across the windshield. The empty passenger seat where courage ought to sit.

He reached for the hymnbook again and let it fall open on its own.

Be Still, My Soul sat at the top of the page, faint and holy.

He mouthed the first line.

"Be still, my soul: the Lord is on thy side."

It wasn't comfort. It was a dare.

He closed the book and gripped it tight enough to leave marks on his palms.

His reflection in the window looked back — ghostlike, layered over the image of the house. Two versions of him, one still inside the world that fit, one already outside of it. For a second, he couldn't tell which was which.

He practiced again, whispering into the steering wheel.

"I'm gay."

This time it didn't sound like surrender. It sounded like survival.

The motion light above the garage blinked on. His whole body flinched. For a half-second he thought someone had opened the door — that the light was judgment made visible. But no — just the wind, or the universe catching its breath. The beam glowed steady, pale gold, casting the frost in halos. For a moment it looked like the world wasn't warning him at all. It was welcoming him.

He laughed under his breath, shaky but real. "If that's a sign," he murmured, "it's a lazy one."

Still, it was enough.

He rested his forehead on the steering wheel, the vinyl cold against his skin. His breath came slow and deliberate, counting like Mrs. Whitaker had taught them before a solo — inhale, two, three, exhale, two, three.

Only this time, the stage was his life.

He remembered the youth retreats — the sermons about purity and sin and the way words like *unnatural* had rolled too easily off tongues that also preached love. He remembered the notes he'd crumpled before they could reach Jeremiah's locker. The nights he'd stared at the ceiling, bargaining with a God who already knew the truth.

Every moment of hiding pressed against him now, dense and heavy, a weight he couldn't carry back through that front door.

Through the windshield, the house looked the same as it always had: siding faded to beige, porch railings flaked from summers of humidity. The "Bless This Home" mat sat crooked, the *B* nearly rubbed away.

Maybe blessings wore out. Maybe they had to be earned back.

His father shifted in the recliner — just a shape in the windowlight — but Van could feel it, that old gravity. His mother's stillness. The house waiting for him to step wrong.

He whispered to no one, "Please let me get it right."

Then, quieter: "Even if it breaks everything."

The cross on his keychain caught the glow of the dashboard. He turned it between his fingers until it left an imprint in his skin. He didn't know if it was faith or habit that made him say, "Wish me luck."

The heater coughed once, then died. Cold seeped into the cabin, sharp enough to make his eyes water. Outside, the air shimmered with frost — thin lace along the edges of the glass. He traced a small circle with his fingertip and looked through it. The front porch looked closer now. The light made the paint chips shine.

He pictured his mother's smile — the tired kind that meant

she was trying to hold two truths at once. He pictured his father's eyes, steady, disappointed, always searching for something to fix. And he thought of Jeremiah's hand closing around his, thumb brushing his pulse. "You've already survived worse."

He reached for that memory like an anchor.

"You can do this," he whispered, but then corrected himself. "You *have* to."

The words steadied him. Not hope exactly — just direction.

He turned off the key. The dashboard light faded, leaving him in the hush of the night, lit only by the house and the motion light above it. The silence pressed in around him until even his breath sounded too loud.

He opened the car door. Cold air rushed in — sharp, clean, alive. Gravel popped under his shoes as he stepped out. The motion light caught the edge of his hair, gilding it. Every step toward the porch felt louder than it should've. He half-expected the world to stop him — some cosmic warning, thunder, or even a shout from the house.

But the only sound was his own heartbeat and the faint hum of a TV preacher's voice fading through the walls.

He stopped at the porch steps. Frost glittered along the rail like a warning written in glass. He reached for it anyway. The wood burned cold against his palm.

Up close, he could see everything he'd tried not to notice — the loose board near the third step, the way the wreath on the door hung just slightly off-center, one bow loop drooping. His mother would fix it in the morning. She always did. She could make anything look better — except what people refused to see.

He looked up at the sky. The stars were faint, blurred by fog, but still there. Maybe that was enough proof.

He took one last breath that scraped his lungs raw, and whispered, "Alright, Grandma. Alright, God. I'm walking in."

Then he did.

The door gave under his hand, the hinges creaking like an old hymn starting up again.

Warmth spilled out — the smell of Pine-Sol, fried chicken, and the faintest trace of his mother's perfume. The TV flickered blue across the living room, catching his father's outline, his mother's profile.

Neither looked up yet.

He stepped inside, closing the door behind him. The sound of it shutting was small, final, sacred.

The moment held — still and trembling — before the storm found its voice.

PART II: THE CONFESSION

The door sighed open—the same wooden moan that always meant sand and spring and coming storms. Warm air met him, thick with leftover barbecue, Pine-Sol, and the faint tang of lemon dish soap. It smelled like ordinary life — the kind that didn't know it was about to change.

Van hesitated on the threshold. The house glowed the same soft amber as always — table lamp humming, TV murmuring from the corner, a clock ticking somewhere in the kitchen like a pulse that had forgotten who it belonged to. He rubbed his palms on his jeans and stepped inside.

His mother sat on the couch in her robe, legs tucked neatly under the crocheted afghan his grandmother had made when Van was a baby. She was folding a towel, small and deliberate, smoothing each corner as if order could keep the world steady. The TV's blue flicker crossed her face in stripes of light and shadow.

His father sat in the recliner, Styrofoam takeout container balanced on his knee, fork tapping against the edge in a lazy rhythm. The remote rested in his other hand like a scepter —

casual, sure, familiar. He didn't look up right away, but Van could tell he'd already noticed him.

His father always noticed things first.

"Hey, sweetheart," his mother said finally, voice soft but careful. "You're home later than usual."

Van's throat felt tight. "Yeah. Lost track of time after my shift."

His father's eyes lifted. "You eat?"

"Not really hungry."

"Suit yourself." The fork kept tapping. One, two, pause. One, two. Like the sound of a clock that didn't want to count down the next five minutes.

Every motion in that room felt rehearsed — a play they'd all been performing for years.

Van moved toward the couch, the floor creaking beneath his weight. "Can we... talk for a minute?"

His mother folded the towel again, aligning the edges like scripture pages. "Of course, honey. Everything alright?"

"Yeah. I just—" His voice caught. "There's something I've been needing to tell y'all."

His father set the fork down, leaned back, half amused, half suspicious. "You're not in trouble, are you?"

"No, sir."

"Then sit down, son. You're hoverin' like you're waitin' for an altar call."

The humor landed flat.

Van sat at the edge of the couch, knees pressed together, hands clasped so tightly they trembled.

His mother smiled faintly, the way she did when she sensed something brewing but didn't want to name it. "Start wherever you need to."

"I've been praying a lot lately," Van said.

"That's good," his father offered. The tone was routine, approving — the reflex of a man who'd spent years grading virtue like a test.

"It's more about what I've been praying for," Van said, eyes fixed on the towel in his mother's lap.

"Something bothering you?" she asked.

He swallowed. His throat felt dry as paper. "I've been asking God to help me understand myself. And what I'm supposed to do with the things I feel."

His father leaned forward, elbows on knees. "What things?"

Van's stomach knotted. "The things that make me… different."

His father's voice flattened. "Different how?"

Van looked up. The words were there, caught in the air between his teeth. His whole life had led to this breath. "I'm gay."

The word filled the room like smoke — not loud, but everywhere.

The fork hit the takeout box. The Styrofoam lid snapped shut.

"What did you just say?"

"I said I'm gay."

The house seemed to inhale and hold it.

The TV light blinked once, flickering against the glass of the family photos on the wall — summer vacations, Sunday suits, smiles that suddenly felt staged.

His mother's lips parted but no sound came. His father stood up slowly, the recliner groaning under the shift of weight.

"No," he said. "No, you're not. You're confused."

"I'm not." The words shook, but he didn't take them back.

His father's jaw tightened. "You think this is brave? This isn't confession, it's rebellion."

"I've prayed for it to go away," Van said, voice cracking. "Begged God to make me different. He didn't. Maybe because there's nothing wrong to fix."

"Blasphemy," his father muttered.

"It's truth."

"Truth?" His father's laugh broke open like thunder. "You're standing in my house talkin' about sin like it's birthright."

"It's love," Van said quietly.

"Love," his father repeated, like he was testing poison. "Love is man and woman before God."

His mother whispered, "Jeff—please—"

But Jeff Shelton had already crossed into sermon.

"You listen to me, son. You've been led astray by this world. Those people out there — they confuse sin for freedom. You're not one of them."

Van felt his pulse rising, heat creeping up his neck. "You don't get to decide who I am."

"I'm your father," Jeff said sharply. "God gave you to me to raise right."

"And I'm trying to *be* right," Van said. "Just not your version of it."

His mother's voice trembled. "Van, please—"

But it was too late. The words had left his mouth. They hung in the air like sparks, bright and dangerous.

His father slammed his palm against the armrest. The fork clattered to the floor, sauce splattering across the rug.

"You will not bring that filth into my house."

"It's not filth," Van said. "It's me."

"You'll *repent* of it."

Van stood, the world tilting around him. "You can't pray away who someone is."

His father stepped closer. "You think you know better than the Word of God?"

"I think the Word's been twisted by people who needed it to sound like them."

For a moment, the only sound was the hum of the refrigerator in the kitchen.

His father stared at him, chest rising and falling hard. "You watch yourself. You're crossing a line."

"I've been standing on that line my whole life," Van said. "You just never looked down to see it."

Jeff's face reddened. "You're talkin' like a stranger."

"Maybe that's what happens when someone finally speaks for himself."

His mother started crying quietly, pressing the towel to her face. "Please stop," she whispered. "Both of you."

But the words couldn't fit back in.

Jeff's voice lowered to a calm that was worse than yelling. "You'll go to that camp Pastor Rich mentioned. The one in Boone. They help boys who lose their way."

Van blinked. "You mean they *fix* boys like me."

"They help them remember what God made them to be."

"I don't need remembering," Van said. "I need to breathe."

His father took a step closer. "You'll go, or you'll pack your things."

"Jeff," his mother said, standing now, voice sharp through her tears. "Don't you do this."

He didn't look at her. "He's my son."

"Then act like it," she said.

That stopped him.

For one second, something in his expression cracked — not softened, but faltered. He turned his head toward her like he didn't recognize the woman standing there. "You'd take his side over mine?"

"I'm not choosin' sides," she said. "I'm choosin' love."

He stared at her, jaw working, then turned back to Van. "You'll regret this."

Van met his eyes. "Maybe. But at least it'll be mine to regret."

He reached for his keys on the counter. The metal cross keychain clinked against the granite — the sound sharp, bright, final.

"Where are you going?" his mother asked, voice shaking.

"I don't know," he said. "Just not here."

"Van—"

The door opened. Cold air flooded in, lifting the curtain edges like the house was gasping.

His father's voice followed him, loud enough to break the quiet. "You walk out that door, don't expect it to open again!"

Van turned once, hand on the frame.

"You didn't open it for me in the first place."

Then he stepped into the night.

THE COLD HIT LIKE WATER, shocking and pure. The air smelled of pine and woodsmoke. His breath came out in clouds. The driveway gravel crunched beneath his boots, each step too loud, too final. He made it halfway to the car before he heard the door open again.

"Van!"

His mother's voice. He turned.

She stood in the doorway, framed in the porch light, robe pulled tight, tears shining on her cheeks. "Please don't drive angry," she said.

"I'm not angry," he said softly. "I'm just tired."

She stepped forward onto the porch, bare feet on cold wood. "You have your grandma's heart, you know. Too brave for your own good."

"Then you know I have to go."

She nodded once, the motion small but certain. "Then go where love is, baby. Not where fear wins."

He wanted to hug her, to make this moment enough to undo everything, but he couldn't move. He just stood there, nodding, eyes burning. Then he got in the car.

When the engine turned over, the dashboard light caught her face one last time — a mother torn between faith and her child, standing in her doorway like a sentry of both.

Van backed out slow. Gravel popped beneath the tires. He didn't look back again.

. . .

HE DROVE NOWHERE IN PARTICULAR. Past the church where the cross still glowed white against the steeple. Past the diner with its neon sign still humming. Past the ball field where the lights were off but the bleachers still smelled like rain and metal. The night swallowed him, wide and familiar.

The hymnbook lay on the passenger seat, sliding with every curve of the road. He touched it once, then let it fall open on its own. The page read: *It Is Well With My Soul.*

He laughed — a broken sound that wasn't joy, not yet. "Maybe one day," he said.

The world outside blurred into streaks of gray and yellow. Houses gave way to trees. He didn't know where he was headed — maybe Aunt Shelia's, maybe just anywhere the air didn't taste like judgment. The road curved, the tires hummed, and for the first time in years, there was no one telling him which way to face.

When he reached the bridge that crossed the Briar River, he pulled over. The headlights painted the guardrail in gold. He turned off the ignition and let the quiet take him. The water below shimmered faintly, black and silver in the moonlight.

He rolled down the window. The cold rushed in, cutting clean through the heat still clinging to his skin. The night smelled alive — wet earth, pine sap, faraway smoke.

He sat there for a long time, forehead resting against the steering wheel. The sound of the river filled the space his father's voice had left behind.

"Grandma," he whispered, "if you can hear me, I hope I didn't break what you loved."

The wind through the trees sounded almost like a reply.

He looked up at the stars — faint, distant, but steady. Somewhere back in town, a house had gone quiet again.

He didn't know what tomorrow would bring. Only that he couldn't go back.

He reached for the hymnbook and read aloud into the dark:

"Though trials should come, let this blest assurance control."

The words shook, but they didn't fall apart.

He started the car again, headlights washing over the trees, and drove into the unknown — not away from home exactly, but toward something that might one day become one.

"Sometimes truth burns before it blesses."

THE LONGEST DRIVE

The cold hit harder this time — not the kind that stings skin, but the kind that settles behind your ribs like grief wearing gloves.

It wasn't wind or temperature. It was the air itself — hollowed out, waiting for something it couldn't name.

Van didn't remember crossing the porch, didn't remember unlocking the car, just the sound of gravel under his shoes and his breath ghosting in the dark. His hands were shaking before he even turned the key. The old engine coughed once before catching, a low hum filling the space his heartbeat used to.

The dashboard light painted everything in amber and shadow. His grandmother's hymnbook lay open on the passenger seat, a page bent by the seatbelt. Her handwriting glimmered in the glow:

When you can't hear Him, breathe slower. He's still there.

He stared at that line until it blurred.

Then he reversed too fast, tires spitting gravel. The rearview mirror caught one last slice of home — the warm windows, the flicker of the TV, the blinking pulse of the Christmas tree — and then the curve of the street took it away.

The road swallowed him whole.

HE DROVE through familiar streets made strange by frost and absence. Streetlights bowed over the asphalt, halos fractured by ice. The world looked dipped in pewter.

Every mailbox, every porch he passed carried the same quiet geometry of small-town life — tidy, predictable, unaware that someone had just undone an entire family inside a living room three blocks away.

The heater moaned weakly. He rubbed his palms together, tried to pray, but the sentences tangled.

Lord, I told the truth. Isn't that what You wanted?

Only silence answered — not cruel, but heavy, listening.

He whispered into the dark, "Jere…"

The name came out half-breath, half-plea.

He remembered Jeremiah's hand on his shoulder earlier that day, the steady voice, the quiet certainty.

"I told it," Van said to the windshield. "And it broke everything."

He laughed once — sharp, cracked — and it turned into a sob. The sound startled him. He pressed his fist to his mouth until the ache subsided.

The bridge lights passed in streaks. The church marquee still read **O COME LET US ADORE HIM.** The words looked holy and hollow at once, like a song you once knew but couldn't sing anymore.

Heritage Baptist Church stood at the northern edge of Briar Hollow, white clapboard walls creaking with every winter gust. The stained-glass windows glowed faintly from the streetlight — Mary, Joseph, the shepherds, each caught mid-reverence. Van had sat beneath those panes his whole childhood, believing color could sanctify pain.

The building had seen floods, weddings, revivals, funerals, and more whispered apologies than it would ever confess.

In Briar Hollow, faith wasn't just believed; it was *inherited* — like land, or shame.

PAST THE COUNTY LINE, the world opened. Pines replaced streetlights. The sky went ink-blue, almost violet where the clouds thinned. The yellow lines blurred under the tires, steady and endless. The hum of the engine became the only rhythm he trusted.

He started talking again — to the dark, to God, maybe to his grandmother.

"I did it," he said. "He was so angry. You'd have told him off, wouldn't you? You'd have said love isn't a sin. You always said God didn't need middlemen."

His throat tightened. "Why didn't You stop him from sayin' what he said? Why let it be *this* hard to be honest?"

The steering wheel vibrated under his grip. His knuckles were white, joints aching.

He slowed when the road bent toward the river. Frost shimmered on the guardrail, glinting like salt under the headlights.

Then — a light ahead. Soft yellow through the trees.

Jeremiah's porch.

The sight hit him like warmth remembered.

He didn't even remember turning down the driveway — just the crunch of gravel, the sudden wash of the truck in the beams, the silhouette on the porch steps.

Jeremiah was already outside, sweatshirt half-zipped, hair messy from pacing. The second the headlights caught him, he stepped down, sneakers sinking into frost-dust grass.

Van parked crooked, left the engine running. His forehead dropped against the wheel. He breathed once, twice, then a soft *knock* on the window.

"Hey," Jeremiah said, voice low, warm.

Van looked up. His eyes were rimmed red, lashes wet. He didn't try to speak.

Jeremiah opened the door. The cold rushed in, smelling like pine and night.

"Come here," he murmured.

Van fell into him before he could think. Jeremiah's arms came around him — firm, certain, anchoring.

Van's breath hitched against his chest. The heat of another human being was too much and not enough.

"It's okay," Jeremiah whispered.

"No, it's not. I told them." The words cracked apart halfway through.

Jeremiah didn't ask *who.* He didn't have to.

"My dad said he'd send me away," Van said. "Some camp. Said they could fix me."

Jeremiah's jaw tightened against Van's temple. "You're not broken."

"Then why does it feel like I am?"

"Because they made you think being loved comes with terms."

Van's laugh came out strangled. "You sound like my grandma."

"Smart woman," Jeremiah said, still holding him.

For a moment, neither moved. Only their breaths, syncing slowly, the sound of the truck engine idling steady as a heartbeat.

"I didn't plan this far," Van admitted.

"You don't have to," Jeremiah said. "Just breathe."

"What if I can't go back?"

"Then you stay here tonight. We'll figure it out tomorrow."

Van shook his head weakly. "I can't explain this to your parents."

"You don't have to. They're asleep." He smiled faintly. "Or pretending to be."

"Jere—"

"Just let me sit with you," Jeremiah said.

So they did. He slid into the passenger seat, closed the door softly, and turned off the ignition. The hum faded; silence rushed in. The only light came from the dashboard, faint and golden, pooling over their hands.

MINUTES PASSED. Maybe an hour. The world outside was nothing but wind and frost.

Jeremiah's fingers drummed lightly against his knee — the same rhythm he used before a game, the one that meant *stay calm, stay grounded.*

Van stared at the hymnbook between them, at the thin gold edges glinting in the dash glow. He traced one corner absently.

"You did the hardest thing," Jeremiah said finally.

"Then why does it feel like I lost?"

Jeremiah exhaled, fogging the windshield. "Because sometimes truth burns before it blesses."

Van turned to look at him. Jeremiah's profile was a study in contrast — sharp jaw, soft eyes, the faintest tremor in his lip when he thought too hard.

"How'd you get so calm about all this?" Van asked.

"I'm not," Jeremiah said. "I just learned to hide it better."

"From who?"

He smiled faintly. "Everyone but you."

The silence that followed wasn't heavy; it was *alive.*

Outside, the wind moved through the pines like an old hymn — tired, beautiful, unbroken.

"You're still here," Jeremiah said.

"Yeah," Van whispered. "Still here."

He leaned his head back against the seat, the exhaustion catching up at last. The heater's after-warmth faded, replaced by the quiet thrum of the night. The windows fogged from their breathing. Stars blurred at the edges of frost.

Somewhere, a dog barked once, then stopped.

Jeremiah reached over, his hand finding Van's on the console. Fingers brushed — tentative, familiar. Van didn't pull away.

They sat like that, the two of them framed by the truck's cabin — a sanctuary carved out of darkness.

Van's eyelids grew heavy. His thoughts drifted, dissolving into shapes and memory: his grandmother humming over dishwater, his mother's tired smile, his father's raised hand. All of it collapsing into the single, simple truth of Jeremiah's thumb tracing small circles over his knuckle.

For the first time since leaving home, Van's breathing slowed.

He woke to gray light bleeding into the sky. The world outside had turned to glass — frost sheathing the windshield, coating every branch in white shimmer. The engine was off. Jeremiah sat beside him, half-asleep, head tilted back, breath clouding faintly in the cold.

Van blinked, disoriented. "How long—?"

"A few hours," Jeremiah murmured. "You crashed."

Van rubbed his eyes. "You didn't have to stay out here."

"I wanted to."

The sincerity in his tone made Van's throat ache. He nodded toward the glove box. "You've got church clothes in there, right?"

Jeremiah laughed softly. "You quoting my mom or yours?"

"Both."

They smiled — small, tired, but real.

He looked out at the pines beyond the driveway, silvered in frost. The horizon was just beginning to soften with dawn. "Feels like a new world out there," Van said quietly.

"Maybe it is," Jeremiah answered. "You left something behind last night."

Van nodded, though he wasn't sure what he'd left or what had followed him. "You think they'll ever forgive me?"

Jeremiah considered. "Maybe. Or maybe they'll just learn how to love you different."

Van looked down at their intertwined hands. "And if they don't?"

"Then you've still got me."

It wasn't dramatic when he said it. It was just true.

THEY WENT INSIDE as the sun came up, shoes crunching across the frozen porch boards. The house smelled faintly of cinnamon and wood polish.

The Davis home always looked like a photograph — tidy, symmetrical, the kind of clean that meant someone was always waiting for company.

Mrs. Davis's voice came from the kitchen, surprised but not sharp. "Jeremiah? That you?"

"Yeah, Mama."

She stepped into the doorway, robe tied tight, hair pinned up. Her eyes flicked from Jeremiah to Van, then to the truck still running a faint line of exhaust in the drive.

"Morning, Mrs. Davis," Van said quickly. His voice was too polite, too careful.

She studied him a moment, then nodded once. "Morning, Van. You boys get some sleep?"

"Sort of," Jeremiah said. "He—uh—needed somewhere to crash."

Her gaze softened, just a fraction. "Coffee's on. You both look half-frozen."

That was all she said. She turned back toward the kitchen. The smell of percolating coffee followed her.

Van exhaled. "She's nicer than I deserve."

"She's smart," Jeremiah said. "Knows when to wait for explanations."

They sat at the kitchen table. Steam curled from mismatched

mugs. The clink of spoons against ceramic filled the silence. Jeremiah's father was already gone for early service; the house carried that Sunday-morning hush of routines happening elsewhere.

For a long time, neither spoke. Then Van said, "I don't think I can go back."

Jeremiah stirred his coffee. "Then don't. At least not tonight."

"Sheila'll take me," Van said, half to himself. "She always said her door was open."

"Then go," Jeremiah said. "You'll be safe there."

"Safe," Van repeated, as if testing the word. "That'd be new."

Jeremiah smiled. "You get used to it."

WHEN HE LEFT THAT MORNING, the frost was melting off the hood of the car. The sun had found its way through the pines, cutting long streaks of gold across the driveway. Van turned the key, then hesitated.

"You sure you'll be okay?" he asked.

Jeremiah leaned on the open window, grin small and sleepy. "You forget who taught half this town how to throw a punch? I'll manage."

"Don't make me laugh. I'm already halfway to crying again."

Jeremiah's grin faded into something softer. "Hey." He reached through the window, touched Van's cheek with the back of his hand — barely a brush. "You told the truth. That's what makes everything possible now."

Van nodded, unable to answer.

As he pulled away, Jeremiah's reflection stayed in the mirror until the bend in the road took him out of sight. The hymnbook slid forward on the seat again. The page still marked read: *When you can't hear Him, breathe slower. He's still there.*

He smiled through tears he didn't bother to hide.

The drive stretched out ahead — long, uncertain, but brighter somehow. The sky had cleared completely, a pale Carolina blue opening over the ridges. He rolled down the window and let the cold whip through his hair, sharp and clean.

For the first time, the air didn't feel like punishment.

It felt like possibility.

And when the wind moved through the trees, it sounded almost like a hymn — tired, beautiful, unbroken.

"Homes have lungs. They inhale family, exhale history."

THE HOUSE THAT WAITED

The drive back felt longer.

Not in distance—in gravity. Every mile had weight now, every landmark a witness. The water tower with its chipped blue paint; the half-lit gas station where the clerk read paperbacks and rang you up without looking; the church sign with its plastic letters rearranged into FAMILY CHRISTMAS SERVICE — ALL ARE WELCOME. Each one watched him pass and said nothing. Even the ditch by the pecan grove looked like it had an opinion.

Van's headlights carved a tunnel through the dark. For a minute he let himself believe that if he just kept going, the road might forget where home was. But his hands knew the turn before it came—the right curve past the trees that always rattled in a north wind; the dip where rain gathered and held on. His body had learned this path too well to unlearn it now.

Briar Hollow slept. Christmas lights blinked in windows like small faithful hearts. Frost silvered mailbox flags and the tops of low hedges. Someone's porch still wore a blow-up snowman that wheezed when the compressor cycled off, leaning as if tired of smiling. The whole street looked rehearsed—tidy, peaceful, a portrait that didn't ask questions. It felt almost cruel, how calm everything appeared.

He turned into the drive. The gravel answered him the way it always did, popping beneath the tires like a string of dry corn in a skillet. The house sat there with its same two gables and the porch light that had been flickering for months. Inside, only one glow: the Christmas tree, pulsing a soft amber in the living room corner like a heartbeat you could see.

He cut the engine. Silence arrived in a rush—sharp, clean, cold. He kept both hands on the wheel after the key turned, as if loosening his grip might let the whole night slide out of control. His breath fogged the glass. He wiped a crescent clear with his sleeve, then wished he hadn't. The clear spot made everything more real—the drooping wreath, the sag in the porch rail where his father said he'd fix it every spring.

The small cross on his keychain caught the dash light and flashed once like a tiny lighthouse. He thumbed it until the metal warmed. "I wish you were here," he whispered to the empty car, meaning his grandmother, meaning God, meaning anyone who might answer with gentleness.

The house did not call to him. It waited.

He opened the door. Cold rushed his ankles. The air outside smelled like pine and someone else's laundry vent and the thin chemical sweetness of de-icer. Gravel was loud under his shoes, the kind of loud that makes you look over your shoulder even when you know no one's there.

He paused at the bottom step. The door stood cracked just enough to show tree-light smudging the hallway. He half expected voices—his father's low baritone, his mother's soft answer—but the only sound was the refrigerator's old steady hum, the house's metronome reminding everything to keep time.

He went in.

Warmth folded over him—thick, stale, inhabited. The tree blinked in patient loops: gold, red, green, gold. Its reflection fluttered on the blank TV screen like a tiny map of fire. The smell of reheated barbecue still clung to the room, that sweet vinegar tang riding above Pine-Sol and old carpet.

His shoes felt like noise. He toed them off by habit and slid them into the gap beneath the coat rack. Every object looked both familiar and wrong—the recliner too big for its corner now, the crocheted afghan too small for the back of the couch, the family photographs one degree askew. Even his own face in those frames seemed to watch him with news he hadn't delivered yet.

Down the hall, his parents' door was cracked, their voices a low seam in the dark. Not fighting—worse. The rhythm of disappointment turned into prayer and back again. He couldn't catch words, only the shape of them. He didn't lean closer. He didn't need to.

He went to his room.

The door stuck like always, then gave with a little sigh. He stood in the threshold a second, letting his eyes adjust. No lamp was on. Only the spill of colored light bleeding from the tree down the hall, flickering stripes of green and red across his carpet and dresser like stained glass laid on its side. His bed was unmade, covers twisted from the morning rush. A Bible lay open to Psalms on the nightstand, the thin pages ruffled, his grandmother's quilt-square bookmark still standing like a small flag. He sat on the edge of the mattress and let his body be heavier than the springs wanted.

The quiet did what it wanted.

He didn't cry at first. He didn't do anything but breathe and listen to the way the house breathed back. Pipes settling. The click in the thermostat. The slow, tired wheeze of the vent in the hallway that always whistled on cold nights. Homes have lungs— he'd always thought that. They inhale family, exhale history. Tonight the house felt like it was holding its breath.

He slid the hymnbook from his jacket pocket and held it with both hands, thumb on the soft leather, the corner worn to suede where his grandmother used to flick it with a nail while she thought. Her note was tucked inside, the one he'd read so often he no longer needed to unfold it: *Listen between the sounds. That's where He lives.*

The words lifted off the page and hovered over the room like steam.

He laid back without meaning to, his heels still on the floor, shoulders in the sag of the mattress. Somewhere between the sigh of the vent and the clock on the dresser ticking its thin metal heart, a drowsiness came like tidewater. He didn't want sleep, but sleep wanted him. It found him the way a well-trained dog finds its master—quietly, directly, as if it had been waiting at the door.

It wasn't the kind of sleep that erases you. It was the kind that sets the scene, pulls a chair out in another room, and invites someone you miss to sit down.

The dream arrived like a film reel warming up—colors too saturated at first, focus softening as it leaned into clarity. He was in his grandmother's kitchen. Not the last weeks version, when everything was measured and careful. The older one, when she was herself completely—rose powder and fried chicken grease and that little electric hum of the percolator meaning afternoon was on its knees.

The vinyl tablecloth was floral, pale green with little pink roses that looked almost embarrassed to be there. The cigarette burn near the edge, perfectly round as a coin, peeked from under the sugar bowl. The overhead light was yellow and kind; it always made you look like you'd been forgiven.

Perry Mason mumbled from the living room where the volume had stayed for years, the exact number on the dial that kept company without interrupting.

She was there.

Hair in soft curls, glasses at the end of her nose, cardigan buttoned crooked because she'd stopped looking at buttons a long time ago. She poured coffee into two mismatched mugs—

the blue chipped one for herself, the one with the state bird for him. Steam rose up between them, carrying the smell of Sundays.

"You been cryin' again," she said, like she'd caught him with a finger in the icing.

Van laughed and it came out as a hiccup. "I thought you'd be mad at me."

"Mad? For what?" Her chuckle was a sound you could put on toast. "For bein' honest with the Lord? Baby, He's known who you are longer than you've had the words for it."

"I told them tonight," he said, and discovered the telling still hurt, even in dreams. "I said it out loud."

"I know," she said. She didn't blink like people do when they're lying about comfort. She stirred her coffee, spoon clicking the cup rim like a small clock.

"They didn't take it well."

"I know that, too."

He looked at her hands. He'd always loved her hands—strong, with that one knuckle swollen from an old jar that wouldn't open. Flour lived in the lines, even when she wasn't baking. "I just wanted them to see me," he said. "To not be ashamed of me."

"They will," she said, setting the spoon down soft. "One day." She pushed his mug closer, as if coffee could shorten distances. "But it might take time. The kind that hurts while you wait."

He pressed his palms around the mug. It was almost too warm to hold—almost. "I don't know if I can wait that long."

"Then don't wait for *them*." She said it like a recipe everyone forgets. "Wait for peace. That's the one that shows up when nobody else does."

Her hand came across the vinyl and covered his. He felt the weight of her wedding ring through the dream—cool metal, worn thin. It anchored him like a dock line.

"Grandma," he said, voice smaller than he wanted. "Do you think God still—"

She smiled before he finished. "Oh, honey. You could set the whole hymnbook on fire and He'd still love you. You think He made all *that* beauty"—she motioned broadly, as if meaning all of Carolina, the rosebush by her back door, the ache in someone's throat when they sang right—"just to be stingy with grace?"

He laughed through his nose; tears made small tracks without permission. "You always did have better sermons than Pastor Rich."

"That's 'cause I don't get paid to scare people." She took a sip, then set the cup down with both hands like a benediction. "Now go rest. You've got more truth to tell before this story's done."

The kitchen began to dim, not like a light going off, but like afternoon moving politely into evening. Her hand slipped away last—of course it did—and the TV's low courtroom voice turned into wind in pines.

"Remember, Van," she said as everything softened to the color of memory, "you don't need permission to be loved."

He woke to daylight—the dull winter kind that makes every surface look as if it's thinking.

For one suspended minute he did not move. The dream lay across him like an old quilt—patched, warm, smelling faintly of cedar and lavender water. Then came sound. Voices. Close.

His parents stood at the foot of the bed.

His mother looked pale, the delicate kind of pale that meant she hadn't slept, the kind of pale that made you want to wrap her in a better life. Her hands were clasped like she was holding the last of her patience between them so it didn't spill. His father stood just behind her, arms crossed tight enough to strain the church-logo jacket he wore when he did men's ministry work in the yard. Morning light found the gold thread and made it a thin stripe of armor.

Van's heart stumbled. The calm from the dream seeped away through the seams of the day.

"We talked last night," his mother said, and even her softness sounded disciplined. "And again early this morning. We called Pastor Rich and Lane. We're going to figure this out as a family."

"Figure what out?" He pushed himself against the headboard, felt how the slats bit into his shoulder blades. The sheets made a twist at his waist as if they, too, wanted him to pick a direction.

"This *confusion*," his father said, flat as cut wood. He didn't sit. He didn't come closer. He stayed in the stance of a man already sure. "We'll meet this week. Get you some clarity. Direction."

"You think this is confusion?"

"You're young," his mother rushed in, cushioning the word like you do when the table edge is sharp and a child is running. "You don't have to decide who you are right now."

"I didn't decide," Van said, and his voice surprised him with how steady it came. "I just *am*."

"Watch your tone," his father snapped, as if sound itself could be rebellious.

A new sound creaked the doorway open more. "Van?"

Emmalee stood there in her pink Disney bathrobe, the hem dragging, hair sticking up like a dandelion that refused to make a wish. Her socks didn't match. Her face did the open thing children's faces do when they haven't learned how to lie and don't want to.

"Emmy, sweetheart," their mother said, too brightly, "go get your bath started. We'll be done in a minute."

"But—"

"Now," their father said. Not loud. Firm enough to make the moment flinch.

Van's chest tightened at his sister's unsure mouth, the way her fingers worried the robe belt. "It's okay, Em," he said gently, throwing a rope across the space. "Go get ready for your party, alright?" He reached to his nightstand and pulled a folded five-dollar bill from under the Bible. "Get an extra ice cream for me."

She came close, wary, as if she'd get in trouble for accepting anything from him. She took the bill like it might dissolve, then leaned and kissed his cheek quick, the kind of kiss that says *I choose you* without paperwork. "Okay," she whispered, and padded down the hall, slippers scuffing.

When she was gone, the room felt smaller, like the walls had scooted a little, eager to hear how this would play out.

"She's not your secret to keep," Van said into the narrow, not looking away. "And neither am I."

"Van, please—" his mother started, the please a frayed ribbon, a steadying hand he loved and resented in the same breath.

"I'm not asking your permission anymore." He swung his legs to the floor. Carpet nap changed direction under his feet, a small rebellion. "Talk to the pastors if you want—that's between you and them. But this—" he pressed a palm to his chest, felt the honest pound there "—this is between me and God. And we already talked."

"Don't you walk away from me again," his father said, and the sentence came out of an older century, the place where obedience earns room and board.

"Then stop giving me reasons to."

He stood. The room felt like a shirt that had shrunk in the wash. He moved past them without brushing, the way you pass a stranger in a low aisle. In the hallway, the thermostat ticked and the vent whistled and the house finally exhaled, as if someone had cracked a long-stuck window.

The Christmas tree still glowed in the corner when he reached the living room, one strand blinking slower than the rest like a tired pupil. The TV screen, black now, held a faint ghost of last night's images. The Styrofoam container still sagged open on the side table, sauce a dark dried comet on the lid.

He took his shoes. He didn't put them on until the threshold. He heard his mother's voice behind him—"we're not done talking"—and heard everything else inside it: fear, habit, love trying to find a tone it hadn't practiced. He didn't turn.

Cold found his face when the door opened, honest and clean.

The sun was up enough to silver the frost on the mailbox and turn the neighbor's bare crepe myrtle branches into a sketch against a washed sky. Somewhere, a dog barked like punctuation.

He slid into the car, wrapped both hands around the wheel, and let himself shake once, the way a runner does at the starting line to remind the body it belongs to them. The engine caught on the second try, low and rough like an old hymn sung by a tired choir.

"Yeah," he murmured, watching his breath cloud and dissolve. "We're not done. Not yet."

He didn't know where he'd go next. He only knew where he wouldn't. The keychain cross warmed against his palm. He tucked the hymnbook onto the seat and backed out slow, gravel giving way the way it always had, the street opening like a page he'd read a hundred times and was finally ready to annotate in ink.

Behind him, the house watched with all its windows and said nothing. Ahead, Briar Hollow stretched out in pale winter light, ordinary as ever, waiting to see what truth would do when it refused to be put away.

THE SANCTUARY OF SMALL EYES

The church lot was half-empty, salt dusted across the asphalt like frost that hadn't decided whether to stay. A line of minivans cooled in place, engines ticking themselves quiet. From the fellowship hall came laughter in uneven bursts—the sound of teenagers trying to sound like everything was fine.

Van eased the BMW under the old live oak that loved to spit sap every Advent. The windshield already wore a scatter of resin stars. He sat a beat with the engine off and his breath fogging the glass, watching the steeple cut a pale seam against a December sky. The cross at the top glinted in a way that made you think of knives before you remembered you were supposed to think of mercy.

Hot chocolate hit him before the door—cocoa powder, scorched milk, the faint metallic tang from a dented pot that had survived more church winters than most marriages. Someone had propped both glass doors open, and a stream of tinny carols spilled out—*Hark! The Herald Angels Sing* performed by a children's choir slightly behind the beat, determined and breathy.

Inside, the fellowship hall had on its best thrift-store Christmas. Folding tables wore garlands that didn't match, tinsel shedding like a nervous cat. Styrofoam cups waited in towers beside sugar cookies glazed in bold faith and bolder food coloring—neon holly leaves, Rudolphs with cinnamon red hots for noses that promised to crack a molar. A plastic nativity perched on the upright piano, Joseph's head still tilted from last year's drop; one wise man had lost his gift and now cupped invisible frankincense like an apology.

"Hey, Van!" Colby called across the room, cider held aloft like a trophy. He wore his letterman jacket even indoors, sleeves pushed to his elbows to show forearms he'd noticed girls noticed. "Where you been, man?"

"Working," Van said, forcing a smile that hoped to be casual. "Not sleeping much."

"Same," Colby lied, grin sharp. "Coach had us run suicides till we saw Jesus."

Dana slid in behind him, her eyes scanning Van's face with the radar she kept tuned to her friends. "You okay?"

"Define okay."

"Alive?"

"Barely."

She nodded once, asking nothing more—her particular kindness. "Come on. Avery staked out the good chairs near the cocoa cauldron."

Avery was mid-monologue to a half-circle of youth about the tragic underfunding of Christmas sweaters. "You'd think a choir this good would at least get sequins," he was saying, tugging at the reindeer knitted into his own. He saw Van and lit like a marquee. "Ah, the tenor with emotional range! Come sit in our circle of semi-functioning saints."

"You realize no one knows what to do with you, right?" Van said, easing down into a metal chair that had lost a rubber foot and wobbled like a prayer life.

"Good," Avery replied, pouring hot chocolate to the brim. "That's how prophets work."

They talked grades and finals and the time Dana got caught trying to weave tinsel into the choir robes ("I was going for celestial!"), and the haircut Seth had given himself with clippers and denial. For a minute—an honest minute—Van let himself believe this could be normal: the furnace clicking on and off, sugar dissolving on his tongue, Dana laughing her laugh that made other people brave. Jeremiah wasn't here yet, which made the air easier and harder in ways Van didn't try to name.

The double doors thumped and Youth Pastor Lane entered with his clipboard and his posture. He had the air of a man who ironed sweatshirts—clean-shaven, hair that defied humidity by sheer will, smile calibrated and holy. He moved through the room like a shepherd at a county fair, clapping shoulders, praising a caroling duet ("excellent blend, girls!"), taking too long to adjust the plastic nativity so Joseph's head leaned less heretically.

He stepped to the front and lifted the clipboard like it contained scripture not schedules. "Alright, guys," he sang, his voice achieving cheerful without letting joy touch it. "Quick announcement before we head over to the sanctuary for music practice."

Chairs creaked as bodies settled. Van's stomach twitched before he knew why—some animal part of him that recognized a tone he'd learned on Wednesday nights and long altar calls.

"As you know, we're preparing for our Christmas Eve service," Lane continued. "Scripture readings, ensembles, and a solo during 'O Holy Night.'" He let the words hang like ornaments, his eyes skimming the room, pausing on Van as if the look were rationed, then moving on. "After praying this morning, we've decided to have Evan sing the solo this year."

A ripple went through the circle—surprise passing for polite. Evan, a baritone whose mother brought lemon bars to every potluck, looked briefly stunned and then deeply pleased, the way people do when picked by God's representative and also their youth pastor.

Van sat still enough to look carved. Under the table, Dana's hand found his knee and pressed twice: *I see you.* Avery didn't move at all, which told Van more than words.

Lane smiled the smile of a man who believed his choices were kindness. "We're excited to celebrate the birth of Christ as one body."

One body. Van bit the inside of his cheek until he could taste iron and something older than shame.

Someone plugged in a string of lights that decided to flicker with a vengeance. Papers shuffled. Chairs scraped. Lane dismissed them toward the sanctuary with a clap that echoed longer than the room. As people funneled toward the double doors, the air filled with polite congratulations and the clatter of plastic cookie trays being over-believed in.

Van waited until the noise was thick enough to cover him and then crossed the space to Lane, who'd paused to add "NO LIQUIDS ON THE PIANO" to a sheet of unheeded instructions.

"Lane?" Van kept his voice low, polite. Too polite. "Can we talk a minute?"

"Of course," Lane said with a pastoral tilt of the head. "Let's step down the nursery hall. Less traffic."

They walked past the coat rack shedding mittens like dandruff, into the dim hall whose walls still wore faded murals of animals that did not appear together in reality—giraffes with penguins, lions with lambs, a koala waving above a verse about Noah that had been misattributed to Proverbs for ten years. A vending machine hummed by the door to the old nursery, now storage; its glowing window promised a cold Mountain Dew to anyone with exact change and questionable judgment.

It smelled like disinfectant, dust, and something sweet that had lived too long inside a plastic cup.

Lane folded his arms in that way that meant *I'm open* while closing. "What's on your mind?"

"When did you decide about the solo?" Van asked. He didn't recognize his own voice. It sounded like the kind he used when managers asked why he needed another Saturday off.

"This morning," Lane said evenly. "We want everything to reflect the right heart posture for the service."

"The right heart posture," Van repeated like he was trying out a guitar string. "You mean me."

"I mean the spirit of the season," Lane replied. "You've been under... strain." He placed the word down gently, like it might break on the floor. "We want to give you space to—"

"To be quietly replaced?"

"That's not what this is."

"Feels like it," Van said. He let the words sit in their coats.

Lane pinched the bridge of his nose, that public act of private patience. "You're loved here," he said in the voice he used for altar calls. "You're valuable. But leadership carries example. When someone's walking through something, it's best to focus on healing before stepping up front."

"Healing from what?"

"You know what I mean."

"I really don't."

He looked then—really looked—and for a second his expression was almost naked. Not cruelty. Fear dressed up as certainty, the kind people wear when they're convinced faith is a glass they're responsible for keeping from cracks. "You're choosing a path that's not in line with God's design."

"You mean I'm not straight."

"I mean you're struggling with sin."

"I'm struggling with shame," Van said. "There's a difference."

Silence inflated the hall. The vending machine coughed a soda with a hollow thud like a bad amen.

"Do you still want to sing, Van?" Lane asked finally.

"Yes."

"Then sing to Him in your room, when no one's watching. Sometimes that's the purest offering."

"And sometimes," Van said, "it's just hiding."

Lane's voice softened into sympathy's shape. "Be careful. Pride is slippery."

"So is hypocrisy."

Lane flinched—barely, but enough to register. "I won't argue Scripture."

"I'm not asking you to," Van said. "I'm asking you to stop using it as a fence."

A thousand sermons walked between them and straight out the side door into air that didn't care what you believed. Lane looked down the hall at the dark nursery door, at the mural lamb that smiled like an advertisement, and back at Van. Regret flickered—there and gone, like a moth flirting with a lamp you couldn't see.

"You're angry," he said.

"I'm awake."

A voice carried down the hall then—Ms. Denise's soft command: "Jeremiah, sweetheart, bring those handbells to the front." Van went still without meaning to. The sound of his name said by someone else's mother always did something to him.

Lane stepped back a half inch, pastoral radius complete. "We should head in," he said. "Rehearsal's starting."

They reentered the fellowship hall, now emptying. The cocoa pot steamed on without audience, a fogged mirror for a world not thirsty enough. Van paused at the doorway to the sanctuary, hand on the frame, and straightened his shoulders like you do before someone takes your picture. Then he stepped into the light.

The sanctuary smelled like old wood and new perfume, poinsettias bristling along the platform the way tradition likes to. Stained glass threw diluted color across pews—enough to halo, not enough to hide. The choir loft was already a quilt of red and black and seasonal sweaters, teenagers squirming into spots according to the shifting logic of friendship and crushes and alto lines.

Dana intercepted him at the end of the aisle. She didn't waste a question. "Well?"

"He gave it to Evan," Van said.

Avery, hovering behind her with three sheet-music folders like a slightly gay music stand, lifted his eyebrows to the line reserved for scandal. "Because of the scandalous vibrato or the scandalous sexuality?"

"The second one."

Avery's jaw worked. It smoothed into something dangerous and bright. "Then we clap louder for you than for him. That's gay revenge, baby."

Van's laugh startled him. It came out like a breath he hadn't known he'd held too long. "Thanks, Ave."

"Anytime," Avery said, handing him *Angels We Have Heard on High* like it was a weapon. "Now let's out-sing the entire fundamentalist South."

From the other aisle, Jeremiah slipped into the tenor row three spots down, eyes on the floor, Ms. Denise a pew back with a handbell case and the kind of smile women wear when keeping everything upright. Pastor Rich stood at the back of the sanctuary, shaking hands he'd already shaken, his gaze drifting now and then toward the loft as if sound could sin.

Jeremiah's eyes found Van's for a half-second—just long enough to say *I see* and *I'm sorry* and *be careful* without moving his mouth. Van felt the look land in his chest and settle there like warmth.

Rehearsal began with a prayer that asked God to inhabit their praises and avoid their politics. They launched into *Joy to the World*, the tempo dragged as it always did under fluorescent lights. The sopranos over-sparkled. The basses under-committed. The tenors did what tenors do—tried to keep the middle beautiful while the edges argued.

Van sang quiet at first, then less quiet. His harmony threaded under the melody like something responsible and aching. He watched the lyrics climb the screen and felt how easy it would be to let words do the lying for you. *Let every heart prepare Him room.* He told the truth to vowels and nothing else—how his heart had prepared room and been told to go sleep in the shed.

Between songs, Lane gave notes that pretended to be about diction. "Watch those consonants, folks," he said. "We don't want *peace on Herd.*" The room giggled; the joke was old and reliable. He added, "Let's keep faces open—worship should show." Van thought of how worship that showed had been used to hide worse, and swallowed that heresy with his water.

They rehearsed *Silent Night* with the lights dimmed to Christmas Eve levels, candles passed unlit down the rows to practice the choreography of reverence. The sanctuary took on that soft midnight hush that made even the HVAC respectful. Van held the unlit candle and imagined the heat of it anyway, the way a flame glows your knuckles more than your face.

"Let's take it a cappella," Lane said, and his hands rose to that small, floating press that starts a hundred years of tradition at once.

Van let his breath go and sang.

Not loud, not showy. Just enough to make the air pick up what he offered. The harmony folded under *round yon virgin,* found the minor where the lyric would not. He felt his voice travel to the back pew and settle on the lap of an old woman who hadn't been touched kindly all week. He felt it whisper along the rafters where spiders had built fortresses the deacons didn't see. He felt it go to the parking lot where small eyes rolled at the sight of two boys laughing and come back unashamed.

Sleep in heavenly peace.

Peace tonight felt like something he would have to build with his own hands and then defend. He sang anyway. He sang because it was the truest thing he knew how to do that didn't require someone else's permission.

When the last chord sighed into the wood, the room held silence for a second that felt like mercy. Lane blew out an imaginary candle and smiled toward the altos. "Beautiful," he said, and it was. Beauty often is even when it's being misused.

As the choir shuffled music, Evan turned and caught Van's eye —awkward, kind. "Hey, man," he said, sotto voce. "You know I didn't ask for it."

"I know," Van said, and meant it.

"Your note on 'divine'—that third—" Evan lifted his hand, unable to find the word he wanted. "It did the thing."

Van smiled, small and real. "Thanks."

Avery elbowed him. "See? Even usurpers can have taste."

"Shut up," Van whispered, and Avery preened.

From the aisle, Ms. Denise called, "Jeremiah, baby, help me with these programs," the *baby* sugarcoated and sharpened at once. Jeremiah gave Van one more glance that held a whole conversation, then went. Pastor Rich's Amen voice filled the back of the room for a benediction to the rehearsal that made it sound like they'd accomplished something God had been waiting on.

They hadn't. But Van had.

After, the fellowship hall returned to its hum. Cocoa cooled into a skin no one loved. The cookie tray wore one mangled tree with too much icing in place of a star. Dana collected discarded bulletins and stacked them with the efficiency of a woman who will one day run a town. Avery filched a second candy cane like it was a sacrament.

"Where to now?" Dana asked, bumping Van's shoulder with hers.

"Home," he said, and tried the word on for size. It fit different every day. "Or—maybe the long way around it."

"Swing by the diner," Avery said. "Marlene will put whipped cream on something and call it pastoral care."

Van's laugh felt like it belonged to him. "Maybe I will."

They stepped out into late afternoon light the color of pewter and regret. The wind cut in around the building, pushed through his coat to his bones like it knew the address. Across the lot, Jeremiah was loaded down with handbell cases, Ms. Denise adjusting her purse strap and not missing a thing. Pastor Rich stood by a deacon's truck, smiling with his eyebrows while his jaw did other work.

Van slid behind the wheel and sat a second with the door shut, the world reduced to glass and frame. He let his head hit the rest and watched the steeple through the windshield. The cross glinted again—hard, beautiful, unholdable.

Maybe peace, he thought, wasn't something you were handed in a sanctuary. Maybe it was something you smuggled out under your coat, piece by tiny piece, and shared in parking lots and diner booths and the front seats of cars where hands touched without permission slips.

He started the engine. The radio came on low—some station halfway to static playing a hymn he knew so well he barely heard it. He pulled out from under the old oak slowly, pine sap catching the light in a constellation that hadn't been named. As he turned toward the road, the church slipped into the side mirror and got small. He let it.

He did not have the solo. He did not have the blessing he'd been taught to want. He had his voice, and he had the knowing that came after someone tried to take it.

For tonight, it was enough.

"It wasn't rebellion. It was survival."

THE WEIGHT OF CHOIR LIGHT

The week before Christmas stretched like the pause between verses—
that silence that hums with everything unsaid.

Outside, Briar Hollow glittered the way small towns do when they want to look brave against winter: lights strangled in the oaks along Main, a storefront nativity glowing pale blue through fogged glass, a blow-up Santa bowing perpetually to passing cars. The air smelled like pine sap and fried onions from the diner vent, and somewhere a porch radio crooned Patsy Cline, soft as prayer through the static.

Inside the Shelton house, light behaved differently. Dimmer. Careful. As if even the bulbs knew better than to burn too bright.

VAN'S FATHER had made the season a performance.

He whistled carols in the kitchen, too loud, too cheerful. Hauled boxes of decorations he hadn't touched in years, untangling lights with military focus. He even volunteered to place the star—a job that had always been Van's.

"Gotta make it nice for Emmalee," he said, balancing on the step-stool. "She deserves a real Christmas."

Van handed him the extension cord and didn't answer. Conversation had splinters lately. Everything you said risked blood.

His mother floated between rooms like a peacekeeper in a war both sides pretended wasn't happening—adjusting ornaments, refilling cocoa, humming through her own exhaustion. The smell of cinnamon and sugar drifted through the house, sweet without landing anywhere. Every surface gleamed with effort.

Emmalee, small enough to believe in the best, carried most of the joy herself. She hummed while wrapping gifts for her dolls, wore a Santa hat to breakfast, taped paper snowflakes to every door. When she tugged at Van's sleeve to help her set out cookies for Santa, he couldn't tell her no.

They sat on the couch together, the tree painting their faces gold and green.

"You think he'll still come?" she whispered.

"He always does," Van said. And though he wasn't talking about Santa, he hoped it was true.

THE CHURCH PULSED every night that week.

Rehearsals spilled through the sanctuary, filling it with brass and candle wax, pine and floor polish. Chairs creaked like polite prayers.

Van still came.

Not because he felt welcome—because leaving would feel like surrender.

He tuned guitars, straightened hymnals, helped the younger kids find their notes. Mrs. Whitaker pressed peppermint bark into his hand "for bravery," eyes full of a compassion she disguised as mischief. "Don't you let that Lane boy tell you where

God won't sit," she whispered once, and winked like rebellion was just another carol.

Jeremiah was there every night. Not touching, not lingering—just close enough that their glances could do the speaking: *I see you. I'm still here.*

Sometimes that was enough to keep breathing.

One evening, setting candles for the Christmas Eve service, Jeremiah caught him at the base of the choir-loft stairs. "You holding up?" he asked softly.

Van smiled without humor. "Define holding up."

"Breathing?"

"Mostly."

They stood in the half-light, wax and pine heavy in the air. Jeremiah reached out and straightened Van's choir stole—carefully, his fingertips grazing the fabric near his collar. The touch burned like a blessing no one had sanctioned.

"He took the solo," Van said.

"I know."

"Guess the Lord works in mysterious exclusions."

"You deserved better."

"I just wanted to sing without being a sermon."

"You still can," Jeremiah said. "Just not from *their* stage."

From the next room, the choir's warm-ups rose—voices finding each other like incense climbing invisible stairs. Jeremiah leaned in close enough for Van to feel his breath.

"You're the reason half of us show up," he said.

"Because I keep snacks in my bag?"

"Because you make it feel like grace might still live here."

Van's throat went tight. "Don't say stuff like that."

"Why not?"

"Because it'll make me believe it."

Jeremiah smiled, a quiet kind of ache. He brushed Van's shoulder as he passed, whispering, "Then maybe it's true."

. . .

By Friday, the house smelled of ham and the record player spun carols no one truly heard. The lights glowed dutifully. His father's mood had turned syrupy—too bright, too forced—as if cheerfulness were a form of penance.

"You excited for Christmas Eve service?" his father asked, carving ham with the precision of avoidance.

"Sure," Van said, pushing potatoes into constellations on his plate. "Watching other people sing songs meant for me sounds great."

"Van—" his mother began.

He cut her off gently. "I'm kidding. Mostly."

His father set the carving fork down, all patience and warning. "Maybe it's good you're sitting this one out," he said. "Gives you time to think."

"About what?"

"Direction. Where you're headed before you get too far down the wrong road."

Emmalee piped up through a mouthful of rolls. "But Van's a singer. He's not on a road."

"Eat your green beans, sweetheart," their mother said softly.

Van stood. "May I be excused?"

His mother nodded, her eyes full of things she didn't have the courage to name.

His father muttered something about respect, but Van was already gone.

In his room, the air felt colder than it had any right to. He sat on the bed and looked at the cross-stitch above the desk—his grandmother's handwriting turned to thread: *Surely goodness and mercy shall follow me.*

He traced the uneven letters with his thumb. The words looked tired. They were still holding.

He opened his hymnbook. Pages smelled faintly of candle

smoke and time. He turned until he found *O Holy Night*—the one that had been his. He hummed quietly, his voice small and sure, the sound catching on the edges of the room. It wasn't rebellion. It was survival.

Down the hall, his parents' voices murmured—a rhythm of concern and doctrine. He could tell which lines belonged to Pastor Rich and which were his mother's softer copies. He closed his eyes and let the hum drown them out. He imagined singing in the dark sanctuary after everyone left, filling it with the kind of sound that didn't ask permission.

The house settled. Pipes sighed. The wind shifted in the eaves like an old organ wheezing awake. Somewhere a car passed, its headlights painting brief constellations on his wall.

He lay back, the hymnbook still open on his chest.

And sleep came, slow but kind.

HE DREAMED NOT of his grandmother this time, but of *light.*

An empty sanctuary. Candles lining the aisle. His own voice in the air—not loud, not perfect, just true. Every note another small star. The pews filled, one by one, with the people who had stayed when it mattered: Jeremiah in his choir robe, Dana clutching sheet music, Avery pretending not to cry, Mrs. Whitaker mouthing harmony like a prayer. None of them judging. All of them listening.

The sound rose—not performance, but confession.

He sang until the roof lifted and the night outside leaned in to listen.

When he woke, his throat was sore from something that might have been crying.

But for the first time in days, he didn't feel hollow.

Just full of an ache that meant there was still a voice left to use.

And maybe, he thought as morning bled through the blinds, that was enough to begin again.

56

"Maybe grace wasn't a place you stood. Maybe it was a person who stayed."

SILENT NIGHT, STANDING ROOM ONLY

The sanctuary glowed like a jewel box that night—brass candelabras trembling at the altar, stained glass throwing shards of color across the pews like blessings scattered too wide to aim. In the foyer, winter air slipped in every time the outer doors opened, meeting perfume and hairspray and the faint singe of wicks caught on the first breath of flame. It smelled like Advent always smells: wax and pine, paper bulletins, old wood warmed by bodies and hope.

Choir room chaos pulsed behind the stage door. Robes rustled like restless doves. Someone's bobby pins pinged against the tile. Mrs. Whitaker leaned into the altos, whispering in a conspirator's hush, "Eyes up on my cut-off, ladies—don't marry your music." Dana pinned back a stray curl, handed Van a safety pin, and didn't say the thing living behind her eyes. Avery stared into the cracked mirror, smoothing his robe like a magician readying a cape.

"You good?" he asked Van's reflection.

"Define good."

"So… devastatingly handsome but spiritually complicated?"

"That's closer," Van said, and the corner of his mouth lifted.

He'd ironed his robe that morning—not out of pride, but ritual. Neat seams when the rest of life refused to line up. The collar still felt a half size too tight; his pulse thudded against it like something trying to hatch.

Youth Pastor Lane poked his head in with a smile polished enough to see your face in. "Ten minutes," he said. "Let's remember what tonight is really about—light in the darkness."

Avery muttered, "Some of us carry our own flashlights," and Dana stifled a laugh that turned into a cough.

Van avoided Lane's eyes and focused on breathing. In for four. Out for six. Like Mrs. Whitaker taught him before a solo he wouldn't be singing.

"Van." Mrs. Whitaker materialized at his elbow. Up close, her perfume smelled like peppermint and mercy. "You sing the inner line on 'Silent Night'? The quiet one that floats under the melody?"

"Yes, ma'am."

"Good. Let it be honey, not molasses." She squeezed his hand. "And remember—truth doesn't need volume to be heard."

The stage door opened; a draft of cold and hymnals swept in. They processed down the side aisle to the loft in pairs, hemmed robes whispering. The sanctuary was beyond full—extra chairs down the transepts, toddlers in velvet clamped to their parents' hips, coats slung across pew backs, bulletin corners folded into swords by bored children. Van's parents sat three pews from the front. His father's arm rested across the bench like a claim; his mother's smile was too bright, the kind people wear when a camera might be watching. Emmalee turned and waved—small, brave—like a little lighthouse.

The organ trembled into the first chords of "O Come, All Ye Faithful." The congregation rose like a single body—and yet Van heard fractures: Mrs. Peterson's alto quaver; a line of tenors a breath behind; the word faithful hanging in the rafters like a dare. He sang anyway. Not loud, not for attention—just enough to feel the note move through him and leave something honest behind.

From the loft, he could see Jeremiah—end of a pew, posture perfect, candle still unlit, eyes forward until they weren't. Their glance met and slid away, quick but anchoring. Two beats. Enough.

Children's choir came first: winged sleeves and stage-fright bravado, halos crooked, shepherds whispering urgent theology about sheep. Scripture readers followed—Luke and Isaiah by memory, each comma rehearsed, each silence held with the rustle of bulletins. Van mouthed along, the words fitting in his mouth even as his trust in their messengers thinned.

Aunt Shelia sat halfway back on the aisle, sunflower scarf bright against a winter sea of charcoal and navy—the lone slice of July in a room built for December. When she caught Van looking, she tipped her chin: I see you. Behave? Maybe. Be small? Never.

Lane took the pulpit. The hush he wanted fell. He preached gentle: light in darkness, birth as beginning, purity rescued in a world that forgets. Van felt each phrase like a splinter. He could see the bones of the outline: metaphor, parable, subtext. The message inside the message: You can be redeemed if you stop being yourself.

From the front row, Pastor Rich nodded along, jaw set in righteous agreement. Ms. Denise's smile could have propped up a roof. Their son stared at the hymnboard like it contained coordinates out of here.

Then the solo.

Evan walked forward, hands perfectly still against his robe, eyes lifted toward the loft edge like the note might be waiting there. The first phrase of "O Holy Night" rang unbroken to the ceiling. The congregation sighed—moved by beauty, by relief that beauty still existed. Van didn't hate Evan. The boy sang well. But the sound scraped against something deeper, because this song was a weary world rejoicing, and Van knew what it meant to be the weary world.

His hands trembled. He laced his fingers to keep them quiet. Beside him, Mrs. Whitaker slid a peppermint into his palm without looking. He let it anchor him.

At the back of the sanctuary, the ushers readied candles. Lights dimmed until stained glass glowed like a memory of color. Evan reached fall on your knees with a shine that would be remembered and forgotten in equal measure by morning.

And then Jeremiah moved.

From the pew's end, he stood—quietly, deliberately—holding his unlit candle before anyone else. He struck the match early. Flame leapt, small and brave in a dark sea. A few people frowned, unsure if he'd missed the cue. Van knew he hadn't. It wasn't defiance. It was solidarity. One light before the rest. A witness.

Van's breath snagged. The ache cracked open; something living stepped through.

When the usher reached their row, Jeremiah tipped his flame to the usher's wick instead of taking from it—reversing the direction without ceremony—and then turned forward, waiting. A small, stubborn geometry of grace. By the time the slow river of fire reached the loft, the sanctuary had become a galaxy—tiny suns passing, faces softened to their best selves.

"Silent Night" began as a thread and gathered into fabric. Van sang the inner line—low at first, then stronger—threading a line no one could confiscate. He watched his candle flicker against Jeremiah's two pews ahead, a heartbeat of flame echoing back to him.

Sleep in heavenly peace, he sang, and for a breath he believed the imperative might be a promise.

The last chord faded like breath on a mirror. In the deliberate quiet that followed, a baby somewhere cooed, and four pews chuckled softly as if holiness had just waved.

"Receive now the benediction," Lane said, smoothing the moment back into order. His eyes did not land on Van.

Robes rustled. Coats shrugged into. "Amens" tinkled like sleigh bells in the aisles. Van sat until his candle shortened to a guttering stub. Wax pooled warm at the web of his thumb. He let it hold him there one beat longer, then pinched out the flame and watched the final ribbon of smoke curl toward the rafters like a prayer brave enough to be seen.

In the receiving line, Van kept to the choir's side door, but the currents of after-service traffic tugged him briefly into the flow. Pastor Rich's grip was a vise; his smile was porcelain. "Merry Christmas, son," he said in a tone built to bless and warn at once. Ms. Denise's hand landed on Jeremiah's shoulder with weight that meant *remember whose you are.*

Aunt Shelia cut across the current like a tugboat. "Best candlelight I seen in years," she announced to no one and everyone. "Some folks even found the flame before the program told 'em to." The sentence floated sugar-sweet; the edge underneath could slice paper.

Van's father steered their family toward the side doors, palm hovering at Van's back like a traffic cone. Van stepped out of reach.

Outside, cold air snapped clean. Families spilled into the night —laughter tumbling in clouds of breath, car locks chirping like metallic birds. The church sign hummed under a halo of frost. Jeremiah waited beneath it, robe over one arm, hair catching streetlight. Neither spoke when Van reached him. They stood borrowed-close, breath weaving.

"You sang anyway," Jeremiah said finally.

"Not loud enough to be noticed."

"That's not the same as not being heard."

Van looked at him—really looked—and felt the smallest shift in gravity. Maybe grace wasn't a place you stood. Maybe it was a person who stayed.

Across the lot, Avery flung his scarf like a banner. "Pilgrimage to Waffle House!" he announced. "Grease is the truest sacrament."

Dana groaned. "Somebody stop him before he writes that on a T-shirt."

Van almost laughed. "Of course he does."

They walked toward their cars. Behind them, church lights dimmed to the kind of glow that belongs to after. Van glanced once toward his family. His mother lifted a hand—half-wave, half-blessing. His father tightened his jaw; the motion could have been a shiver, could have been fury.

"Ride with me?" Jeremiah asked, already unlocking the truck.

Van nodded and didn't bother inventing a reason why yes felt like oxygen.

They slid into the bench seat, breath fogging the windshield. Jeremiah cranked the heat; the vents coughed then sighed. For a few seconds, they just listened to the fan and their pulse.

"You lit early," Van said.

Jeremiah's mouth twitched. "Some things don't need permission."

They pulled out behind Avery's truck, taillights smearing red on wet asphalt. The giant star on the church roof shrank in the rear-view until it was a pinprick caught in black lace branches. Briar Hollow unspooled around them—porches, pawn shop, the dark bend by the river where fog liked to gather. The world looked almost gentle from inside a warm cab with the right person.

"You okay?" Jeremiah asked, eyes on the road.

"Define okay."

Jeremiah smiled the same tired smile he'd been wearing all Advent. "Breathing?"

"Yeah," Van said. "And singing under my breath."

"That counts," Jeremiah said. "Maybe that counts more."

They didn't say anything else. They didn't need to. Between them, the silence took its coat off and stayed.

"Peace isn't the absence of a fight. It's knowing you're still standing after one."

HALLELUJAH DINER

The Waffle House crouched at the edge of town like a chapel built from caffeine and stubbornness. The F in the sign flickered, resigning every third second so it read WAFLE HOUSE, like grammar had surrendered at midnight. Inside: syrup, fryer oil, and the kind of stories people tell when they think no one important is listening.

Heat slapped their faces as they pushed through the door. The place thrummed in that 11:30 p.m. way—truckers baptizing pie in coffee, two teenagers arguing with theological zeal about whether smothered hash browns counted as a vegetable, the jukebox crackling out an old country hymn dressed as a heartbreak song.

"Look what the Advent wreath dragged in," Avery announced from the back booth, lifting his mug. "Our tenor of sorrows. And his heroic candle-bearer."

"Praise be," Dana said, scooting over. "Sit before he starts quoting Liza."

"I would never," Avery sniffed. "Not before the first waffle."

Jeremiah slid to the end seat. His white shirt had traded for flannel that still remembered candle smoke. He didn't say anything at first—just met Van's eyes for a beat too long and then studied the laminated menu like it might absolve him of something. No one called it out. Their kindness had become a practiced art.

The waitress—hair piled high and name tag JUNE—arrived with an order pad and the authority of an archangel. "Y'all the church kids?" she said, pen poised.

"Guilty," Avery said. "We bring hunger and moral complexity."

June didn't blink. "Hash browns fix both. What'll it be?"

They ordered everything they didn't need—waffles lacquered in syrup, eggs, bacon, grits that gleamed like polished pews. When the plates landed, the table became a small weather system: syrup bottles passing, salt sliding, inside jokes clattering like forks.

Van laughed—really laughed, the kind that starts in your ribs and shakes stiffness out of your shoulders. Dana watched him over her straw with a look that said there you are.

Colby sat across from Avery, arms folded, face carrying the gospel of disapproval. He'd shown up late, still in church clothes, tie loosened just enough to prove he was mortal. "You see Coach?" he asked no one. "He cried during the shepherds."

Dana snorted. "He has three boys under six and an infant. He cries when he sees a pillow."

June returned with more coffee, refills sloshing like a tide. "Y'all want whipped cream on them waffles?" she asked.

Avery clasped his hands. "Sister June, we desire abundance."

"Thought so," she said, and swept away like a benediction with sensible shoes.

"I'm stealing that," Dana said. "Desiring abundance."

"Put it on a mug," Avery said. "We'll sell 'em to Lane to fund sequins for the choir."

Van kept tracing the condensation on his glass, lines turning to shapes turning to nothing. "It's strange," he said quietly, "singing about peace when everything feels like a war."

The table fell into a gentle hush. Even Avery let the line sit.

"Maybe peace isn't the absence of a fight," Jeremiah said after a moment. "Maybe it's when you're still standing after one."

"You sound like my grandmother."

"She must've been smart."

"She was."

The quiet that followed wasn't heavy. It was the kind that pulls chairs closer. Then Avery broke it with holy foolishness. "Well, if we're doing grandma proverbs: mine said never trust a man who says 'trust me,' and always order extra bacon, because tomorrow is hypothetical."

"Your grandma was a prophet," Dana said.

June slid a plate between them with the practiced accuracy of a short-order saint. "Y'all need anything else?"

"Hope," Avery said.

June nodded toward the griddle where a man in a paper hat flipped a pancake with sacramental solemnity. "We got that too. It just looks like breakfast if you squint."

They ate. Syrup made little glass rivers on the Formica. Grease beaded the edge of the paper placemats in a halo. The cook yelled "Order up!" with the same rhythm a deacon uses for *Amen.* Somewhere by the windows, a woman laughed until she had to press a napkin to her eyes.

When the plates settled to half-empty, questions took the seat between them.

"Y'all see those candles from the loft?" Dana asked. "Looked like a star map."

"I lit early," Jeremiah said.

"We noticed," Avery said, eyes soft with mischief. "Half the congregation clutched their pearls with both hands. The other half smiled into their hymnals."

Colby rolled his eyes. "You're not supposed to draw attention during worship."

"Light is attention," Avery said. "That's literally the point."

Colby stabbed at his eggs. "Not *your* light."

Van's fork paused. Jeremiah's hand, under the table, found the edge of Van's napkin and held it still. Dana shot Colby a warning look. He looked away, jaw tight as scripture.

June returned with a pot of coffee and a look that could read a page at a glance. "That time of year again," she said, topping cups. "Y'all sing yourselves hoarse and then come here to put back what the sermon took."

"June," Avery said reverently, "preach."

She smirked, not unkind. "Baby, I preach by keepin' this place open."

Van smiled into his mug. The warmth stretched his chest like a new shirt.

Avery lifted his glass. "A toast," he said, because of course he would. "To candlelight and rebellion, to hash browns as therapy, to friends who clap loudest when they're not allowed to."

"Add 'to June,'" Dana said.

"To June," Avery echoed, and she waved it away like she didn't collect toasts, just tips.

"Also," Dana said, leaning her chin into her palm, "to this one." She jerked her head toward Van. "For singing anyway."

Van ducked his head. "Y'all are ridiculous."

"Correct," Avery said. "And yet somehow necessary."

By the time they tumbled back into the cold, frost had needled the lot. Their breath hung like a string of white psalms. Avery staged a tableau beneath the flickering sign. "Behold," he declared, arms outstretched, "the night of our deliverance!"

Colby lobbed a napkin. "Get in the car, prophet."

Dana climbed into her Honda and rolled down the window. "You okay?" she called to Van.

"Better than I was," he said, surprised to hear it ring true.

"Progress," Jeremiah said, appearing at his elbow with the truck keys.

"Ride with me," he added, soft as a suggestion that already knew its answer.

They rode with the window cracked, radio low, the town sliding by like a set from a play they'd already seen. The squeal of the old swing set at the park. The pawn shop's sign buzzing. The pharmacy's snowman blinking one eye like a conspirator.

"Do you think people ever stop talking?" Van asked.

Jeremiah considered. "They get tired," he said. "Or they start talking about something better."

"What's better?"

"You," Jeremiah said. "Us. Whatever this is when we stop apologizing for breathing."

Van didn't answer. He reached across the bench seat, let his fingers find Jeremiah's in the space where the gearshift wasn't. Jeremiah didn't look down. He just squeezed, knuckles warm and certain.

They pulled into Van's drive. The house sat quiet, the tree in the window blinking a slower pattern than the rest of the world. The porch light had burned out sometime between evening and mercy.

"Thank you," Van said, hand still caught in Jeremiah's like a promise you don't need to write down.

"For what?"

"For the match," Van said. "For the light before the cue."

Jeremiah smiled into the dark. "Anytime."

Van started to open the door, then stopped. "Merry almost-Christmas."

"Merry almost-Christmas," Jeremiah said, and if his voice thickened, the night kept its secrets.

Inside, the house smelled like ham and silence. Van stood in the entry until his eyes adjusted. The tree clicked softly. Somewhere down the hall a floorboard sighed like tired timber. He climbed the stairs, hymnbook under his arm, candle smoke still folded in the folds of his robe. In his room, he sat on the bed and let the day collect itself, then fall away.

He pressed his grandmother's book flat. The page found him: *All is calm, all is bright.* It wasn't true yet, not quite. But for the first time in weeks, the sentence didn't sound like a lie. It sounded like something that might arrive if you kept a light on and didn't flinch.

Down the street, a train horn tilted into the cold. Somewhere else, June refilled a cup for someone sitting alone. In a little house on a quiet road, a boy who had been told to be less sang the inner line to an empty room, and the room learned it by heart.

When sleep came, it didn't bang on the door. It slid in beside him like a friend who knew the way.

And in the last thin band of waking, Van understood this much: he had not been noticed, maybe. But he had been heard.

"Some truths don't ask for applause—they just wait for you to
stop whispering."

THE MORNING AFTER BETHLEHEM

Christmas morning came soft and gray—the kind of light that looks like it's been prayed over before it dares to touch windows. The house smelled faintly of cinnamon and wood polish. Down the hall, Emmalee's hum rose in a sugar-rush scale—half carol, half countdown.

Van lay still, tracing ceiling cracks like constellations. *Christmas*, he remembered, and the word felt too bright for the heaviness behind his ribs.

He dressed quiet. The green sweater his mother folded last night still held the scent of lavender and starch. In the living room, the machine of the day already ran: his mother in a red turtleneck arranging deviled eggs with surgical focus; his father tightening his tie in the shine of the microwave door.

"Morning," Van said.

"Morning," his mother answered, not looking up. "We need to leave in twenty."

"Don't drag your feet," his father added. "Your uncle doesn't like late blessings."

"I know," Van said, softer than he meant.

Emmalee spun in—nightgown, ribbon listing in her hair, joy full to spilling. "Santa came! He left crumbs everywhere!"

"Messy man," Van said, and meant it like a benediction. For a moment, almost—almost—normal.

The drive to Uncle David and Aunt Leslie's was a hymn in minor key. *Joy to the World* on the radio sounded like a dare. Frost etched the mailbox flags; the sky wore porcelain.

Inside, the house gleamed. Garland disciplined to symmetry. Poinsettias obedient at the stairs. Candles practicing posture on the table set with the same gold-trimmed plates as always.

"There's my favorite choir boy!" Aunt Leslie sang, kissing beside his cheek. "Mrs. Whitaker must have you leading half the hymns by now."

"Something like that," Van said, wearing the smile that fits the family frame.

Uncle David's hand landed heavy on his shoulder. "Good to see you, son."

Cousins swarmed—tearing paper like pirates dividing treasure. Emmalee gasped at her doll like it had risen from the dead. Van let himself enjoy it for a breath before loneliness folded back over him like a coat.

Prayer lasted a chapter too long: blessings named and renamed, gratitude for the faithful departed, a nod toward "unity in our household" that made Van's stomach tighten. Forks clinked in unison at *Amen*, the performance back on beat.

He ate quietly. Smiled when required. Felt his father's eyes grazing him from across the table—storm not yet, but near. Every time Van looked up, his father was either staring or pretending not to.

By noon, dessert plates clinked into the sink. Aunt Leslie planned lunch out loud like liturgy. His mother wrestled with a sleeve, already halfway to the door.

"Van," she said, "you're coming home for lunch, right?"

He hesitated. "Actually... I might skip."

"Skip?"

"I told Jeremiah I'd meet him. Quick drive out to the overlook." He made it sound like nothing and meant everything.

His father's head lifted from his coat buttons. "You're what."

"Meeting a friend."

"You mean that pastor's boy," his father said, gravel finding shape.

"Yes, sir."

"Maybe invite him by later—" his mother tried.

"No," his father cut in. "Let the boy eat with his family." *Family* cracked like a whip. "You'll eat where you belong."

"I belong where I'm wanted," Van said, too low and too true.

"Don't start."

"I'm not. I'm just done pretending."

From the kitchen: "Dessert's ready!" as if the world refused to stand still for drama.

"Maybe after lunch—" his mother tried again.

"No, Mama," he said gently. "I'm going."

Emmalee clutched her doll in the doorway. "Where are you going, Van?"

"Out for a bit," he said, crouching. "Keep an eye on Dad for me, okay?"

"I always do," she grinned. He kissed her hair and left before courage had time to reconsider.

The sky had opened to wintry blue. The road to the overlook wound through pines and red clay, sun splintering through bare branches. He cracked the window for a lungful of cold clean air— the kind that wakes you against your will.

Jeremiah's car waited by the railing. He leaned against it, hands buried in his jacket pockets, wind combing his hair. When he saw Van, the small, real smile arrived—like a door that didn't squeak.

"Merry Christmas," Jeremiah said.

"If you say so."

Jeremiah reached into the passenger seat and pulled a small box wrapped in brown paper and twine. "It's not much."

"I doubt that," Van said.

"Open it."

They sat on the hood—metal cold through denim, county quiet spreading to the tree line. Van untied the twine, peeled the paper. A hand-carved wooden box warmed his palm. Inside lay a silver pendant on a leather cord: a treble clef, delicate, bright. It flashed the faintest star when the sun found it.

"I found it at that thrift place in Wilmington," Jeremiah said, rubbing the back of his neck. "Guy said seventies. I don't know. It looked like something you'd wear. Like it already knew your song."

Van didn't feel the first tear until Jeremiah's thumb caught it. "Hey," he said, soft as first light. "You don't have to be okay today."

"I might never be," Van said. "Not fully."

"Then I'll meet you halfway."

Jeremiah tied the cord, fingers careful at Van's nape. The cold made every touch ring like a bell. The pendant settled against his sternum—small, defiant note.

"I didn't get you anything," Van said.

"You showed up," Jeremiah answered. "That counts."

They watched the sky drift toward honey-gold behind the trees. Breath rose like smoke; quiet carried.

"You ever think," Van said, "maybe God doesn't live in churches at all?"

"Maybe He's in the space between people trying to love each other anyway."

"That sounds like something my grandmother would say."

"Then she was probably right."

Van leaned a shoulder into him—just enough to know where warmth was. The last light caught the silver note at his throat. It looked like a star learning to stay.

They didn't say goodbye so much as stand at the same time and know. The drive back would be colder. The house wouldn't be easier. But somewhere between a thrifted note of silver and the way another person stands beside you without asking you to shrink, there was a path that felt like mercy.

Van slid into his car and touched the pendant once, as if it were a compass. "Okay," he whispered to no one and to God and to the woman who still visited his dreams. "I can do this."

The engine turned. Headlights cut a clean lane through the paling day. The world kept being the world—imperfect, unyielding. But the note at his chest kept time with his heart, stubborn and true, and for the length of the road home, that was enough.

HYMNS FOR THE HALF-BELIEVED

The house stirred before the sun—

not all at once, but in small proofs of living: the coffee pot clicking toward a boil, a floorboard telling on someone's heel, the low, domestic sigh of warmth pushing back the night. Van lay still and listened.

Down the hall, Emmalee tried *Away in a Manger* around the new gap in her smile. Half tune, half wind—still enough to soften the room. Light seeped beneath his door, gold as memory. Other years that light had meant cocoa and his grandmother's laugh about paint-stripping coffee, his father pretending to hate carols while tapping along anyway. This morning it made him feel like a guest in a house with his name on the mail.

"Van?" his mother called, the old clipped-not-cruel voice. "We're supposed to be at David and Leslie's by eight. Don't make me come down there."

He dressed slow. The green sweater from last Christmas— *brings out the gold in your hair*, his grandmother had said—still held the ghost of lavender and starch. In the kitchen, cinnamon braided with bacon. His mother wiped a clean counter. His father studied the sports page without reading. Emmalee spun in a red dress that made its own weather.

"Morning," Van said.

"Morning," his mother answered, a smile drafted for photo frames. His father: "We leave by seven-thirty." No one asked if he slept.

The drive ran on AM 540's sermon about joy that sounded more like a bill come due. Frost feathered the glass. Fields went by in long pale ribs. Everyone in the car seemed to be taking careful breaths, as if the air could break.

Aunt Leslie's house gleamed by the rules. Garland disciplined to symmetry, candles set at obedient intervals, poinsettias stationed like polite soldiers. "Y'all made it," she said, as if punctuality were a sacrament. She kissed his mother, dusted herself with Em's glitter, and told Van he looked taller or thinner—"I can't tell."

At the table, Uncle David folded his hands as if guarding a secret. The cousins whispered. The chair at the far end—the one his grandmother used to fill with cardiganed warmth—held a poinsettia on its seat, petals already curling. The prayer ran long enough to lap itself, gratitude widening to include weather and "unity in our household." At that, something in Van pulled tight.

Plates moved. Words became static. "Still in choir?" Aunt Leslie asked.

"Yes, ma'am."

"Wonderful to see a young man using his voice for the Lord. We need more of that—for the right reasons." The smile had sugar in it and a little sermon.

Under the table, his mother's fingers closed around his knee— *let it go.* He did. Emmalee rescued them anyway. "I'm gonna sing too," she announced. "Van teaches me."

"Right," he said, and for a beat his own voice felt like a place to stand.

After dishes, he slipped to the porch. Air bit clean. Trees wrote their bare hands against pewter sky. Somewhere a neighbor burned oak, and the smoke stitched its way into his coat. From the dining room came laughter that didn't bend much; Aunt Leslie's crystal voice directed seconds like traffic.

Grandma, you'd hate this silence, he thought, and then—because hope was a habit she'd taught him—*or you'd fill it.*

The screen door rasped. Em padded out in socked feet, carrying a cookie like contraband. "You hiding?"

"Maybe a little."

"I don't like raisins," she said, giving him the cookie without ceremony.

"Brave choice," he said. They watched winter breathe through the yard.

"Do you think Grandma can see us?" she asked.

"Yeah," he said, swallowing. "She would've liked your dress."

"She'd say it's too fancy for breakfast."

"Then you'd tell her I picked it."

Em grinned. "Yeah."

Down the block, bells wandered into an almost-hymn, a half-minute late to the hour. The sound moved through the cold like something honest. Van leaned on the rail and whispered the line his grandmother used when days were heavy: "Even a cracked bell can call you home."

By the time pies were scraped clean and small talk thinned to polite echoes, his nerves felt worn to thread. "We should head home," his mother said, practical as a list. "The roast will be ready at two."

"I might skip lunch," Van said lightly, as if it were nothing. "Dana mentioned people dropping by." Half-true. Harmless sounding.

His father looked up. "You'll eat with your family. Christmas is about family."

"I did," Van said. "Twice, if breakfast counts."

Chairs breathed. Aunt Leslie realigned napkins. Uncle David found a cough. His mother gave him a look with hurt braided into warning. His father's fork clicked hard against porcelain and then, after a beat, he said, "You can do what you want." The tone made permission feel like a door closing.

Van folded his napkin. "Thanks for breakfast," he told Aunt Leslie—relief flashed across her face, grateful for a sentence she could nod at.

Outside, the air did what air is supposed to do. He sat in his car until his heartbeat climbed down from its rung. The cracked bells down the street kept ringing themselves right, late and loyal. *Sometimes leaving's not rebellion, baby. It's protection,* he heard in his grandmother's voice. He left.

The back roads toward Stillwater Creek curled like old thoughts you can't rush. Patches of snow sulked in ditch shade. The radio floated in and out of a station where carols sounded like they'd been recorded under quilts.

Jeremiah's truck waited behind the little white chapel. He sat on the tailgate, collar up, breath making scripture in the air. When Van pulled in, that slow, real smile appeared—the kind that didn't pretend to be bigger than it was.

"You made it," Jeremiah said.

"Barely. The roast escaped without me."

"Heroic," Jeremiah said, and the edge in Van's body eased.

They stood too close for friendship and far enough for public, the air between them bright with unsaid things. Snow began the lazy kind of falling, wide flakes deciding on them. Jeremiah reached—careful, ordinary—to brush a flake from Van's sleeve, and did not snatch his hand back.

"Can we—" Jeremiah nodded toward the car. "Hang it?"

The **treble clef pendant** he'd given Van at the overlook sat in Van's palm like a small star that had decided to be metal. "Yeah,"

Van said, and the word carried more than permission. He looped the leather cord over the rearview. It settled there, bright as if it had always belonged.

They slid onto the front seat, doors not quite closed, snow whispering against the roof. For a while they watched the pendant sway itself to stillness. A few kids on bikes cut across the far lot, bundled to the eyebrows, not looking their way.

"You okay?" Jeremiah asked finally.

"Define okay."

"Breathing?"

"Mostly."

"Then that's enough for today."

They didn't kiss. They didn't need to remake the moment they'd already trusted the world with. On this day, this small chapel lot, sitting shoulder to shoulder watching a silver note learn the car's particular gravity felt holy enough.

Van pressed his forehead lightly to the steering wheel. "I don't know what happens next."

"Next is not today's problem," Jeremiah said. "Today we install hope on a string and call it décor."

Van huffed a laugh that almost became a sound like relief. "Okay."

When the snow thickened and the light dipped toward honey-gray, they said the kind of goodbye that isn't a goodbye so much as an agreement to keep arriving. Jeremiah tapped the pendant once—*stay*—and then was gone in a twin trail of taillights.

Van drove home through a town lit up like it believed itself. Window strands blinked in slow motion, reds bleeding into greens on the glass. He parked and let the engine tick itself cool, watching the living room tree blink against the windowpane. Inside, shadows crossed—the shape of his father's shoulders, his mother folding a dish towel small. Emmalee laughed somewhere deeper in the house.

He touched the pendant with his thumb. "Okay," he said, to the note, to the air, to the woman who'd taught him how to listen between sounds. "I can do this."

He turned the key. Headlights faded. Snow kept doing what snow does—covering the tracks behind him as if the day itself believed in mercy and resets.

"Every generation rewrites the same prayer, hoping this time it'll be answered with gentleness."

THE MORNING AFTER GRACE

*H*e dreamed warmth that wasn't real.

The living room that always smelled a little like lemon oil and something baking even when nothing was. Perry Mason doing its grayscale hum. His grandmother's floral chair and its wooden arms worn smooth by elbows and prayer. The soft click of knitting needles keeping time with the judge's gavel. He was ten again, knees under his chin, small enough to fit in the curve of things.

"You look tired, baby," she said, the way people ask when they already know.

"I am."

"You been carrying too much again." She touched his hair. "You don't have to prove you're worth loving. Stop running from who you already are."

He tried to answer, but the picture rolled. The sound thinned like wind through blinds. Her hand lifted away first, then her voice, and then—

"Van?"

Waking. Cold breath in his room, December thin. Coffee brewed. His father's aftershave too clean for the hour. His mother sat on the edge of his bed, hands folded; her hair already done—the first sign of a hard conversation. His father stood in the doorway, arms folded like the frame needed help.

"Morning," his mother said, too even. "We wanted to talk before the day gets going."

Talk meant something else. It always had.

He saw where he'd tucked the box from last night—empty now, the pendant safe on the rearview. He sat up, bones aware of themselves. "What time is it?"

"Early," she said. "We didn't sleep."

His father cleared his throat. "We've been making plans."

Warning gathered behind Van's ribs. "For what."

"For help," his mother said quickly. "Pastor Rich is back tomorrow. Lane's available tonight. They'll pray with us, lay out next steps. There's a men's retreat in the mountains right after New Year's—good counselors, accountability, structure."

The word *mountains* dropped like a coin in a deep glass.

"We already talked about this," Van said, voice hoarse. "Before Christmas. I told you no."

"You're young," his mother said, soft like a bruise. "Grief makes people lose their footing. We can find it again together."

"I didn't slip," he said. "I stood up."

His father stepped in, shadow shifting on the carpet. "God fixes anything a man will let Him fix."

"I talked to God," Van said. "For months. I tried to pray it away until I couldn't stand. He didn't change me. Maybe because He made me right."

"Watch your tone," his father snapped, reflex hard as oak.

Van flinched and then didn't. "Stop calling it confusion. Stop calling me a problem you can outsource to the woods."

"It's not punishment," his father said. "It's direction."

"It's conversion," Van answered flatly.

Silence spread thin enough to see the seams of it. The clock in the kitchen took on the sound of a metronome Mrs.

Whitaker would love. Van slid his legs out of the covers and found the floor with his feet. Cold woke him the rest of the way.

His mother stood, adjusting herself into the doorway without quite blocking it. "Please don't make this harder than it has to be."

"Harder than being told your love is a disease with a zip code?" Van's voice cracked and re-formed. "You keep acting like God's love is a bandage. You're using it like a blade."

"Van," she whispered, the kind of whisper that wants to pull everything back into the box.

A small voice behind them: "What's going on?" Emmalee— Disney robe, hair a storm cloud, doll by the arm. Her eyes were too big for the hallway.

"Get your bath for church, sweetheart," their father said, too fast. "Go on."

"But—"

"Now," sharper.

She looked at Van. He lowered himself to her height, the room easing around the simple act. "You're gonna have so much fun today," he said. "Mini-golf in the fellowship hall? Arcade? Save me some tickets."

She frowned. "Are you mad?"

"No," he said, making it true for a second. "Just grown-up stuff."

She didn't buy it, not fully, but she took the folded five he slipped her and let the ritual ease her face. "Thanks," she whispered. "Love you."

"Love you more," he said, and meant it until it hurt.

When she padded away, Van stood again. His mother's lip trembled. His father's jaw set. From the living room, the tree did its patient blinking—red to green to gold to red—like time won't be hurried.

"You can meet with Pastor Rich," Van said, voice steadier. "If that helps you. But that's your plan. Mine is... not that. I'm not confused. I'm not ashamed. I'm not going to a place that tells me to be."

His mother blinked when he said, "I already talked to God. And Grandma still listens." As if two kinds of listening couldn't both be true.

His father stepped closer, a hand lifting like it might find his shoulder or the doorframe—Van didn't wait to learn which. He took his jacket from its peg, his keys from the bowl, the treble clef on the ring nicking light. His mother's voice tried to catch him. "Van, wait—We're not finished."

He turned at the threshold. "Neither am I."

The cold outside felt like a statement. Sun snagged on last night's thin crust of snow. Somewhere down the hall behind him, Emmalee started *Joy to the World,* each word a little lantern. It put a hurt under his ribs.

In the car, he let the heater cough itself warm. Through the window, he could see his mother's shoulders fold; his father became the shape of a man refusing to sit down. Van set both hands on the wheel and whispered, "Don't let me break." He wasn't sure if he meant himself or all of them.

He backed out slow, tires grinding old ice. The radio found a hymn without asking—*Come, Thou long-expected Jesus*—and for once he didn't argue with the irony. Expected nowhere, he drove toward the only place that had ever made sense and not, all at the same time.

He drove toward the church.

"Some storms don't break things. They reveal what was never nailed down."

THE SANCTUARY OF DUST AND LIGHT

Heritage Baptist smelled like dust and evergreen—the kind that settles into hymnals and refuses to leave even after the calendar turns. Afternoon light fell through stained glass and lay across the carpet in slow colors: cobalt, wine, a honeyed gold that made the dust look briefly holy.

Dana stood on a step stool with a string of garland and a losing argument. "If one more person tells me to 'straighten it out,' I'll straighten them out."

Avery drifted past in a choir robe he wore like a cape, a box of spent, wax-scalloped candles in his arms. "Reverence, saints. This is the Lord's tinsel."

"You've said that three times," Van called from the communion table, where he was coaxing a velvet ribbon into a bow around a pillar candle rescued from Christmas Eve.

"And I'll say it a fourth," Avery replied without breaking stride. "Artistry is repetition with better lighting."

The sanctuary hummed with small obediences: robe fabric whispering, a metal ladder grazing wood, a vacuum muttering then giving up. Someone at the sound board tested a track; *O*

Come, All Ye Faithful wobbled out of tired speakers like a home movie.

Van straightened a poinsettia that preferred its own direction. His hands trembled—not from cold. The last two days had been too crowded: his father's silence that felt like a verdict, his mother's half-smiles stitched to hold, Lane's new way of looking at him as if he were a project that had gone wrong at the factory.

Lane stood near the pulpit with a clipboard, conferring with a deacon about Sunday's order. When he called Van's name, it wasn't unkind. It had that careful tone people use when the decision already happened in a meeting you weren't invited to.

"Hey, Van—got a minute?"

Van brushed wax from his fingers and crossed the aisle. Pine and candle smoke rose as he moved.

"I wanted to touch base for the next few weeks," Lane said, polite smile snug as a tie. "You've led really well this fall. But I've been praying about direction, and I think it's wise to give you a breather from up-front roles—testimony night, small ensemble rotation, that kind of thing. Just a short reset."

Van blinked. "A reset."

"Yeah," Lane said, voice warmed to pastoral. "Not about talent. It's about guarding witness. After the holidays, people look for… clarity. We want the right heart leading the room."

There it was, the unsaid thing wearing church clothes.

Van nodded once, eyes on the varnish that showed the room in broken reflections. "Right. Heart."

"I know that's disappointing," Lane continued, gentling his tone like he was bringing a skittish animal to water. "Sometimes God redirects us to refine us. You understand."

Van's throat tightened and then steadied. "Actually," he said quietly, "I do."

Relief glanced across Lane's face. Lesson landed, paperwork filed. "Good, good. That's all I wanted to share."

Van turned down the aisle, walked three pews, and then

turned back. Light made a mosaic of his shoes. "Lane—can I ask you something?"

"Of course."

"If the church says 'come as you are,' why does it only mean *come as you are* until you find out who I am?"

Lane opened his mouth. The air between them waited. Nothing came out that would help.

Van didn't wait for what wouldn't arrive. He stepped into the narthex and then outside, where the air had that clean, blue edge. The sky was slipping toward evening; the stained glass behind him held its colors like a breath. From inside, a muffled *Silent Night* began as the youth choir warmed up without him.

He walked around back where the field sloped toward the creek and the holly bushes kept their red like a secret. Frost outlined each blade of grass in glassy grammar. He stood there until his breath made its small bright ghosts.

The door hinges breathed. "Hey," Jeremiah said, voice low, sure.

"You shouldn't be out here," Van said, not turning yet.

"Neither should you," Jeremiah answered, shoes crunching until he stood beside him. "It's freezing."

"Feels honest."

"What happened?"

"Lane," Van said. He offered the shape of the conversation: the friendly exile, the way *guarding witness* could mean *sit down,* how blessing could be made to sound like a benching.

Jeremiah's jaw tightened, then loosened. "You did nothing wrong."

"I know," Van said, watching his breath vanish. "It still feels like I did."

Jeremiah hesitated only long enough to be careful. His fingers found Van's sleeve and rested there, warm through the fabric. "They don't get to decide who you are. Not anymore."

"They think God's disappointed in me."

"Then they've forgotten who God is."

Inside the wall, the choir reached *sleep in heavenly peace*—thin through plaster, still somehow enough.

Van closed his eyes. "Sometimes I wish faith were easier."

"Maybe it's not meant to be easy," Jeremiah said, breath fogging between them. "Maybe it's meant to make us brave."

They stood with the wind pulling at their jackets, the world briefly small and exact. When Van finally turned, Jeremiah gave him the kind of smile that doesn't promise—only stays.

"Come on," Jeremiah said. "Before you turn into a choir-cicle."

"You first," Van said, and almost smiled.

They walked back toward the spill of light, their shadows long and sensible across the frost. Inside, someone struck the opening chord again—*Christ the Savior is born.* For the first time, Van didn't mouth the words. He let the room carry them without borrowing his throat.

AND HE LISTENED

The church was different after everyone left.

Still holy, maybe — but not in the way the sermons described. It was the kind of holy that came from emptiness, from the echoes that lingered when sound had already gone.

The air inside Heritage Baptist smelled like dust and evergreen — that quiet, stale sweetness that sank into hymnals and never left. The heat had kicked off hours ago, and the temperature had settled into that deep winter stillness that made wood creak and breath bloom white.

Van stood in the back doorway for a moment, watching the light pool through the stained glass. The afternoon sun had dropped low enough that the windows painted the air in slow colors: cobalt, burgundy, and the softest amber — a light that made the dust itself shimmer, as though the world had forgotten to stop being beautiful.

He walked down the aisle slowly, fingertips brushing the tops of pews. The varnish was worn smooth where years of hands had rested. He could almost see them — the congregation that filled this place week after week, bowing, murmuring, believing.

He envied how simple it looked when they did it.

Every echo sounded alive here: the faint buzz of the exit sign, the heater's sigh through the vents, the soft groan of the pulpit settling in the cold. Somewhere in the darkened choir loft, a single bulb flickered, throwing long shadows across the baptistry.

When he reached the front, Van stopped beside the communion table. A stray poinsettia leaned too far over the edge, its petals browned and curling inward. He set it upright, careful not to crush the stem. Small gestures mattered here. They had to.

He sat down on the front pew and let the silence press around him. His hands twined together out of habit, but the movement felt clumsy.

He hadn't prayed since Christmas Eve — not really. Not the kind of prayer his grandmother taught him.

When he finally slid from the pew onto his knees, it wasn't graceful. His jeans caught on the edge of the wood, and the carpet's roughness bit against his skin. He leaned forward until his forehead almost brushed the rail.

"Hey," he said softly. "It's me again."

His voice cracked the silence, too thin to stay steady.

The words hung there and fell flat. He cleared his throat.

"I don't really know what I'm doing anymore," he whispered. "I keep trying to be what they said was good. But every time I try, I feel less like myself and more like a story someone else wrote for me."

The air seemed to shift with each word. Not in any magical way — just the kind of stillness that made you notice your own heartbeat.

He glanced up toward the stained glass — toward the figure of the shepherd holding his staff, the blues so deep they looked wet. His grandmother used to sit right below that window. She'd called that shepherd *her proof.*

Said she liked knowing someone was out there looking for the lost things.

"I think about Grandma a lot lately," he said. His breath rose in small, ghostly wisps. "How she prayed for everybody — even the people she was mad at. How she made forgiveness look like something you could hold."

He laughed once, short and shaky. "I miss her so much it aches in places I didn't know could ache. I wish she were here to tell me I'm not crazy. To tell me I can love You and still be… me."

His voice trailed off, but the building creaked like it was answering — wood expanding, air shifting. Somewhere near the side door, a draft found its way through and made the garland sway.

The bulb above him flickered twice, then steadied again.

"I know the verses," Van whispered. "I know what they'll say. I know how they'll say it. But what if I'm not broken? What if I was made this way on purpose? What if You knew and loved me anyway? What if You always did?"

He paused, hands pressed tight together until his knuckles went pale. His eyes burned, but he didn't wipe them. "I don't want to fight You. I just don't want to disappear trying to please everyone else. If there's something in me that You hate, I don't understand why You'd make it so full of love."

The sanctuary held its breath.

He thought of his grandmother again — how, one Christmas Eve long ago, she'd stayed behind after service to blow out the candles. He'd been nine. He remembered asking her why she didn't let them burn out on their own.

She'd smiled and said, *"Even the light deserves to rest before it goes out."*

That memory rose now, soft as the flicker of those old candles. He could almost smell her perfume — faint rose powder mixed with peppermint. He turned his head slightly, and for a second, he swore he caught a shimmer of light bend toward him.

He didn't move. Didn't speak. Just let it be.

"If this is You," he whispered, "don't speak. Just stay. That's enough."

He stayed like that — hands folded, forehead pressed to his arm — until the ache in his knees became part of the prayer itself.

The wind outside picked up, making the stained glass hum faintly. The colors shifted — gold bleeding into blue, blue into crimson. One beam stretched across the floor and landed on his shoulder. He didn't know what that meant, but he felt it.

When he finally opened his eyes, the air looked different. Not brighter, just steadier. The kind of light that didn't demand to be noticed, only accepted.

He stood slowly, brushing dust from his jeans, and looked around. The sanctuary had gone half-dark — only the tree near the baptistry still glowed. Half its lights had gone out, but the rest blinked stubbornly on.

Van walked over and adjusted one of the wires. The strand steadied, burning soft and even.

"Guess You're not done yet," he murmured.

He reached for one of the unlit candles sitting on the communion table — small, white, its wick still clean — and set it in the brass offering plate. He didn't light it. Just left it there, a quiet gesture of something unfinished.

As he started down the aisle, he trailed a hand along the pews again. Each step felt heavier and freer at once.

By the time he reached the door, the church had gone completely still.

He turned once more toward the cross above the baptistry. Its wood caught the last bit of the light, glowing faint and old and steady.

"Okay," he said softly. "If You're still here, I'll stay too."

He pushed the door open, and the night greeted him — sharp, pine-scented, alive.

Outside, frost was settling along the steps, catching bits of light like scattered glass. He stopped there, just breathing, letting the cold undo him a little.

From somewhere down the hall, a faint hum floated through

the walls — someone in the choir room humming "O Holy Night," off-key and half-asleep. The sound was imperfect, human, beautiful for it.

Van smiled. Not because he believed everything would be fine, but because maybe it didn't have to be tonight.

He brushed his hand along the doorframe one last time and whispered, "Merry Christmas."

It was meant for his grandmother. For God. Maybe for himself.

Then he stepped into the dark, where the air smelled of pine and wax and the fragile promise that something could still grow in the cold.

WOULD you like me to add a **short reflective transition paragraph** at the end — Van driving home under the Christmas lights, setting up the emotional tone shift that leads into Chapter 13 ("The Quiet Between Years")?

It would bridge this quiet, sacred solitude into the returning tension of the home scenes beautifully.

THE NIGHT WRAPPED around him like something almost kind.

The parking lot was empty now, the asphalt glossed with frost and the orange halo of streetlights. His breath hung in front of him, silver and soft.

When he reached his car, the metal was cold beneath his fingers. He sat for a moment before starting the engine, watching his reflection in the dark glass — the faint outline of his face caught between the lights of the church behind him and the night ahead.

When he turned the key, the heater coughed awake, humming low like it was remembering how to breathe. The radio came alive with static before finding a station. A man's voice was reading the Gospel of Luke, the Christmas story one more time, his tone tired but tender.

Van let it play, though he didn't listen to the words. He just watched the church through the windshield — the faint glow of stained glass, the flicker of the Christmas tree inside, still blinking steady.

As he pulled out of the lot, the tires crunched over ice. The town was quiet — windows glowing with the kind of yellow light that made everything look smaller, safer, unreachable.

He passed the diner where he worked, its neon sign buzzing faintly in the cold. The "E" in *Coffee* still flickered — it had for years — but he'd always liked it that way. Imperfect. Honest.

A few blocks later, he slowed as he turned down his street. The houses wore their decorations like reminders: wreaths leaning, strings of lights drooping, blow-up Santas half-deflated but still trying.

In his mother's window, the tree glowed warm and steady, the angel on top tilting slightly to one side.

Van parked at the curb and sat with the engine running, the heater rattling, his hands still around the steering wheel. The church lights were far behind him now, but the peace of that silence — fragile and flickering — hadn't gone out.

He whispered, "Thank You," though he wasn't sure to whom. Maybe that was the point.

Outside, a single snowflake drifted onto the windshield and melted in the warmth of the glass. He watched it fade to nothing and thought —

Maybe that's how grace works. Quiet. Ordinary. Enough.

Then he turned off the car, stepped into the night, and walked toward home.

THE QUIET BETWEEN YEARS

The week after Christmas always felt like a ghost — not gone, just quieter.

The streets were half-empty, the wreaths on doors turning brittle, lights still glowing even though no one was looking at them anymore. Time itself seemed to hesitate, unsure if it should move forward or wait for permission.

Van woke late most mornings, sunlight slicing thin across his room, catching on the dust that hung in the air. The house smelled faintly of leftover pine and reheated casseroles. His mother had stopped playing Christmas music, though sometimes he caught her humming the tunes anyway — the sound more habit than joy.

In the living room, the tree still stood. Its needles had begun to fall, leaving tiny green reminders scattered like confetti across the rug. His father kept threatening to take it down but never did. It felt like no one wanted to be the one to end the season, as if doing so would make the silence afterward too sharp to bear.

Van sat on the couch one afternoon, thumbing through a hymnal his grandmother had left him — the one with her name scribbled inside the cover in blue pen. She'd circled verses and written notes in the margins: *for strength, for patience, for Van.*

He smiled at the last one, though it made his throat tighten.

From the kitchen came the familiar click of his mother's heels on the linoleum. "You working today?" she asked, not looking up from the sink.

"Yeah," Van said. "Double shift."

She nodded, drying her hands on a towel. "That diner'll wear you out."

"It's not so bad," he said. "The jukebox works again."

That got the smallest smile from her — real, tired, and gone before it could stay. "Be careful driving. The roads are slick."

He nodded. "Yes, ma'am."

From the recliner, his father grunted without looking away from the TV. The sound wasn't approval, but it wasn't argument either.

Van took it for peace — or something near enough to pass.

THE DINER SAT on the edge of town, tucked between a shuttered hardware store and a car wash that hadn't worked since summer. Its windows fogged with every cup poured, the smell of bacon grease and coffee permanent as wallpaper.

Inside, time didn't move so much as hum quietly in place.

Van had been working there since summer — part-time during school, full-time on breaks. His boss, Doris, was the kind of woman who said grace over her cigarettes and meant it. She ran the place like a confessional: everyone came in needing something, and she knew exactly when to listen and when to tell them to hush and eat their pie.

"Morning, preacher boy," she said when he clocked in. "You ready for the post-holiday hangover crowd?"

Van tied his apron. "As ready as anyone can be for coffee refills and regret."

"That's the spirit." She smirked. "Table three wants extra syrup. Don't argue theology about it."

By noon, the diner filled with the usual chorus — spoons clinking, boots scraping, Doris shouting orders through the pass-through window. The radio played old hits just a hair off frequency.

Van moved between tables like muscle memory, pouring, clearing, smiling when he needed to.

When the bell over the door jingled, he looked up and found Dana and Avery sliding into a booth like they owned it.

"Well, if it isn't Saint Van of the Short Order," Avery said, draping his scarf dramatically over the seat. "Does this establishment serve anything besides existential dread and bad coffee?"

"Just the dread," Van said. "The coffee's extra."

Dana rolled her eyes, grinning. "He's been like this all morning. He needs fries and salvation."

"Fries I can do," Van said, scribbling on his pad. "Salvation's management's department."

"Tell Doris I'm open to either," Avery said, then lowered his voice. "Also, there's a very attractive man working the fryer. Does he come with the combo meal?"

Van smirked. "He's seventeen and has a tattoo that says *Born to Fry*. Pretty sure that's not what you think it means."

"Tragic," Avery said, sighing. "God gives with one hand, burns with the other."

Dana snorted soda through her straw, coughing. "Avery, for the love of—"

"What? I'm appreciating local art," Avery said. "Support small business."

Van shook his head, biting back a laugh as he walked away to place their order.

It struck him how different the world felt when he was with them — brighter, looser, easier to breathe in. Avery's flamboyant ease, Dana's dry wit — they filled the air with life, the kind that didn't apologize for existing.

From behind the counter, he could see them still talking, heads leaned together over the Formica table, light catching in Avery's hair like static. They were both laughing again — a sound too big for the diner, but nobody minded.

Doris leaned on the counter beside him, watching them too. "Your friends are loud."

"They tip well," Van said.

She smirked. "Good answer."

THE AFTERNOON SLID by in syrup and steam. When his shift ended, Dana and Avery were still there, picking at cold fries and arguing over whether Mariah Carey should be considered a Christmas prophet.

"You closing?" Dana asked.

"Half hour," Van said. "You two need a ride?"

"We took the bus," Avery said, dramatic sigh included. "Because apparently Dana thinks we're poor."

"I think," Dana said, "that Avery shouldn't drive after last night's punch bowl."

"I had two glasses!"

"You had five and called the snowman 'Daddy Frost.'"

Van choked on a laugh. "I'm not sure I want to know."

"No one does," Dana said flatly.

Avery put a hand to his chest. "It was performance art."

Van grabbed his jacket. "I'm heading out. You coming to the mall tomorrow?"

Dana perked up. "You mean the glorious after-Christmas clearance pilgrimage? Of course. I need new boots."

"And I," Avery said, "need to bask in the radiant glow of boys who work in the food court. It's practically religious."

Van grinned. "I'll meet you there."

"Bring a flask," Dana said. "It's our only defense."

THE NEXT AFTERNOON, the mall looked like someone had shaken a snow globe and forgotten to stop. Glitter, sale signs, half-dead garland, and the faint electric hum of too many fluorescent lights. It smelled like cinnamon pretzels, bad cologne, and nostalgia.

Van found Dana and Avery in the food court, seated beneath a fake palm tree and a blinking sign that said *Taste the Season*. Avery was stirring his lemonade like it had offended him. Dana was halfway through a slice of pizza that defied physics.

"Behold," Avery said when Van arrived, "the temple of consumer despair."

Dana grinned. "He's been like this since Claire's closed."

Avery placed a hand on his chest. "It was the only place in this godforsaken town that understood my aesthetic."

Van laughed and sat. "You could always try Hot Topic."

"I did," Avery said solemnly. "They feared me."

A group of teenage boys in matching mall uniforms passed by — khaki pants, name tags, the whole thing. One of them, tall and sharp-jawed, laughed a little too loud at something, brushing his friend's shoulder as they walked.

Avery's eyes followed them openly. "Well, Merry Christmas to me."

Dana snorted. "You're ridiculous."

"And observant," Avery said. "The Lord works in mysterious hotness."

Van tried not to smile too wide, but couldn't help it. The ease of it — the freedom in Avery's lack of pretense — hit something deep in him.

He wanted to be that unguarded. To look without scanning the room first.

Dana leaned over. "You okay?"

"Yeah," Van said, pulling his attention back. "Just thinking."

"Dangerous hobby," she said.

Avery perked up. "About what?"

Van hesitated. "About how some people just get to be themselves."

Avery's smile softened. "And some of us are learning."

It wasn't heavy when he said it — just true.

They spent the rest of the afternoon wandering stores, trying on hats they couldn't afford, taking Polaroids in the photo booth until the strip jammed. For a few hours, Van forgot how much he was holding inside.

He even laughed — really laughed — when Avery managed to knock over an entire rack of scarves and declared it "performance rebellion."

It felt like breathing again.

THAT NIGHT, at home, the air had cooled back into the quiet that lived between holidays. His parents were in the living room — his father reading the paper, his mother folding laundry with a precision that looked like penance.

"You were gone late," his father said, not looking up.

"Mall with friends."

His mother smiled faintly. "Did you find anything?"

"Just trouble," Van said, and she laughed — a real laugh, surprised out of her.

It startled both of them. His father looked up, his mother's smile fading as quickly as it came. The silence that followed wasn't sharp this time — just tired.

She brushed a strand of hair behind her ear. "I'm making coffee. You want some?"

"Sure," Van said, but he knew it wasn't about coffee. It was her peace offering — the ritual that stood where words failed.

As she moved to the kitchen, his father folded the newspaper with a sigh. "We spoke to Pastor Rich this morning," he said. "He wants to come by this week. Says it'd be good to talk."

Van exhaled slowly. "About me, I'm guessing."

His father didn't answer. He didn't need to.

"Dad," Van said, tone steady but not cruel, "I'm not doing another sermon in the living room."

His mother returned then, setting a mug on the table between them. "That's enough," she said quietly.

His father frowned. "I'm just saying—"

"I know what you're saying," she cut in, her voice tighter now. "And maybe you can give it a rest for one night."

The surprise of it filled the room like heat from a struck match. She turned to Van, her tone softening. "Drink your coffee before it gets cold."

He nodded, grateful and aching all at once.

As the house settled into its uneasy peace, Van sat by the window. Outside, the last of the Christmas lights blinked along the neighboring houses, soft and tired. Somewhere, a dog barked once and fell silent again.

The calendar on the wall still read December, though the days were already running out. He traced the edge of the page, wondering what the new year would even mean.

Somewhere deep inside, he hoped it might mean *becoming*.

"There's no sound quite like truth hitting a wall of fear."

THE FIRST SUNDAY OF AFTERWARDS

The last morning of the year came quiet — the kind of quiet that held its breath.

The sky was pale and patient, a soft gray stretched thin over the rooftops. Frost covered the yard like sugar, and the trees stood still against it, thin and waiting, as if they too were listening for something that hadn't yet been said.

Van started the car while the air still carried its bite, the heater coughing to life with a low hum. His breath fogged the windshield before the vents chased it away. He rubbed his palms together, not for warmth but to keep his nerves from showing.

Footsteps thudded on the porch — quick, uneven, familiar.

Emmalee came bounding down, her scarf half-tied, the bow in her hair already slipping sideways. She held her Bible to her chest like it might fly away.

"Can I ride with you?" she asked, breath puffing out in clouds.

Van smiled. "You don't want to ride with Mom and Dad?"

She wrinkled her nose. "They talk too serious. And you play better music."

Their mother stepped into the doorway, coffee cup in hand, eyes soft but guarded. "That's fine," she said. "We'll see you there."

Their father adjusted his collar, nodding once before following her inside. His silence carried down the porch steps, lingering even after the door closed.

Emmalee slid into the passenger seat, kicking her boots against the mat. "Can we listen to something happy?"

Van turned the dial until static gave way to a soft country song about home and heartache — the kind that didn't pick sides. "That happy enough?"

She grinned. "Close."

THE ROAD WOUND through frosted fields, pale and endless. The car heater buzzed, filling the silence with its steady hum. Outside, the light grew brighter — all soft golds and gray mist rising from the ground.

Emmalee pressed her mitten to the glass, tracing crooked stars into the fog her breath left behind. "It's funny," she said after a minute, "how everyone dresses up for church even though God already saw us in our pajamas."

Van laughed quietly. "Maybe He likes surprises."

"Or maybe He likes pajamas better."

He smiled. "You might be right."

They passed through town square — storefronts still half-decorated, wreaths drooping, a faded banner clinging to a lamp-post that said *Merry Christmas* even though Christmas was already gone. The radio crackled as a DJ talked about resolutions, fireworks, and the promise of starting over. Van turned it down.

Emmalee kicked her feet lightly, then said, "Can I tell you something? Or maybe ask you something?"

"Sure."

She picked at a loose string on her mitten. "I heard Mom and Dad talking about you one night. I wasn't supposed to, but I was in the hallway getting my blanket off the couch. They didn't see me 'cause they were sitting in the kitchen with the light over the stove. Mom had her tea — the chipped cup — and Dad was reading the paper even though he wasn't really reading it. He was doing that thing where he stares at it but doesn't turn the page."

Van's grip on the steering wheel tightened. "What were they saying?"

She took a breath, watching the trees blur past. "They said you were… different. That maybe you liked boys instead of girls. Mom said it like she was sad, and Dad said it like it was heavy. Then Mom told him to stop, and he said something about it not being right, and she told him he didn't even know what right was anymore."

She nodded solemnly, as if replaying it perfectly. "Then it got real quiet. I could only hear the fridge buzzing."

Van's chest ached. "And what did you think?"

"I thought it was weird," she said honestly. "They talk about love all the time — that it fixes things, that it's what makes God happy. So why whisper about it like it's bad?" She glanced over at him. "They whisper loud, you know."

He smiled softly, eyes on the road. "Yeah, they do."

She was quiet a moment, then said, "So… what does *gay* mean?"

Van blinked, searching for words that wouldn't break her small, trusting world. "Well," he said finally, "you know how in stories, sometimes the princess falls in love with the prince?"

"Yeah."

"Sometimes," he said, "the story just changes. Maybe it's two princes, or two princesses. Or maybe it's just two people who see each other and think, *you make the world less lonely.* It's still love, Em. Still magic. Just written a little differently."

She tilted her head, considering. "So, like a fairy tale remix?"

Van laughed quietly. "Exactly. Same song, just a new verse."

"That doesn't sound bad," she said.

"It isn't."

She looked out the window again, thoughtful. "Then why do people whisper about it?"

"Because," Van said softly, "sometimes people forget that love doesn't need their permission."

She nodded slowly, like she understood. "Grandma said God *is* love," she added, "and she never said He was picky."

Van's throat tightened. "Grandma was right."

Emmalee turned toward him, eyes wide and serious. "So if you're that word, then that's fine. I just wanted to know if you'll still love me."

He smiled, voice low. "Always."

"Okay." She nodded once, decisive. "Then I'm happy."

The air in the car shifted — lighter now, softer somehow. Then, as quickly as a child's mind changes course, she brightened. "You know who's nice?"

"Who?"

"Jeremiah," she said instantly. "He always brings hot chocolate for the kids when it's cold. He lets us stir it with the tiny spoons, even though everyone spills it. He helped me find my glove last week too. He said maybe it ran away 'cause my hand was too loud."

She giggled. "He's funny. And he talks to the little kids like they're big kids."

Van smiled, trying to hide the warmth spreading through his chest. "Yeah. That sounds like him."

She nodded. "He's nice to you, too."

Van's voice softened. "Yeah. He is."

"You like him, don't you?" she asked, as easily as if she were asking about ice cream flavors.

He hesitated, then said, "He's my friend."

She looked satisfied. "Good. He's a good one."

She turned back to the window, scarf shifting as she leaned closer to the glass. "Do you think he'll bring hot chocolate tonight?"

"I bet he will."

"Good. Maybe I'll get two cups."

"You always do."

She laughed, high and bright, her joy filling every small corner of the car.

And as they drove, frost glittering along the roadside, Van realized that sometimes grace didn't come as a sermon or a hymn.

Sometimes, it came wearing mittens, with a crooked ribbon in its hair, speaking truth like it was the easiest thing in the world.

THE CHURCH APPEARED over the hill, white steeple cutting through the pale sky. Frost gleamed across the parking lot like crushed glass. The nativity still stood on the lawn, though one of the wise men had toppled face-first into the grass — an oddly fitting metaphor for the year.

Emmalee unbuckled before the car stopped. "Race you to the door!"

"Hey—careful!" Van called, but she was already halfway across the lot, her laughter echoing in the cold.

His parents' car pulled in beside his. Their mother's smile was tight but polite; his father's nod carried the weight of a thousand unspoken expectations.

The church bell rang overhead — deep, imperfect, steady.

Inside, Heritage Baptist glowed with soft, amber light. The air smelled of evergreen and candle wax. Poinsettias drooped beneath their own beauty. People moved like ghosts of celebration — smiles stretched, conversations brief, laughter practiced.

His father's hand found his shoulder. "Pastor Rich wants to see you," he said quietly.

"Now?"

"Better sooner than later."

Pastor Rich stood near the altar, shaking hands and blessing babies, his voice carrying the warmth of someone who'd practiced it long enough to believe it.

Beside him, Jeremiah was stacking hymnals, sleeves rolled to his elbows, hair falling across his brow.

Van's heart stumbled in his chest. Their eyes met for the briefest second — a flicker of recognition, small but grounding.

Then Pastor Rich turned toward Jeremiah, leaning close to whisper something. Jeremiah nodded, quietly setting the last hymnal down before slipping through the side door, disappearing into the hall.

By the time Van reached the front, Pastor Rich's smile was fixed and polished. "Good morning, son," he said. "Haven't seen you since Christmas Eve. The Lord must've missed you."

Van shook his hand. "I've been around."

"Well, I trust you're ready to start the new year right," the pastor said, voice smooth. "We all stumble, but grace gives us another chance."

His father's grip on his shoulder tightened — a silent reminder to stay small.

Van kept his tone even. "I've learned grace doesn't always need someone else to hand it to you."

Pastor Rich's smile faltered, just slightly. "We'll pray on that."

"You do that," Van said softly.

He turned away, scanning the pews until he found Emmalee waving at him, her bow crooked again, her grin unbothered by the tension that had followed him in.

He sat beside her, and she whispered, "Jeremiah said he made extra cocoa for the youth group. I'm getting two cups."

He smiled despite himself. "You always do."

Her laugh chimed like a bell, pure and unashamed.

The organ began to hum the opening chords of a hymn as his mother slipped into the pew behind them, posture perfect, eyes tired.

As the music swelled, Van looked up toward the stained glass — ribbons of blue and red bending across his hands like light finding its way through fracture.

He thought of Emmalee's small voice in the car:

"If you're that word, then that's fine. I just wanna know if you'll still love me."

And then:

"He's nice to you, too... you like him, don't you?"

He smiled faintly. For the first time in weeks, the ache in his chest didn't feel like something to hide — just something human.

The congregation stood. The first notes rose — soft, full, unsteady.

And somewhere between the melody and the silence that followed it, Van whispered under his breath,

"I'm still here."

"Even broken glass can catch light."

WHERE THE NIGHT BREAKS OPEN

By the time the last hymn faded and the organ gave its tired sigh, the air inside Heritage Baptist felt over-filled — too many bodies, too much perfume, too much grace trying to crowd the same space. The new year waited just beyond the frosted glass doors, but no one seemed in a hurry to reach it.

The congregation moved in slow waves toward the vestibule — all wool coats and polite laughter, the soft percussion of hand-shakes and compliments. Every "Happy New Year" came wrapped in the unspoken understanding that most resolutions would dissolve by February.

Van lingered near the back, half-hidden behind the bulletin board that still read *Unto Us a Child Is Born* in glittery gold letters shedding onto the carpet. He crouched as though adjusting his shoelaces, though his attention wasn't on his shoes.

Across the room, Jeremiah stood with his parents beneath the chandelier that buzzed faintly with age. Pastor Rich — crisp, rehearsed, spotless — spoke to a deacon with a tone that could've blessed or condemned with equal polish. Ms. Denise, immaculate in her winter-white coat, offered smiles like benedictions to anyone within reach.

Jeremiah stood between them, hands in his pockets, face easy, posture obedient. He looked like a boy who knew exactly how to survive under scrutiny — steady, kind, safe. Van could see the tiny movements of restraint: the too-measured breath, the jaw unclenching only when his father turned away.

Avery's voice broke Van's focus.

"This punch tastes like bad decisions and powdered sugar," he said, grimacing.

Dana appeared beside him, holding her own paper cup. "That's impressive, considering it's ninety percent ginger ale."

"Maybe they blessed it too hard," Avery muttered.

Van smiled, still half-distracted. "You're terrible."

"I'm observant," Avery corrected. "And so are you. Quit staring before Ms. Denise starts an intercessory prayer circle."

Van looked down, pretending to laugh it off. But when he lifted his eyes again, Jeremiah's gaze had found him across the vestibule. Not a long look — just long enough to say *wait*.

The moment vanished as Pastor Rich turned back toward his son.

THE CONVERSATION between Jeremiah and his parents was a quiet war fought under smiles.

"I was thinking," Pastor Rich began, tone syruped with authority, "you could help us set up the fellowship hall for the midnight service. We'll need strong hands for the tables."

Jeremiah's answer was polite, even. "Actually, some of us from the youth group were going to Avery's. Just snacks, games, nothing wild."

Ms. Denise's eyebrows arched in perfect skepticism. "Avery?" she asked, stirring his name like sugar into suspicion.

"Yes, ma'am," Jeremiah said. "Dana, Colby, Van— a few others."

His father's voice thinned. "Van Shelton?"

The name landed like a dropped hymnbook.

Jeremiah hesitated — just a flicker. "Yeah. He's going. It's a group thing."

Pastor Rich smiled the way people do when they've stopped listening. "I think you'd be better off bringing in the new year with prayer."

Jeremiah's own smile matched his father's, but the meaning was reversed. "Then I'll pray on my way."

Ms. Denise stepped forward, fussing with the collar of his coat, her fingers trembling just slightly. "Be home before one," she said quietly. "And remember, people talk."

He leaned closer, voice low and certain. "They talk anyway, Mom."

For half a second, her mask faltered — fear and pride tangled into something human — then she let him go.

Mrs. Lambert appeared just in time to rescue him. "Pastor Rich!" she said brightly, holding out a tray of leftover fudge. "We just *have* to thank you for that message tonight. You've really blessed us."

He turned, smile snapping neatly into place. "All glory to God, Sister Lambert."

Jeremiah slipped through the small opening like a practiced escape artist.

As he passed Van's table, he didn't look up — just brushed a hand against the edge of the cup sitting there, fingertips glancing Van's knuckles.

"Ten minutes," he murmured.

Then he was gone.

THE NIGHT AIR outside was sharp, the kind that tasted like tin and freedom. The parking lot shimmered under the halogen lights, every car haloed in frost. The faint hum of "Auld Lang Syne" drifted from a passing car radio somewhere down the road.

Van stood on the steps for a moment, hands in his pockets, letting the cold bite through his sleeves. He could still hear his father's laughter echoing faintly inside the church — the way he always sounded most at home behind a pulpit or a conversation about someone else's sins.

Avery appeared, shaking his keys like sleigh bells. "Alright, party caravan departs in five. Get in losers, we're reclaiming New Year's Eve."

Dana rolled her eyes. "You're not Regina George."

"I'm the Baptist version," he said. "Less pink, more trauma."

They piled into cars — too many people, too much noise, the familiar chaos of kids desperate to feel older than they were. Someone cranked the radio to a pop station. Someone else unwrapped candy that immediately got passed around like communion.

Van drove, his sister's old car rattling at every stoplight. He watched the town slip by — closed diners, blinking stoplights, storefronts dark except for the glow of plastic nativity scenes. Briar Hollow in winter had a kind of tired beauty; the kind that belonged to places that kept their secrets well.

He thought of Jeremiah in the vestibule light, the quiet defiance in his voice when he said *Then I'll pray on my way.*

He didn't realize he was smiling until Dana elbowed him lightly. "Whatever that is," she said, "you're thinking about it too hard."

AVERY'S BASEMENT smelled faintly of popcorn, Pine-Sol, and the ghosts of old sleepovers. Christmas lights looped the ceiling like a half-finished halo. Someone had dragged the couch from the den, and the floor was a quilt of mismatched rugs.

Colby was in charge of music, which meant it sounded like a 1999 skating rink — loud, nostalgic, slightly terrible. Dana was pouring off-brand cola into Solo cups. Avery, naturally, was orchestrating chaos.

"Welcome to the sacred space," he declared, gesturing wide. "Leave your inhibitions and parental approval at the door."

"You're such a drama major," Dana said.

"I prefer prophet," he replied. "Now: who wants to embarrass themselves first?"

The room filled with laughter, the kind that made the walls feel closer in a good way.

When Jeremiah arrived, his coat half-buttoned and cheeks pink from the cold, Van felt the air change. Not dramatically — just that quiet tilt of the world when someone you've been waiting for walks into it.

Jeremiah found Van instantly. He didn't smile big, didn't wave — just a small lift of the corner of his mouth that said *I made it.*

Van's own grin was small but couldn't be helped.

Avery clapped his hands. "Alright, saints and sinners, it's almost midnight. And the Holy Spirit demands entertainment. Truth or Dare!"

Groans, cheers, mock prayers. Someone dimmed the lights. The heater clicked on with a groan.

The air shifted — warmer, closer, filled with the soft electricity of being almost grown.

They formed the circle. The bottle waited in the center, gleaming under Christmas lights like a sermon wrapped in glass.

The first few rounds were harmless — laughter, inside jokes, Avery's endless one-liners. Dana dared Colby to sing Britney Spears in a gospel vibrato; he did it too well. Avery dared Dana to text her crush and she threw a pillow at him.

It was silly. Human. The kind of noise that made the world feel safe for once.

But beneath it all, Van felt something humming — the soft ache of things unsaid.

Every time Jeremiah laughed, Van felt it in his chest. Every time their knees brushed, something in him sparked and then settled.

The bottle spun again.

The heater hummed louder.

Upstairs, the clock began to strike twelve.

And in the blink between seconds, Van thought — *maybe grace looks like this too.*

Not pews or sermons or confessions.

Just this.

Warm light, soft laughter, and the slow turning of a bottle that could change everything.

TRUTH OR CONSEQUENCE

The old wall clock upstairs struck midnight.

The sound wasn't sharp — just a slow, uneven toll, the kind of chime that's lived too long in a house that doesn't know what to do with silence. Each note sank through the floorboards into the basement, meeting a chaos of laughter, sugar, and fluorescent light.

The basement of Avery's house looked exactly like what it was — the kingdom of teenagers who'd been allowed too much soda and too little supervision. The couch sagged in the middle like it was praying for retirement. The snack table had collapsed into a small battlefield of chip crumbs and empty cups. String lights hung unevenly across the ceiling, half of them blinking like they couldn't decide whether to hold on or give up.

Avery stood in the center, holding an empty Sprite bottle like a relic. "Ladies, gentlemen, and Dana," he announced, "welcome to the final judgment of 2002."

Dana threw a pretzel at him. "You're insufferable."

"I prefer 'anointed,'" Avery replied. He bowed, grinning. "Now — before we all fall asleep from too many cans of Surge and unresolved trauma — I declare one final round of Truth or Dare."

Groans and cheers collided. Someone clapped. Someone else knocked over a Dr Pepper.

Van sat near the end of the circle, legs crossed, back against the arm of the couch. Jeremiah was beside him, leaning forward on his knees, laughter slipping from him so naturally that Van couldn't stop watching. The air smelled like sugar, damp carpet, and teenage perfume — the scent of borrowed freedom.

"Alright, saints," Avery said, crouching dramatically as he set the bottle down on the floor. "Prepare your souls."

He gave it a spin.

The bottle twirled wildly, catching flashes of red and green from the lights. A blur of glass and motion, humming faintly as it spun across the rough carpet. The circle leaned in, collective breath held.

It slowed, wobbled once—

and stopped.

Pointing directly at Van.

"Ah," Avery said, grinning like a cat that had been waiting all night for this. "Our golden tenor."

The laughter came light and teasing. "Yes, Van!" "About time!" "He can't dodge forever!"

Van rubbed his palms together, trying to hide the tremor in them. "Alright," he said, smiling faintly. "Let's get it over with."

"Truth or dare?"

"Truth."

Avery made a show of sighing. "Always truth. You're gonna make it hard to ruin your life, man."

Dana reached over, nudging him. "Don't be mean."

"Me?" Avery said, feigning offense. "I'm an emissary of honesty."

The others giggled and murmured among themselves. Someone whispered something into Avery's ear, then another leaned in to add to it. Their laughter was nervous, conspiratorial, the kind of laughter that happens before someone asks the question everyone's been pretending not to.

Avery's smile faltered for the first time that night. He looked at Van — and something in his face softened. He ran a hand through his hair, exhaled, and said quietly, "Okay… I think we all kinda know the answer. But I wanna hear it from you."

Van blinked, unsure if he'd misheard. "Hear what?"

Avery hesitated, voice lower now, careful. "Are you… gay?"

The laughter stopped so suddenly the silence felt alive.

It wasn't cruel. It wasn't even teasing. It was just… *bare*.

A truth laid on the table like something holy and fragile.

Van's first thought was how loud everything had become — the hum of the old space heater, the fizz of an open soda can, the ticking of the wall clock overhead. The air thickened, close and electric, as if every sound in the world had stepped aside to make room for this one.

He could feel everyone's eyes, waiting. Dana's hands twisting her ring. Avery's wide-open expression, part apology, part curiosity. And Jeremiah — motionless, breath caught, eyes fixed on Van's face.

The world tunneled. He couldn't tell if the heat in his cheeks came from shame or just the sheer weight of the moment pressing against his ribs.

And then — the smallest thing.

Jeremiah's hand brushed his under the couch cushion, hidden from view. Just a touch, soft and steady.

That single contact — warm, real — brought him back into his body.

He realized he'd been holding his breath. He let it out slowly.

He could lie. He could laugh. He could say *no* and the night would move on, and everyone would pretend to believe him.

But what if he was done pretending?

He looked at Avery, then around the circle. These were the same people who'd seen him in choir robes and cafeteria lines, who'd shared youth trips and inside jokes and long, bored Wednesday nights.

Maybe it was time to let them see all of him — even if it meant risking the rest.

He swallowed hard, voice shaking. "Yeah."

He cleared his throat, forced the words to be steady. "Yes. I'm gay."

Across the circle, Colby shifted, his expression tightening like someone had just cursed in church. Daphne's hand froze around her drink, her knuckles pale against the red plastic cup. The silence stretched too long, sharp enough to hear every blink.

Colby finally exhaled, muttering under his breath, "Man, that's not… right."

Daphne's lips pressed into a thin line. "It's just not what God wants," she whispered, eyes dropping to the carpet.

The words weren't loud — they didn't have to be. They landed anyway, the way judgment always did: softly, but with precision.

Avery shot them a look, his voice edged but even. "You two can keep your theology for Sunday morning. This is Saturday night, and nobody's dying from honesty."

Daphne glanced away, cheeks flushed. Colby shifted again, retreating behind the safety of silence.

Van caught all of it — the discomfort, the small flickers of fear and faith clashing in the same faces that had been laughing a minute ago. His chest ached, but Jeremiah's hand stayed steady against his, hidden and sure. The room felt divided — not cleanly, but like a sheet tearing down the middle.

Then Avery broke the silence with a grin. "Called it."

Dana smacked his shoulder. "Avery!"

"What?" he said, laughing, relief loosening his voice. "We *knew*! The hair alone gave you away, bro."

Laughter broke through the tension — awkward, too loud, but real. It rippled around the circle like oxygen.

Van's heart pounded, and then — unexpectedly — he started laughing too. It came from somewhere deep, something cracked and uncoiling, like laughter was the only thing big enough to carry the weight out of his chest.

Dana leaned forward, smiling. "We love you, Van. You know that, right?"

He nodded, voice thick. "Yeah. I do."

Avery raised his soda can like a toast. "To honesty and better hair products!"

The laughter came again, louder this time.

Van wiped at his face, not sure if he was hiding tears or trying to look busy.

Jeremiah's hand still held his under the couch, firm now. A quiet promise.

And just like that, the room felt different — lighter, safer, real.

Like he'd been holding his breath for years and someone had finally told him it was okay to exhale.

He didn't want to linger too long in the heaviness. He smiled, shaky but genuine. "Alright," he said, "before this turns into an after-school special — my turn to spin."

"Coward," Avery teased.

"Efficient," Van said, grabbing the bottle. He gave it a strong flick.

The bottle spun fast, flashing under the string lights — a blur of plastic and reflection. The room leaned in, half-dreading, half-praying.

"Please not me again," someone said.

"Come on, fate, give us drama."

"Spin of destiny!"

It slowed. Wobbled.

And stopped.

Pointing straight at Jeremiah.

The room erupted. Shouts, laughter, the kind of noise that

comes from knowing exactly how much this means without saying it.

"Oh, this is *fate!*" Avery crowed, clutching his chest.

"Rigged!" Jeremiah said, laughing nervously. "Absolutely rigged!"

Dana was already clapping. "Oh, this is going to be good."

"Unanimous vote?" Avery shouted.

"DARE!" came the chorus, loud enough to rattle the string lights.

Jeremiah met Van's eyes. The noise blurred.

Behind them, the furnace kicked back on with a soft groan, and outside, fireworks began — faint cracks and whistles somewhere beyond the cold window glass.

Van's pulse thudded against the quiet. Jeremiah's thumb brushed the back of his hand again, invisible to everyone else.

And in that single, suspended heartbeat — as the laughter filled the room, as confetti lights flickered and the new year hummed through the walls — Van realized something simple and terrifying.

The truth had set something in motion.

And it wasn't stopping now.

The bottle gleamed between them, its glass catching the faint shimmer of gold light — one small, spinning mirror of what had just changed forever.

\Chapter Seventeen – The Dare

For a few seconds after Avery yelled *"DARE,"* the room just blinked—

a collective pause suspended between laughter and disbelief.

Jeremiah gave a slow, nervous grin, running a hand through his hair.

"You're serious?"

"Completely," Avery said, spreading his arms like a revival preacher at the end of a sermon.

"Final dare of the night—final dare of the year. Kiss the person you've got a crush on."

The air in the basement shifted, as if everyone suddenly forgot how to breathe.

The laughter thinned into whispers, soft and electric.

The string lights hummed above them, their uneven flicker reflecting off the empty Sprite bottle like a warning flare.

A few of the girls giggled, exchanging glances, suddenly hyperaware of themselves—of posture, of smiles, of how their hair looked under the colored bulbs.

Dana crossed her legs and leaned forward, elbows on her knees, eyes bright with curiosity.

Colby let out a low whistle and muttered, "Lord, help us," earning a sharp elbow from Daphne. She gave him that pinched church-lady look that said *this is too far from God's work,* even if she didn't have the courage to say it aloud.

Jeremiah exhaled through a nervous laugh, looking around the circle.

"Man, you guys don't make this easy."

"You've got five seconds!" Avery said, holding up his fingers like a countdown clock.

"Make it count before the year turns over!"

Jeremiah's eyes swept the room. "Alright," he said, half-smiling. "Got it. I know exactly who that is."

Every girl straightened. One adjusted her sweater. Another tucked hair behind her ear.

Daphne folded her arms like she was bracing for blasphemy.

Van's pulse thrummed low in his chest. His hand—hidden beneath the couch—was still where Jeremiah had brushed against it earlier.

He didn't dare move. Didn't dare hope.

Jeremiah stood.

The light caught him just enough to draw gold along the edge of his jaw, turning him momentarily into something almost divine.

Instead of walking directly toward anyone, he began circling the group.

The laughter picked up again—thin and nervous.

"Oh, he's making it dramatic."

"Pick someone already!"

"Here comes heartbreak!"

He ignored them, the teasing grin curling at one corner of his mouth.

He stopped behind Dana, placing a hand lightly on her shoulder.

"Tempting," he said, playfully.

She laughed and shoved him off. "Not my type, preacher's kid."

He kept moving, stopping behind Avery next.

"You?"

Avery clutched his chest. "Not unless the Lord Himself writes it in lightning."

The room burst into laughter, a mixture of relief and nerves.

But beneath it, something else pulsed—an awareness no one wanted to name.

Jeremiah moved slower now, fingertips trailing along the wood paneling like he was tracing the perimeter of a confession.

The sound of the old clock upstairs began to seep through the ceiling—

a slow, hollow toll.

Eleven fifty-eight.

Jeremiah's shadow crossed Van's shoes. He was behind him again.

The circle fell quiet.

Even Avery stopped grinning.

"Well?" someone whispered. "Don't keep the congregation waiting."

Jeremiah leaned forward, voice low.

"I'm not."

He stepped around the couch, now facing Van directly.

The laughter drained from the room entirely.

He extended his hand. "Come on," he said softly. "You know the rules."

Van froze. The air seemed to thicken until even breathing felt disobedient.

"Jeremiah…" His voice broke against the name.

But Jeremiah just waited—hand outstretched, steady.

For a heartbeat that felt longer than a year, Van didn't move.

Then, almost on instinct, he reached up and took it.

Jeremiah pulled him gently to his feet.

The circle widened just enough to make space for whatever this was becoming.

They stood there, framed by the blinking Christmas lights and the hum of a tired space heater.

Jeremiah's hand didn't let go.

"I know only one person I have a crush on," he said, voice calm but shaking at the edges.

Then, quieter—almost swallowed by the air—

"No one else has even caught my attention."

The old clock struck **eleven fifty-nine.**

Van could hear everything—

the creak of someone shifting on the couch,

the fizz of a half-open soda can,

the faint rustle of someone whispering a prayer under their breath.

Jeremiah's thumb brushed against his hand once, steadying them both.

"Ten!"

Someone upstairs had started the countdown—muffled voices from the living room, the echo bleeding through the floorboards.

"Nine!"

Jeremiah smiled faintly, that same reckless kind of peace he'd worn when he decided to speak his truth.

"Eight! Seven!"

The air was heavy and bright all at once, saturated with the hum of waiting.

"Six!"

"Five!"

Jeremiah leaned in, breath warm, eyes searching.

"Four!"

Van's hands trembled. "You okay?" Jeremiah whispered.

Van nodded, barely. "Yeah. I think so."

"Three."

"Good."

"Two—"

And then, "One."

The clock upstairs struck midnight.

The noise above exploded—cheers, laughter, the rise of a new year.

But in the basement, silence fell like snowfall.

Jeremiah leaned in and kissed him.

The world folded inward.

The heat of it, the quiet courage of it.

It wasn't smooth or cinematic—it was trembling, honest, holy.

For one breathless instant, time held still.

Then the fireworks started outside—soft pops and bursts of gold flickering through the basement window.

The lights shimmered against the walls like stained glass.

They pulled apart. Both laughing, both dazed.

Then came the reaction—

Avery's cheer loudest of all, hands clapping above his head.

Dana gasping, then laughing into her sleeve.

Colby whispering, "Jesus, Mary, and Joseph," before taking another sip of soda.

And Daphne, her expression pulled tight, eyes darting toward the ceiling as if waiting for thunder.

"Oh, this is better than any sermon!" Avery shouted.

"About time!" Dana said.

Jeremiah stood frozen in the center, still holding Van's hand. His cheeks were flushed, his smile soft.

Van felt like the air had turned to light.

Outside, the fireworks flared again.

The room glowed.

Avery raised his can. "To truth, to love, and to a new year that's already holier than the last!"

Everyone laughed.

Even Colby cracked a smile.

But Daphne stayed quiet—her silence heavy enough that Van felt it long after the others had moved on.

Jeremiah leaned closer, voice low so only Van could hear.

"Happy New Year."

Van's chest tightened, not from fear this time, but from the dizzy weight of being seen.

"Yeah," he whispered. "Happy New Year."

The Sprite bottle still sat in the center of the circle, forgotten and gleaming under the lights—

a small glass witness to everything that had just changed.

"Not every distance is a punishment; some are an invitation to breathe."

AFTER THE FIREWORKS

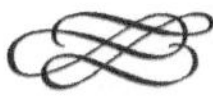

The laughter upstairs had thinned to a tired hum — soft, sugary, and spent.

Somewhere above them, someone dropped a cup; it rolled once and stopped. The music looped through an old pop ballad, too loud for its own sentiment, then faded as if even the stereo was ready for sleep.

The air smelled of candle wax, cola syrup, and confetti. Every sound in the house had taken on that stretched quality that only exists in the small hours after something important has happened — too fragile to name, too new to understand.

Van stood near the bottom of the basement stairs, pulse still beating out of sync with the world.

His lips tingled faintly — not from shock anymore, but from the impossible truth of it. Jeremiah had kissed him. In front of everyone. And somehow the world hadn't ended.

He could still feel it — the tremor of contact, the quiet gasp that rippled through the room, the warmth that hadn't yet cooled from his skin. It was dizzying, the realization that he hadn't been imagining the pull between them. The truth had been waiting all along, just needing air.

He stepped over the mess of paper cups and snack wrappers, found his coat tossed across the railing, and slipped out the back door.

The porch greeted him with cold that bit straight through his shirt.

It was the clean kind of cold — the kind that scraped away the noise and left only what mattered.

The boards creaked under his weight, their rhythm matching his heartbeat.

The sky stretched wide and pale gray, threaded with the last smudges of fireworks — faint pink and gold dissolving into the stars. The air smelled like frost and burnt smoke. Every breath clouded before him, then vanished.

From inside came a muffled roar of laughter. Avery's voice, animated and theatrical: "And then — I swear to God — he *stood up!*" Dana's giggle followed, high and exhausted. Someone clapped. Someone else said, "I knew it!"

The sound was half a world away.

Van leaned against the railing and let the cold burn him clean.

His reflection hovered faintly in the kitchen window behind him — a double image: the boy who'd spent years pretending, and the boy who had finally said it out loud. They didn't quite look like the same person anymore.

The door creaked again.

He didn't turn. He didn't have to.

Jeremiah stepped outside, closing the door quietly behind him.

Warm light spilled across the porch for a moment, then slipped away when the door latched. The night swallowed them both, leaving only the silver wash of distant fireworks.

Neither spoke at first.

Their breaths rose and fell like smoke signals, slow and even.

Jeremiah's voice came soft. "You okay?"

Van huffed a half-laugh, the kind that trembled on its way out. "I think that word's retired for the night."

Jeremiah smiled faintly. "Yeah. Me too."

He came to stand beside him, close but not touching. The space between them hummed.

Together, they watched the last trails of light fade above the rooftops.

"Did you know you were going to do that?" Van asked after a long silence.

Jeremiah's breath fogged white. "No. Maybe. I don't know. I just knew if I didn't, I'd hate myself tomorrow."

Van's throat tightened. "And now?"

"And now," Jeremiah said quietly, "I think I can breathe."

The porch creaked as they both leaned forward, elbows on the railing. The sound of wind moved through the trees — low and steady, like the world exhaling.

"They're all going to talk about it," Van said. "Probably already are."

"I know."

"My dad will lose his mind."

"My dad will quote Leviticus before I finish breakfast."

They both laughed, quietly, like it was the only way to stop from shaking.

"You ever feel like the whole town's one long sermon?" Van asked.

Jeremiah nodded. "Yeah. And we're the footnotes no one wants to read."

Van glanced sideways, catching the faint smirk on his face. "You think it's worth it?"

"I think..." Jeremiah looked up at the fading fireworks, his eyes reflecting the last faint color in the sky. "I think telling the truth is always worth it. Even if no one claps."

The air thickened with something almost holy. Not loud, not cinematic — just real.

They stood there in that kind of quiet that comes after confession, when the only thing left is the hum of the world resetting around you.

Van's voice dropped to a whisper. "Do you regret it?"

Jeremiah shook his head slowly. "No. You?"

"Not even a little."

"Good."

They fell silent again. The last fireworks hissed somewhere far off, faint and ghostly.

Jeremiah shifted slightly closer, their sleeves brushing — accidental, but not unwelcome.

"For the first time in years," Jeremiah said, almost to himself, "I don't feel like I'm lying to God."

Van turned toward him. "You think He minds?"

Jeremiah smiled — that same small, quiet kind of smile that carried more truth than a sermon.

"I think He's been waiting for me to stop pretending."

Van's chest ached. Not from guilt, but from the sheer weight of understanding.

The frost glittered on the railing between their hands. The light from the kitchen cast soft halos on the wood, gold fading to silver.

"What do we do now?" Van asked.

Jeremiah breathed out a long, thoughtful sigh. "We live."

Van almost laughed. "That's it?"

"That's all there ever is," Jeremiah said. "We live, and we don't apologize for it."

From inside came the sound of a camera flash — Avery's voice calling, "Group photo, or it didn't happen!" followed by Dana shouting, "Not a chance, my eyeliner's gone to hell!"

Van smiled at the sound, then looked back toward Jeremiah. "They're going to rewrite this whole night by morning."

"Then we'll write our own version."

"Even if it hurts?"

"Especially if it hurts."

Van's voice trembled. "You think it'll get better?"

Jeremiah looked toward the horizon, where smoke from the fireworks was still drifting into dawn. "Maybe not easier," he said. "But truer. And that's better."

For a long moment, they didn't move. The wind picked up just enough to stir Jeremiah's hair.

The porch light flickered — once, then steadied.

Jeremiah turned to him. "If I lose everything after tonight — the choir, my dad, whatever's left of my reputation — I still won't call this a mistake."

Van's reply came soft but certain. "Then we match."

The fireworks were gone now, leaving only smoke and silence.

Their breaths rose and met in the cold.

"What happens tomorrow?" Van asked.

Jeremiah's answer was the same one he'd given inside.

"Tomorrow comes."

It was the only answer there was.

And it was enough.

The sound of laughter echoed faintly behind them, followed by the clatter of soda cans and Avery's theatrical voice announcing another "round of truth."

The night, as always, carried on without permission.

But out there — under the last ribbons of smoke and color — it felt like something had broken open and made space for the light to finally come in.

Van looked up once more at the sky — pale now, soft with dawn. "You realize this changes everything."

Jeremiah's voice barely above a breath. "Good. I was tired of everything staying the same."

They stood that way until the noise inside faded and the frost began to form again on the railing.

When Jeremiah finally spoke, it was almost lost to the wind.

"Happy New Year, Van."

Van smiled, eyes on the horizon. "Happy New Year."

And as the last spark of light disappeared into the quiet January dark, both of them stood perfectly still — two silhouettes framed by the faint echo of fireworks — standing not in victory or fear, but in truth.

"Even broken glass can catch light."

THE SPACE BETWEEN

The night didn't end so much as dissolve.

One moment the house was full of noise — Avery laughing too loud, Dana swearing she'd never recover from the shock, someone clinking cups in mock toasts — and the next, it was just the sound of bodies settling into fatigue.

Music played low, tinny and half-hearted. The smell of soda syrup hung thick in the air, sweet and tired. The kind of air that only exists in the hour between late and early — when time forgets what direction it's supposed to move.

Van stood in the hallway, coat half-zipped, listening to it fade.

He could still feel the kiss, the weight of Jeremiah's hand, the hum of the room as everything changed but nothing fell apart.

It hadn't been chaos. It hadn't been fire and brimstone or rejection.

It had been quiet — and somehow that made it more real.

He walked back through the living room, past Avery sprawled across the couch like a saint of chaos, arms flung wide, soda can balanced on his chest.

Dana had claimed the recliner, head tilted, eyes fluttering open just long enough to say, "You okay?"

Van nodded. "Yeah. I think so."

"Good," she murmured, eyes already closing again. "It's about time."

He smiled, small and shaky, and kept moving.

By the time he reached the kitchen, most of the lights had been turned off. Only the string of mismatched Christmas bulbs still glowed in the window — one of them blinking sporadically, as though trying to stay awake.

He stepped onto the back porch. The cold hit him clean, sharp enough to sting.

The world outside was holding its breath.

The last fireworks had burned out, leaving thin streaks of smoke curling over the rooftops. Somewhere, a dog barked once, then went silent.

The town, for the first time all night, was still.

Van leaned against the railing, eyes tracing the faint horizon. The air smelled like frost, pine, and something faintly metallic — the scent of winter after celebration.

He could still taste Jeremiah's breath, still hear the catch of his voice saying, *I won't call tonight a mistake.*

Inside, laughter flared again — Avery reenacting the kiss for whoever was still awake. His voice carried through the thin walls, bold and ridiculous:

"And then, he *stood up like a movie!* You should've seen it — Dawson's Creek, but gayer!"

Dana's sleepy voice followed: "Shut up, Avery, I'm trying to have a spiritual awakening."

Laughter broke out, warm and fading.

Van smiled into the dark. For the first time, the noise didn't make him flinch.

He stayed out there until the porch light flickered twice and finally died, leaving him in half-darkness. The sky was beginning to pale at the edges — that thin gray line between night and morning.

When he finally slipped back inside, the house had gone still. Avery was snoring. Dana had curled under a blanket. Someone's phone buzzed faintly against the coffee table, unanswered.

He found his keys, whispered a quiet goodbye no one heard, and stepped into the cold again.

The streets were empty.

Confetti stuck to the curbs, glittering under the streetlights like fragments of a brighter world. The stoplights blinked red-yellow-red, keeping time for no one.

He drove with the window cracked just enough for the cold to thread through his hair.

The radio was on — some late-night station spinning slow country songs about love and loss and promises left in parking lots.

He didn't know the words, but the melody settled into him anyway.

At a red light, he caught his reflection in the windshield — soft, unfamiliar. His hair still mussed from Jeremiah's touch. His eyes brighter, or maybe just clearer.

He didn't look changed. But he felt it — that invisible rear-ranging inside him, like the air in a room after someone opens a window.

He reached up and touched the wooden pendant hanging from his rearview mirror. Jeremiah's gift — the small carved cross with the stars etched in its grain.

It swung gently with the motion of the car, catching the light from a passing streetlamp.

Van pressed it between his fingers, feeling the grooves. "Don't let me regret this," he whispered.

The road curved through the quiet heart of town — the shuttered diner, the gas station with its flickering sign, the church rising in the distance with its white steeple pale against the dark sky.

Even now, it looked both beautiful and suffocating — a place built to hold faith and fear in the same breath.

When he reached his street, the first color of morning had begun to seep into the world. Pale blue bleeding through the black, the edges of trees turning silver.

His parents' house glowed faintly ahead — the porch light still on, as if waiting.

He parked quietly, engine idling. The hum of it filled the car with a low vibration that felt almost like company.

For a long time, he didn't move.

He thought of Jeremiah — the way he'd looked under the last burst of fireworks, the way his words had sounded when he said *truth is always worth it.*

He thought of Emmalee's small voice in the car days ago — *if you're that word, then that's fine.*

He thought of Avery's grin, Dana's laughter, Frank's quiet certainty that truth changed the air.

Everything in his world was rearranging, but not in the way he'd always feared.

It wasn't collapse.

It was opening.

He shut off the car, the sudden silence pressing warm against his ears.

The house was mostly dark, except for one lamp glowing in the living room — the soft amber of a late-night sentinel. The curtains were half-drawn. His father's Bible sat open on the side table, pages rippled from overuse. A coffee mug cooled beside it.

That was how Van knew: his father had been waiting up.

He slipped off his shoes and moved carefully across the floor-boards, each step deliberate, rehearsed.

The old clock on the mantel ticked too loud, counting each breath.

In the mirror by the hallway, his reflection caught him again.

The same face.

But now there was something unhidden behind the eyes — not pride, not fear, something quieter. The look of someone who had finally stopped holding his breath.

He stood there a moment longer, just looking.

Then he whispered to his reflection, "It's okay."

The words didn't sound confident, but they didn't have to. They were real.

Standing at the end of the hallway in front of his bedroom door, the house creaked — the slow shifting of a home turning toward morning.

He slipped into his room. The faint hum of the heater, the soft glow of his alarm clock blinking *2:47 a.m.*

He sat on the edge of the bed, still wearing his coat, the smell of fireworks and cold clinging to it.

For the first time in months, he didn't feel like running.

He just sat there, breathing.

Alive.

When sleep finally came, it wasn't heavy.

It was the kind that waits with open hands.

THE MORNING AFTER

The smell of cinnamon toast drifted through the hallway long before Van opened his eyes.

It was the kind of smell that lied softly — the smell of everything being fine.

It spoke of ordinary mornings and unbroken patterns, of a house still pretending that the world hadn't shifted overnight.

For a few seconds, still caught in the gray space between dreams and waking, he almost believed it.

Down the hall, kitchen drawers opened and closed in rhythm. The faint scrape of plates, the muted hum of the radio tuned to WJRO's morning news.

His mother's voice carried through the house — calm, practiced, the same voice she used to keep peace without ever acknowledging the war underneath.

"Emmalee, stop feeding the dog toast crusts."

His sister's laughter answered back — bright, unconcerned.

Van lay still, eyes tracing the cracks in the ceiling paint that spread like tiny roads — a map of where the house had sighed too often.

His chest felt lighter and heavier at the same time.

Lighter, because he wasn't carrying the secret anymore.

Heavier, because it was now out there, walking around in other people's mouths.

He ran a hand through his hair and stared at the pale light leaking through the blinds.

He thought about Jeremiah's breath in the cold, the touch of his sleeve on the porch, the sound of his voice saying *We live.*

The words still echoed somewhere in his chest, quiet but insistent — a kind of music only he could hear.

When he finally went downstairs, the kitchen was already awake.

Emmalee sat at the table in her pajamas, a pink plastic tiara slightly askew on her head, singing softly to her cereal spoon.

Their mother, still in her robe, stood at the stove flipping pancakes with the precision of someone who used control like prayer.

His father sat at the head of the table, newspaper folded beside his plate, his coffee steaming faintly in the air.

Nothing in the scene looked different, yet everything was.

"Morning," his mother said without looking up.

"Morning."

"Sleep well?"

"Yeah."

He lied out of habit, the word leaving no trace behind it.

His father gave a brief nod. "Big day today," he said, voice clipped, eyes on the paper. "We'll take down the lights this afternoon. Weather's turning."

"Can I help?" Emmalee asked.

"You can hand me the clips," their father said. "No ladders."

Van poured himself coffee — black, bitter, grounding. The mug was chipped, shaped like a shark from a beach trip years ago. He remembered being ten, terrified of the ocean, his father laughing as waves chased them both to shore.

Now the memory felt like it belonged to someone else.

His mother placed a plate in front of him — two pancakes stacked neatly, butter melting in the middle like sunrise.

"How was the party?" she asked.

"Good," he said. "Quiet."

"Quiet?" Emmalee snorted. "Avery doesn't do quiet."

Van smiled faintly. "Okay, maybe not quiet."

His father turned a page of the newspaper. "You behave yourself?"

"Yes, sir."

"Good. World doesn't need any more trouble."

The words hung there — not sharp, but heavy.

Van let them pass, like a bird flying too low.

His mother sat, folding her hands around her coffee mug. "You have work today?"

"Lunch shift," he said. "Double."

She nodded. "Good. Stay busy. Keeps your mind right."

Emmalee, unfazed, reached across the table and stole a corner of his pancake. "Can I come see you at the diner later? Dana says the milkshakes are the best."

"Only if you bring a big tip," Van said.

She grinned. "Deal."

The moment held just long enough to almost feel normal.

Almost.

THE DINER SAT at the bend where Highway 321 met the interstate — a chrome box that glittered even under gray skies.

It smelled like butter, grease, and coffee — a second kind of home for people who didn't know where else to go at ten in the morning.

Van clocked in a few minutes early.

Frank was already behind the counter, coffee in hand, apron hanging crooked. The radio played an old George Strait song low under the hiss of the griddle.

"You look like someone hit reset on your soul," Frank said without looking up.

Van laughed softly. "Morning to you too."

"Sleep?"

"Some."

Frank flipped a pancake, perfect motion, like it had taken him his whole life to learn it. "You make any resolutions?"

"Survive."

"That's the only one worth keeping," Frank said. "Grab the rag. Wipe the booths before the lunch rush brings in their bad decisions."

"Got it."

"Don't call me sir. Makes me sound like I vote on purpose."

Van smiled, grabbed the rag, and started working his way down the line of booths.

By ten-thirty, the diner was alive — orders called out, the bell above the door chiming every few minutes, silverware clinking like wind chimes.

The rhythm soothed him: motion without thought, comfort without question.

He poured coffee for a couple in their Sunday best, topped off a cup for a trucker reading the paper, then wiped crumbs from a corner table near the window.

When he looked up, sunlight was streaming through the glass — weak but steady, turning the chrome trim into ribbons of gold.

Frank leaned against the counter, one hand on his mug. "You look different today," he said.

Van glanced over. "Different how?"

"Like someone took a stone off your chest."

Van chuckled. "Guess I'm sleeping better."

Frank nodded slowly. "Good. You were starting to look like a ghost last month. Now you look like somebody who remembered he's still got skin."

"That's... a weird compliment."

"Most true things are." Frank took a long sip of coffee. "Funny thing about truth. When you finally stop hiding it, the air around you changes. People feel it, even if they don't know why."

Van paused mid-wipe, rag in hand. "What do you mean?"

"I mean," Frank said, motioning toward the window, "a sunrise doesn't make noise, but everything alive still turns toward it."

Van followed his gaze.

Outside, frost was melting on the pavement, dripping in slow silver threads. The morning light caught the diner's sign, making it gleam like something new.

"Whole world's built on folks pretending," Frank went on. "You stop pretending, even for a second, the ground remembers what it's supposed to feel like."

Van stood still, the words landing slow and heavy.

Frank didn't look at him. He didn't need to. Truth, Van was learning, didn't need an audience.

The bell above the door chimed again.

Van straightened, coffee pot in hand.

"Atta boy," Frank said, turning back to the grill. "Keep showing up. That's half the job. Hell, that's half of life."

THAT AFTERNOON, the clouds finally gave up — breaking apart into long streaks of light that spilled across the park. The air was sharp and blue, clean in that way winter sometimes allows when the world has been wrung dry of noise.

The basketball court looked older than it was, lines faded to pale ghosts, the net clanging against the rim with every missed shot. Avery was in full performance mode — spinning, lunging, and nearly falling.

Van leaned against the fence, arms folded. "You play basketball the way my grandma drives," he called.

Avery tripped over his own foot and sent the ball bouncing toward Dana, who caught it neatly against her hip.

"Graceful," she said. "If you ever get tired of comedy, you could go pro."

"I was warming up," Avery said, breathless.

"Sure," Dana said, "warming up for failure."

Colby was sitting cross-legged near the bench, holding up his flip phone. "Don't worry, I got that on video. I'm showing everyone. Somewhere. Eventually."

"You're a menace," Avery said.

Colby smirked. "I'm preserving history."

Van laughed. "It's tragic history, but still."

Dana took a sip of hot chocolate, steam rising in soft curls. "You people are hopeless."

"Correction," Van said. "He's hopeless. The rest of us are witnesses."

The ball rolled back toward Avery's foot. He picked it up, spun, and missed the hoop entirely.

"God left the court five minutes ago," Dana said.

A voice came from behind them, warm and even. "I believe it."

Jeremiah walked across the lot, hands deep in his coat pockets, a quiet smile bending his face. He carried two Styrofoam cups, steam curling into the wind.

"About time," Avery said. "We're holding a championship and you're late."

Jeremiah looked around the cracked court. "Championship? I see more bruised egos than points."

Avery pointed the ball at him. "That's slander."

"It's observation," Jeremiah said. "Big difference."

Van smiled as Jeremiah approached, handing him the second cup. The warmth bled through the cardboard, soft against his fingers. "Still the good kind?" Van asked.

"With the fake whipped cream," Jeremiah said. "The kind that tastes like hope."

Dana groaned. "You two and your poetic nonsense. I'm freezing to death while you flirt with dairy products."

Jeremiah laughed quietly. "You could've stayed home."

"And miss divine comedy?" she said. "Never."

Colby tilted his phone toward them. "Say that again, Jeremiah — about the hope thing. I'm building a quote reel."

"Delete it," Jeremiah said.

"Never," Colby replied.

The sound of their laughter rose into the cold air, echoing faintly against the bare trees. Van leaned against the fence, his shoulder brushing Jeremiah's. The contact was subtle, almost invisible, but it sent a pulse through him — something electric and quiet all at once.

Avery threw another wild shot and missed again. "I think God's not the only one who left," Dana said. "The Holy Spirit's packing too."

Van grinned. "Maybe He's just hiding behind the backboard."

"Or behind you," Avery said. "Ready to smite the mockers."

"Then He's gonna need a bigger lightning bolt," Dana replied.

Jeremiah's laugh came easy this time, warm and human. Van caught the sound and tucked it somewhere deep inside.

For a moment, the scene slowed — like a frame from an old film: Avery's wild gestures, Dana's grin, Colby's phone glinting in the sun, Jeremiah's hand steady near his. It was ordinary, imperfect, but real.

Jeremiah looked over. "You're thinking again."

"I am," Van said. "Trying to figure out if this is what 'okay' feels like."

Jeremiah exhaled, his breath curling white into the air. "If it is, don't chase it. Just hold it while you can."

Van smiled. "Yeah. I think I will."

School started back the second week of January.

Peidmont Valley smelled like pencil shavings, floor wax, and recycled gossip.

The hallways buzzed with too much noise and not enough meaning.

In English, Mr. Pope stood at the board, chalk in hand, declaring, "Hester Prynne had to suffer before she could be redeemed. You can't rewrite redemption."

Van stared at the text open on his desk, tracing a sentence underlined by someone else years ago: *She had not known the weight until she felt the freedom.*

He murmured, "Maybe forgiveness doesn't belong to anyone else."

From the back row, Jeremiah's voice whispered, "Amen."

Avery elbowed Van from the next desk. "You look like you're narrating your own indie film again."

"Maybe I am," Van whispered.

"Then make sure the soundtrack is a hit," Avery replied, just before Mr. Pope called on him to define "puritanical morality."

Van bit back a laugh, his pulse lighter, his heart louder.

THAT NIGHT, driving home, the world felt endless.

The roads gleamed with dew. Streetlights blurred into long gold lines. The radio played something slow — a song about mercy, motion, and miles to go.

The pendant Jeremiah had carved swayed from the mirror, catching the passing light — silver, gold, silver again.

Van reached up and steadied it.

For once, the silence didn't feel empty. It felt like space — space to breathe, space to live, space to be.

He whispered, half to himself, "We live."

And the words felt true.

THE COMPANY WE KEEP

The morning light came slow through the kitchen window, soft and amber, sliding across the checkered tablecloth like it wasn't in any hurry. The house smelled like toast and dish soap and the faint perfume of yesterday's coffee. Van sat at the table, turning his spoon through a bowl of cereal gone soggy, his mind still caught halfway between dreams and the echo of the night before.

He hadn't expected Aunt Shelia to already be sitting there, elbows on the table, coffee cup in hand like she'd been waiting for him all along.

"Well, if it isn't the sleeping prince," she said, her voice sweet and sharp all at once. She wore her usual Sunday-best-but-I-might-fix-your-fence-in-it outfit — pressed jeans, a tucked-in blouse with embroidered roses, and a red scarf knotted at her throat. Her hair was set just right, curls pinned like they meant business. "You look like somebody who stayed up thinkin' too hard."

Van rubbed the back of his neck. "Morning, Aunt Shelia. Didn't know you were here."

"Course I'm here. I came by to borrow a bundt pan, but your

mama made coffee and started talkin', and, well..." She sipped. "Here I am."

His mother smiled from the stove, flipping a pancake. "You know how she is. Once she starts, the Lord Himself couldn't send her home."

Shelia gave a mock glare. "I'll have you know the Lord likes my company."

Van half-smiled. "You got a sermon for breakfast today?"

"I didn't say I didn't." She leaned forward, lowering her voice just enough to make it a secret shared with the morning. "Now, your daddy's out in the yard fussin' over that busted bird feeder, so you're safe for a few minutes. Eat somethin' before you go starvin' yourself over feelings."

Van stirred his cereal again. "You sure do have perfect timing."

"That's the Lord's gift, baby," she said. "That and discernment. And my discernment says somethin's stirrin' in this town like a wasp nest."

His mother sighed. "Shelia, not at the table."

"I'll hush when they start tellin' the truth in this town," Shelia replied, rising to refill her mug. "I stopped by the grocery this mornin', and half the folks in the checkout line quit talkin' when I walked up. That's never a good sign unless somebody died or somebody sinned — and both make people equally excited."

Van kept his eyes on the bowl, but his chest tightened all the same.

Shelia reached out and rested her hand on his shoulder. "You just keep your head, sugar. Folks love to build bonfires and then act surprised when they smell smoke."

He looked up, caught the warmth in her eyes. "You think it's that bad?"

"I think you're young and honest and this town don't know what to do with either," she said, matter-of-fact, like she was calling the weather. Then she kissed the top of his head, whispering, "You do what's right. God ain't never once regretted honesty."

And just like that, she was gone — coffee cup in hand, scarf fluttering behind her — before his father came back through the door.

The kitchen felt quieter without her laughter, but sharper somehow. His mother set a plate of eggs in front of him and said softly, "Don't let folks make you small, Van. But don't give 'em more to chew on than they already have, either."

He nodded. "Yes, ma'am."

By the time Van pulled into the Peidmont Valley parking lot, the morning haze had lifted. The school stood like a tired monument — red brick, chipping paint, the flag out front tangled in the breeze. The chatter outside carried that strange January energy: everyone back from break, pretending nothing had changed, even when half of them knew something had.

He caught sight of Jeremiah across the lot — hood up, laughing with two varsity teammates from the basketball team. But it wasn't the same laughter as before. It was guarded, shaped to fit what the others expected. When Jeremiah noticed Van, the laughter faltered just enough to show the crack before he turned away.

Inside, the halls buzzed with rumors — whispers too small to name but loud enough to hear. Snippets drifted between lockers and classrooms:

"...at Avery's New Year's thing..."

"...thought I saw them on the porch..."

"...you know how church folk get..."

Each voice seemed to carry another match, waiting for someone to strike it.

Van kept walking, head down, just another student in a sea of denim jackets and half-awake faces. But every step felt like he was walking through static.

The bell rang, and the sound of chairs scraping filled the air.

Mr. Pope stood at the front of the room, sleeves rolled up, a coffee mug that read *World's Okayest Teacher* sitting beside a stack of ungraded essays. He turned from the whiteboard with a grin that said he had plans.

"Alright, Peidmont Valley, time to stretch those brains a little. New project."

He wrote the words *Controversial Research Project* in big, looping letters.

Groans echoed around the room.

Mr. Pope chuckled. "That's the spirit. Pair work, two weeks, worth twenty percent of your grade. You'll pick a modern issue — something people actually argue about. I'm talking gay adoption, the death penalty, animal testing, legalizing drugs, climate change, gun control. You name it."

He tossed the marker onto his desk. "If folks in Briar Hollow would argue about it over cornbread, it counts."

Laughter rolled through the room, nervous but genuine.

"This isn't about what's right," he said. "It's about how you argue, how you listen, and how you make someone think. Consider it practice for living here."

He pulled out a clipboard. "Now — let's see who's fated to suffer together."

Van slumped slightly in his chair, already bracing for the outcome.

"Van Shelton..." Mr. Pope paused for dramatic effect. "... you're with Lisa Cartwright."

A soft wave of murmurs rippled through the class. Lisa was one of the good ones — smart, steady, church-going, the type who always volunteered at the bake sale. Van offered a polite nod as she turned in her seat to smile back at him.

Jeremiah, sitting two rows over, didn't turn at all. But Van felt it — that quiet shift in the air.

Mr. Pope finished calling the pairs and dismissed them with a reminder: "Topic proposals by Thursday. Don't bring me essays about recycling or puppy mills unless you've got something new to say."

When the bell rang, Lisa gathered her books and walked beside Van into the hallway.

"I was thinking maybe something about morality in family values," she said brightly. "Or whether the media shapes belief. Unless you've got another idea?"

Van managed a half-smile. "Honestly? Something lighter sounds good."

She nodded, relieved. "Library after school tomorrow, then? My dad says the house is too noisy for thinking."

"Sure. Library works."

They parted ways at the stairwell. Van lingered, pretending to dig in his backpack until the crowd thinned.

Jeremiah passed by a moment later, books tucked under his arm. "Lisa Cartwright, huh?" he said, voice low but steady.

"Yeah. Just for the project."

Jeremiah nodded once, jaw tightening. "Right."

Van searched his face. "You okay?"

Jeremiah's smile came slow, careful. "Yeah. Just... funny how people start lookin' for ways to test what they already think they know."

Before Van could answer, the warning bell cut through the air, and Jeremiah disappeared down the hall.

That afternoon, the clouds broke apart — the sky a hard, hopeful blue.

Van drove home with the window cracked just enough to let the cold roll in, the BMW humming steady beneath him, low and smooth like a secret he trusted not to tell. The leather still held the faint scent of Jeremiah's cologne from a week ago — cedar and something warm — and it made the drive feel both comforting and dangerous. The backroads of Briar Hollow curved through fields gone winter-brown, and every porch he passed seemed to hold a conversation — neighbors sweeping, heads turning, voices dropping just low enough to stay polite. Briar Hollow had always been small, but lately, it felt smaller.

When he turned onto his street, his father's truck was still in the drive. He found him out back, hammering at the bird feeder Shelia had mentioned.

"Looks like it's fixin' to hold," his father said, not looking up. "Sometimes all a thing needs is to be put back where it belongs."

Van nodded. "Guess so."

His father finally looked up, the lines around his eyes sharp in the cold light. "Don't be draggin' your friends' reputations through the mud while you're tryin' to figure out what's meant for you, son. Folks'll forgive a mistake, but they don't forget what they think they saw."

The words came quiet, not cruel — but heavy in the way only truth or fear could be.

Van blinked. "I'm not draggin' anybody anywhere," he said, his voice low but firm. "People are gonna talk no matter what I do."

His father leaned on the post, jaw working. "Talk's one thing. Belief's another. Once folks believe somethin', it sticks harder than sap."

Van's chest tightened. "So I'm supposed to live small so people don't get uncomfortable?"

His father's eyes met his — not angry, just tired. "You're supposed to remember you ain't the only one that lives with what folks say."

Van let the silence stretch. The wind caught in the branches above them, rattling the feeder chain like it was agreeing with neither of them. "Seems like you care more about what people see than what's real."

His father exhaled slow, the kind of breath that ended a conversation before it ever started. "Maybe you'll understand when you're older."

"Maybe I already do," Van said quietly.

That one landed. His father didn't answer — just picked the

hammer back up, measuring the next nail like precision might fix the world.

"Yes, sir," Van added — not out of respect, but to end it clean.

He turned toward the house, gravel crunching under his boots. The words followed him, looping in his head the way sermons did: *folks'll forgive a mistake, but they don't forget what they think they saw.*

By the time he reached the porch, it felt less like advice and more like a warning he'd already outgrown.

Inside, the house smelled like fresh cornbread and something sweet. His mother hummed over the sink, the radio playing low. Van watched her for a moment, the way light caught the edge of her hair, soft and gold against the kitchen window.

For a fleeting moment, everything looked almost normal — like the world might stay that way if no one breathed too hard.

But somewhere in Briar Hollow, whispers were already growing legs.

WHISPERS AND WEATHER

The morning light came slow through the kitchen window, soft and amber, sliding across the checkered tablecloth like it wasn't in any hurry. The house smelled like toast and dish soap and the faint perfume of yesterday's coffee. Van sat at the table, turning his spoon through a bowl of cereal gone soggy, his mind still caught halfway between dreams and the echo of the night before.

He hadn't expected Aunt Shelia to already be sitting there, elbows on the table, coffee cup in hand like she'd been waiting for him all along.

"Well, if it isn't the sleeping prince," she said, her voice sweet and sharp all at once. She wore her usual Sunday-best-but-I-might-fix-your-fence-in-it outfit — pressed jeans, a tucked-in blouse with embroidered roses, and a red scarf knotted at her throat. Her hair was set just right, curls pinned like they meant business. "You look like somebody who stayed up thinkin' too hard."

Van rubbed the back of his neck. "Morning, Aunt Shelia. Didn't know you were here."

"Course I'm here. I came by to borrow a bundt pan, but your

mama made coffee and started talkin', and, well..." She sipped. "Here I am."

His mother smiled from the stove, flipping a pancake. "You know how she is. Once she starts, the Lord Himself couldn't send her home."

Shelia gave a mock glare. "I'll have you know the Lord likes my company."

Van half-smiled. "You got a sermon for breakfast today?"

"I didn't say I didn't." She leaned forward, lowering her voice just enough to make it a secret shared with the morning. "Now, your daddy's out in the yard fussin' over that busted bird feeder, so you're safe for a few minutes. Eat somethin' before you go starvin' yourself over feelings."

Van stirred his cereal again. "You sure do have perfect timing."

"That's the Lord's gift, baby," she said. "That and discernment. And my discernment says somethin's stirrin' in this town like a wasp nest."

His mother sighed. "Shelia, not at the table."

"I'll hush when they start tellin' the truth in this town," Shelia replied, rising to refill her mug. "I stopped by the grocery this mornin', and half the folks in the checkout line quit talkin' when I walked up. That's never a good sign unless somebody died or somebody sinned — and both make people equally excited."

Van kept his eyes on the bowl, but his chest tightened all the same.

Shelia reached out and rested her hand on his shoulder. "You just keep your head, sugar. Folks love to build bonfires and then act surprised when they smell smoke."

He looked up, caught the warmth in her eyes. "You think it's that bad?"

"I think you're young and honest and this town don't know what to do with either," she said, matter-of-fact, like she was calling the weather. Then she kissed the top of his head, whispering, "You do what's right. God ain't never once regretted honesty."

And just like that, she was gone — coffee cup in hand, scarf fluttering behind her — before his father came back through the door.

The kitchen felt quieter without her laughter, but sharper somehow. His mother set a plate of eggs in front of him and said softly, "Don't let folks make you small, Van. But don't give 'em more to chew on than they already have, either."

He nodded. "Yes, ma'am."

By the time Van pulled into the Peidmont Valley parking lot, the morning haze had lifted. The school stood like a tired monument — red brick, chipping paint, the flag out front tangled in the breeze. The chatter outside carried that strange January energy: everyone back from break, pretending nothing had changed, even when half of them knew something had.

He caught sight of Jeremiah across the lot — hood up, laughing with two varsity teammates from the basketball team. But it wasn't the same laughter as before. It was guarded, shaped to fit what the others expected. When Jeremiah noticed Van, the laughter faltered just enough to show the crack before he turned away.

Inside, the halls buzzed with rumors — whispers too small to name but loud enough to hear. Snippets drifted between lockers and classrooms:

"...at Avery's New Year's thing..."

"...thought I saw them on the porch..."

"...you know how church folk get..."

Each voice seemed to carry another match, waiting for someone to strike it.

Van kept walking, head down, just another student in a sea of denim jackets and half-awake faces. But every step felt like he was walking through static.

The bell rang, and the sound of chairs scraping filled the air.

Mr. Pope stood at the front of the room, sleeves rolled up, a coffee mug that read *World's Okayest Teacher* sitting beside a stack of ungraded essays. He turned from the whiteboard with a grin that said he had plans.

"Alright, Peidmont Valley, time to stretch those brains a little. New project."

He wrote the words *Controversial Research Project* in big, looping letters.

Groans echoed around the room.

Mr. Pope chuckled. "That's the spirit. Pair work, two weeks, worth twenty percent of your grade. You'll pick a modern issue — something people actually argue about. I'm talking gay adoption, the death penalty, animal testing, legalizing drugs, climate change, gun control. You name it."

He tossed the marker onto his desk. "If folks in Briar Hollow would argue about it over cornbread, it counts."

Laughter rolled through the room, nervous but genuine.

"This isn't about what's right," he said. "It's about how you argue, how you listen, and how you make someone think. Consider it practice for living here."

He pulled out a clipboard. "Now — let's see who's fated to suffer together."

Van slumped slightly in his chair, already bracing for the outcome.

"Van Shelton..." Mr. Pope paused for dramatic effect. "... you're with Lisa Cartwright."

A soft wave of murmurs rippled through the class. Lisa was one of the good ones — smart, steady, church-going, the type who always volunteered at the bake sale. Van offered a polite nod as she turned in her seat to smile back at him.

Jeremiah, sitting two rows over, didn't turn at all. But Van felt it — that quiet shift in the air.

Mr. Pope finished calling the pairs and dismissed them with a reminder: "Topic proposals by Thursday. Don't bring me essays about recycling or puppy mills unless you've got something new to say."

When the bell rang, Lisa gathered her books and walked beside Van into the hallway.

"I was thinking maybe something about morality in family values," she said brightly. "Or whether the media shapes belief. Unless you've got another idea?"

Van managed a half-smile. "Honestly? Something lighter sounds good."

She nodded, relieved. "Library after school tomorrow, then? My dad says the house is too noisy for thinking."

"Sure. Library works."

They parted ways at the stairwell. Van lingered, pretending to dig in his backpack until the crowd thinned.

Jeremiah passed by a moment later, books tucked under his arm. "Lisa Cartwright, huh?" he said, voice low but steady.

"Yeah. Just for the project."

Jeremiah nodded once, jaw tightening. "Right."

Van searched his face. "You okay?"

Jeremiah's smile came slow, careful. "Yeah. Just... funny how people start lookin' for ways to test what they already think they know."

Before Van could answer, the warning bell cut through the air, and Jeremiah disappeared down the hall.

That afternoon, the clouds broke apart — the sky a hard, hopeful blue.

Van drove home with the window cracked just enough to let the cold roll in, the BMW humming steady beneath him, low and smooth like a secret he trusted not to tell. The leather still held the faint scent of Jeremiah's cologne from a week ago — cedar and something warm — and it made the drive feel both comforting and dangerous. The backroads of Briar Hollow curved through fields gone winter-brown, and every porch he passed seemed to hold a conversation — neighbors sweeping, heads turning, voices dropping just low enough to stay polite. Briar Hollow had always been small, but lately, it felt smaller.

When he turned onto his street, his father's truck was still in the drive. He found him out back, hammering at the bird feeder Shelia had mentioned.

"Looks like it's fixin' to hold," his father said, not looking up. "Sometimes all a thing needs is to be put back where it belongs."

Van nodded. "Guess so."

His father finally looked up, the lines around his eyes sharp in the cold light. "Don't be draggin' your friends' reputations through the mud while you're tryin' to figure out what's meant for you, son. Folks'll forgive a mistake, but they don't forget what they think they saw."

The words came quiet, not cruel — but heavy in the way only truth or fear could be.

Van blinked. "I'm not draggin' anybody anywhere," he said, his voice low but firm. "People are gonna talk no matter what I do."

His father leaned on the post, jaw working. "Talk's one thing. Belief's another. Once folks believe somethin', it sticks harder than sap."

Van's chest tightened. "So I'm supposed to live small so people don't get uncomfortable?"

His father's eyes met his — not angry, just tired. "You're supposed to remember you ain't the only one that lives with what folks say."

Van let the silence stretch. The wind caught in the branches above them, rattling the feeder chain like it was agreeing with neither of them. "Seems like you care more about what people see than what's real."

His father exhaled slow, the kind of breath that ended a conversation before it ever started. "Maybe you'll understand when you're older."

"Maybe I already do," Van said quietly.

That one landed. His father didn't answer — just picked the

hammer back up, measuring the next nail like precision might fix the world. "Once I get this feeder set up," Van's father not looking up for a response. "Don't be messing around it until the glue is set."

"Yes, sir," Van added — not out of respect, but to end it clean.

He turned toward the house, gravel crunching under his boots. The words followed him, looping in his head the way sermons did: *folks'll forgive a mistake, but they don't forget what they think they saw.*

By the time he reached the porch, it felt less like advice and more like a warning he'd already outgrown.

Inside, the house smelled like fresh cornbread and something sweet. His mother hummed over the sink, the radio playing low. Van watched her for a moment, the way light caught the edge of her hair, soft and gold against the kitchen window.

For a fleeting moment, everything looked almost normal — like the world might stay that way if no one breathed too hard.

But somewhere in Briar Hollow, whispers were already growing legs.

THE WEIGHT OF SUNDAY

Sunday morning came dressed in its usual disguise — pressed clothes, polite smiles, and the sound of hymnals snapping open like wings.

The air outside Heritage Baptist was crisp enough to bite, the kind of cold that carried perfume, coffee, and the faint tang of car exhaust from a dozen idling engines.

Van parked near the far edge of the lot, the old BMW out of place between mud-splattered trucks and hand-me-down sedans. He sat for a moment with the engine off, watching people file toward the sanctuary doors — families bundled together, hands tucked into coats, heads bowed against the wind.

Inside, everything still smelled faintly of poinsettias and pine. The foyer held traces of gold glitter fallen from the now-removed Christmas garlands. The bulletin boards that once sang "Joy to the World" now carried verses printed in looping fonts and sign-up sheets for bake sales and Bible studies.

The holiday season had already been replaced with the comfort of habit — potlucks planned, pews polished, and the quiet pretense that everything holy stayed the same.

He caught sight of Aunt Shelia almost immediately —

standing near the back, fanning herself with a folded bulletin even though the air was brisk.

Her blouse was sunflower yellow, a small rebellion against the winter's dull palette of grays and browns. Her earrings — wide golden hoops — caught the light every time she turned her head, scattering small bursts of brightness through the shadowed pews.

"Well, if it ain't my favorite sinner," she whispered when he passed. "Don't you look like conviction in a suit."

Van grinned despite himself. "You always this reverent in the Lord's house?"

"Only on days that end in y," she said, patting his arm. "Keep that chin up. I see more truth in your eyes than half the choir's hallelujahs."

He laughed softly — the sound small, but it felt like a window cracked open in a room that hadn't breathed in years.

Then Jeremiah walked in.

Even from across the sanctuary, Van felt the shift.

The room didn't fall silent, but the tone turned — like someone had played the right song in the wrong key.

Jeremiah's parents led the way down the aisle — Pastor Rich in his best gray suit, Ms. Denise following just behind, her hand poised on her son's shoulder like a guide and a leash. They passed pew after pew of polite smiles that stopped just short of kind.

Van's mother shifted beside him, glancing down the row toward the pastor's family. The choir began "Leaning on the Everlasting Arms," but the harmony felt thinner than usual — too many eyes turned toward something they weren't supposed to notice.

From the pulpit, Pastor Rich smiled — wide and rehearsed.

"Good morning, church family," he said, his voice booming with the warmth of a man who'd long since learned to perform sincerity. "A blessed start to a new year — a time for reflection, repentance, and righteous living."

The word *repentance* hit like a hammer dressed as scripture.

Van felt it. Jeremiah did too.

He didn't have to look over to know — he could sense the way Jeremiah's shoulders went stiff, how the hymnbook stayed closed in his lap.

Two pews back, Aunt Shelia murmured under her breath, "Well, ain't that convenient timing," and shook her head, fanning herself harder.

The sermon built as it always did — verse, anecdote, metaphor, warning — but tucked between each line was a blade.

Pastor Rich spoke of "young men losing sight of godly examples," of "temptations that disguise themselves as friendship," of "those who mistake kindness for calling."

Every word was broad enough to deny but sharp enough to wound.

Van sat still, eyes fixed on the hymnbook spine in front of him, pulse pounding so loud it drowned out the choir's final chords.

He wondered if anyone else could hear it — the sound of guilt that wasn't his but still clung to him like smoke.

When the final hymn began, he couldn't bring himself to sing. Jeremiah didn't either.

Ms. Denise nudged her son sharply, her lips pressed into the kind of smile that meant *obey now, discuss later.*

AFTER THE BENEDICTION, the aisle turned into a slow-moving current of coats and chatter.

Ms. Denise smiled too hard, the kind of smile that could hold up a house if it needed to.

Pastor Rich stationed himself by the door, his hand warm and heavy on every shoulder that passed — a ritual of control disguised as blessing.

When Van reached him, the pastor's grip tightened just enough to make his knuckles ache.

"Good to see you, Van," he said, voice friendly but fixed. "Hope the new year's treatin' you right."

"Yes, sir."

"Keep your focus, son. The devil does his best work in confusion."

Van nodded, the words sticking in his throat. "I'll keep that in mind."

Before Pastor Rich could add another pointed proverb, Aunt Shelia stepped forward like a storm in pearls.

"Well now, Brother Rich," she said, smile sugar-sweet. "If the devil's work is confusion, this town must be sittin' right on his front porch."

The laughter that followed was nervous — half genuine, half relief.

Ms. Denise's smile faltered, her eyes narrowing like she'd just bitten into something sour.

Pastor Rich's expression didn't waver. "Always a joy to have you with us, Sister Shelia."

"Oh, I know it is," she said, fanning herself again. "And you just keep preachin' the Word, brother — I'll keep remindin' folks that God don't play favorites, no matter how many church keys they hold."

A few pew-side heads turned; someone coughed to cover a laugh.

Ms. Denise's hand shot out, gripping her husband's arm — her version of restraint.

Shelia leaned in just enough to make her point. "You know, preacher, you got a fine pulpit and a powerful voice, but you might remember — God's ears work just as good outside this building as they do inside."

Pastor Rich's smile went brittle. "Bless your heart, Sister Shelia."

"Oh, He has," she said. "Repeatedly."

She turned to Van, looping her arm through his. "Come on,

baby. We're goin' to lunch before I end up rebukin' half the deacons and gettin' myself uninvited to potluck."

O*UTSIDE*, sunlight turned the frost to silver. Cars idled. Breath clouded in the air. The last chorus of the choir still drifted faintly from inside, carried through the heavy oak doors like smoke after a fire. The smell of perfume, exhaust, and fried chicken from the fellowship hall clung to the morning.

They walked toward Shelia's Buick parked by the side fence. Van shoved his hands into his coat pockets, head down, the gravel crunching beneath his boots. She waited until they were clear of the doorway, far enough from the curious eyes and polite smiles.

"Now, don't you let that man's sermon crawl under your skin," she said finally. "That wasn't the Word talkin'. That was fear wearin' a robe."

Van nodded, jaw tight. "Yeah. Guess it just got in deeper than I meant to let it."

Shelia glanced sideways at him, reading what he didn't say. "Something else you're carryin', sugar?"

He hesitated. His breath came out in a thin cloud, his throat suddenly dry. "Aunt Shelia..." He stared at the ground, words slipping loose before he could stop them. "I'm gay."

The sound of it landed between them — small, but sacred. Like a prayer spoken in the wrong room.

Shelia stopped walking. The wind tugged her scarf loose, fluttering it over her shoulder like a flag. Then she let out a slow exhale — half laugh, half sigh. "Well, Lord love ya, it's about time you said it out loud."

Van blinked. "You... you knew?"

"Baby," she said, smiling softly, "I've known since you were six years old singin' Shania Twain into your mama's hairbrush with that apron on backward. You thought you were hidin' it; I thought you were auditionin'."

He huffed out a laugh that shook on its way up. "You're not… mad?"

"Mad?" She brushed his cheek with the back of her glove. "Sweetheart, the only thing I'm mad about is how scared this world made you to be yourself. You hear me? God don't make mistakes. And He sure didn't start with you."

Her words landed like warmth through winter air — the kind of love that didn't need explaining.

Van's voice cracked when he spoke. "I thought you might be disappointed."

Shelia smiled, sad and proud all at once. "The only thing disappointin' about you, baby, is that you been tryin' to fit yourself into a box built for people who never had your kind of courage."

He didn't mean to, but a tear escaped. He swiped it away quick, pretending it was the wind.

That's when the crunch of gravel cut through the moment. Van's father's voice came low and tight — too calm to be safe.

"What's this I'm hearin'?"

Van turned fast. His father stood near the truck, arms folded, eyes sharp under the brim of his cap. That same hard look he wore when talkin' to deacons about roof leaks or money short-falls — the one that meant *this ain't over.*

Millie stood a few feet behind him, coat buttoned tight, her eyes already wary.

Shelia straightened her shoulders, voice even. "It's family talk, Jeff."

"Family talk that don't include me?" His tone dropped. "He tellin' you now what he already told us?"

"Because you don't ask," she said, cool as a judge.

His jaw flexed. "You got no right spreadin' around things that ought to stay in this family. We agreed he was workin' through it — figurin' himself out quietly."

Shelia let out a short, humorless laugh. "Quietly? Baby, secrets don't heal. They rot."

Van's mother stepped forward gently. "Jeff, please. This isn't the place."

Turning his glare toward her. "It's not the place, but it's happenin', isn't it? Right here in front of God and half the congregation's cars."

"Then maybe God's ready to hear somethin' true," Shelia said.

His father's voice rose, barely contained. "You always gotta make a scene. This ain't your business."

"This *is* my business," she said, planting her feet. "He's my blood same as yours. And if you think truth's a scene, maybe that's why you can't stand to watch it play out."

His mother's hand hovered between them, pleading. "Stop, both of you. Please."

His father turned toward Van, his voice sharp but shaking. "Son, I told you this was for us to deal with as a family. Now it's church gossip."

Van's throat tightened. "It's not gossip, Dad. It's just the truth. Aunt Shelia loves me — that's not a scandal."

Pointed toward the church doors. "You think these people care about love? They care about appearances. We don't need to hand 'em more to whisper about." His father says.

Shelia stepped closer, her eyes narrowing. "And that right there is the problem. You're raisin' a boy to fear people instead of trustin' God."

Van's father's face went red. "You think I don't trust God? I'm tryin' to protect him from a town that'll eat him alive!"

"Then maybe it's the town that needs changin', not the boy."

They stood there — four silhouettes now — family bound by blood and unraveling by pride.

Then, mercifully, a syrupy voice drifted from behind the next row of cars.

"Well, if it isn't the Sheltons!"

Mrs. Hattie Brewton tottered toward them, casserole dish clutched to her chest, hat blooming like a rose bush in winter. "Mercy, y'all look serious! Everything all right?"

His father's entire body tensed, smile snapping into place like armor. "Just fine, Miss Hattie."

Hattie blinked between them, sensing the tension but pretending not to. "Well, good! I was just sayin' to Earl how we don't see your boy and that sweet Jeremiah singin' together much lately…"

Shelia didn't miss a beat. Her voice turned sweet as syrup with a bite underneath.

"Now, Miss Hattie, don't you go worryin' about our choir schedules. You just keep that banana puddin' from freezin' in this wind, bless your heart."

Hattie's face twitched between curiosity and compliance. "Well, of course, dear. Y'all have a blessed day." She waddled off, eyes still flickin' over her shoulder.

Shelia waited until she was out of earshot, then muttered, "Nosy as a rooster in a rainstorm."

Van's father let out a hard breath. "You think this is funny?"

"No," she said, looking him dead in the eye. "I think it's *family*. And I think you better start rememberin' that before this boy forgets what home's supposed to feel like."

Van's mother's voice came soft, but there was steel under it. "She's right, Jeff. We can't treat the truth like it's a sickness."

He looked at her then, eyes wet but angry. "You're supposed to be on my side."

"I am," she said quietly. "I'm just tired of pretendin' sides are what keep us together."

The silence that followed was colder than the wind. Van

wanted to reach for one of them — all of them — but didn't know which would pull away first.

A gust swept across the lot, carrying the fading sound of the church bell — one last echo of a sermon that no longer mattered.

Shelia turned toward her Buick, scarf catching the light. "Come on, baby," she said gently, voice steady despite the tremor underneath. "Let's go find somethin' fried and sweet before I say somethin' that gets us both struck by lightnin'."

Van hesitated, then followed, the gravel crunching under his shoes. He looked back once — his father still standing beside the truck, hands on his hips, head bowed just slightly, like he couldn't tell if he'd lost a battle or a blessing. Millie stood near him, quiet, the cold wind catching her hair as she watched them go.

And as Shelia's car door creaked open and the cold air shifted, Van realized something simple and irrevocable:

sometimes salvation didn't sound like a hymn.

Sometimes it sounded like Aunt Shelia telling the truth in a parking lot — loud enough for heaven to hear, but quiet enough to still count as love.

THE TABLE

The house smelled like cornbread and tension —
familiar, heavy, and almost holy.

That Sunday smell that made dinner feel more like obligation than comfort.

His mother moved through the kitchen in practiced silence, pulling casseroles from the oven and setting out the good plates — the ones reserved for holidays or sermons that went too long.

His father sat at the head of the table, fingers laced tight, eyes tracing the tablecloth's faded floral pattern like it might reveal the right words.

Van lingered near the doorway, unsure whether he should help or stay invisible.

Aunt Shelia leaned against the counter, sweet tea in hand, pretending to read the church bulletin she'd tucked into her purse earlier, the paper creasing between her fingers.

Every sound carried too sharply — the scrape of silverware, the hum of the refrigerator, the ticking clock that had survived three houses and two generations.

"Emmalee," his mother called, "tell your brother dinner's ready."

Emmalee came skidding down the hall, socks sliding on the linoleum, hair half-pulled into a crooked ponytail.

"He's right there," she said, pointing at Van with a grin.

His mother smiled faintly. "Then tell your daddy to bless the food."

His father cleared his throat but didn't speak right away.

"Lord," he began finally, "thank You for this meal, for family, for the chance to gather and—"

He stopped. The pause stretched long enough for the silence to breathe.

"—for guidance, even when it's hard to see the right path. Amen."

"Amen," they echoed.

Plates shifted. Cornbread passed. Roast carved. Beans ladled.

The motions were the same as always — the rhythm of routine pretending it could drown out the noise beneath.

"So," Shelia said at last, breaking the quiet, "what'd y'all think of Pastor Rich's sermon today?"

His father didn't look up. "He was clear."

"Clear as mud," she said, sipping her tea. "Sounded to me like he was preachin' to specific pews."

His mother gave her sister a look. "Shelia…"

"What? I'm just sayin'. Mighty convenient time to talk about 'temptations among young men.' Selective scripture ain't exactly new."

The fork in his father's hand hit the plate harder than it should've.

"We're not discussin' church politics at the table."

"Oh, I didn't realize truth was political now," Shelia replied, tone light but blade-sharp. "Guess I skipped that lesson in Sunday school."

His mother sighed. "Please, just eat."

Shelia raised her glass. "Alright. But the day I stop sayin' what needs sayin' is the day y'all bury me twice."

Van tried to swallow a bite of roast, but it turned dry in his mouth.

Emmalee, oblivious to the tension, poked at her mashed potatoes.

"Daddy," she said, "how come everyone at church keeps whisperin' about Van?"

The room froze.

His father's hand paused mid-air. His mother's breath caught. Shelia gave a quiet, humorless laugh that broke apart before it reached her eyes.

Van's pulse thudded behind his ribs. "Em…"

She looked up, brow furrowed. "They were sayin' stuff about him and Jeremiah. I told 'em to hush, 'cause Van's nicer than half those mean girls anyway."

His mother spoke gently. "Sweetheart, sometimes people talk when they don't understand."

Shelia murmured, "Or when they don't want to."

His father's jaw set. "That's enough."

"No," Shelia said softly. "That's exactly what needs sayin'."

His father's palm hit the table, the sound sharp as a slap. "You think you're helpin'? You come in here, stir up talk, and now my daughter's askin' questions I shouldn't have to answer!"

His mother flinched. "Jeff—"

"No," he snapped, pointing at Shelia. "You've been meddlin' since breakfast. If you'd just kept your mouth shut—"

"She's the only one sayin' what you're too scared to," Van said suddenly, voice trembling but loud enough to fill the space.

His father turned, eyes hard. "Scared? You think I'm scared, boy?"

Van swallowed. "Yeah. Of what people think. Of losin' face more than losin' family."

His mother whispered, "Van—"

"No, Mama. I'm tired of pretendin' this is about sermons and secrets. You act like me bein' honest is the sin, not the lie you wanted me to live."

His father pushed back from the table, chair legs scraping the floor. "You don't know what it's like to raise a family here — to live in a town that judges before it forgives."

Shelia's tone cut clean through. "Then maybe it's time somebody stopped carin' about forgiveness from folks who don't know what grace means."

He turned on her. "You always did love to talk. But you don't have a husband, Shelia. You don't have kids who get pointed at."

Her eyes flashed. "No, but I've watched enough children lose themselves tryin' to make their parents look good. And I won't sit here while it happens again — not in my sister's kitchen."

His mother stood then, trembling. "Both of you — enough!"

Her voice cracked like thunder. "This is our table. Our family. And if we can't sit here without tearin' each other apart, maybe we don't deserve to pray over the food."

The silence afterward was heavy and holy.

Van looked at her — hands shaking, tears caught in her lashes — and something in him softened.

She wasn't pickin' sides anymore. She was just tired of holdin' a house together with her bare hands.

Emmalee sniffled, small voice wobbling. "I didn't mean to make y'all mad."

Shelia reached across the table, brushing a curl from her niece's forehead. "You didn't, sugar. You just told the truth. Grown folks forget how sometimes."

Emmalee hesitated, then looked at her brother, eyes wide with certainty.

"I don't care if Van loves Jeremiah," she said. "He's happy when he's with him. And that's good, right? Love's just love — isn't it, Aunt Shelia?"

Shelia's expression softened, the edges of her mouth lifting.

"That's exactly right, baby. Love's the only thing that's ever been worth tellin' the truth about."

The words lingered in the air, trembling between peace and ache.

His father's shoulders dropped slightly, the fight draining from him though the shame still clung.

His mother pressed her napkin to her eyes. No one moved for a long time.

The clock ticked on. The roast cooled.

Outside, a soft wind moved through the trees, brushing the windows like forgiveness trying to find a way in.

When the meal finally ended, Shelia gathered the dishes. "I'll clean up," she said quietly. "Maybe that'll count as my penance."

His mother nodded, voice low. "Thank you."

Van stood, folding his napkin. His father didn't look up.

His mother offered him a faint, weary smile — the kind that said *I love you, but I don't know how to fix this yet.*

Shelia met his eyes across the table. "Go on, baby," she murmured. "Get some air. Let the Lord cool this house off before it catches fire."

Van stepped onto the porch, the screen door sighing shut behind him.

The sky had turned lavender; the last light of day stretched long over the yard.

Inside, voices dropped to a low murmur — a family still trying to decide if truth was the thing that would break them, or the thing that might finally set them free.

THE PORCH

SPRING, 2002 — BRIAR HOLLOW, NORTH
CAROLINA

The porch light hummed against the gathering dark.

It wasn't a steady sound — more a low, flickering drone, like the house itself was sighing after holding its breath all day. Crickets had started their slow hymn in the yard, that whispering rhythm that came only when the world decided to hush. Every chirp seemed to fill the cracks left behind by arguments and prayers.

Van sat on the steps, elbows braced on his knees, his breath ghosting out in faint steam that caught the light before vanishing. The evening had cooled faster than he expected, the kind of chill that carried the sharpness of pine and the ghost of wood smoke. The scent of supper still clung to his shirt — roast, cornbread, and something sweet that had gone untouched after everything fell apart.

Behind him, the house murmured faintly. Water ran. Dishes clinked. Shelia's low voice threaded through it all like a hymn trying to calm the air after a storm. His parents' tones were quieter now, but quiet didn't mean peace — it just meant they'd run out of words loud enough to throw.

He leaned forward, tracing the worn edge of the porch step

with his thumb. The wood had been painted white once, but years of seasons had stripped it down to its bare grain. His father always said he'd repaint it come spring, but somehow spring always brought new excuses.

Storm. Work. Church repairs.

The porch had learned to live unpainted — weathered, honest, and tired.

He exhaled through his nose, slow. The sound of the night filled the spaces where his thoughts didn't dare go.

Storm, stillness, clean-up.

He knew that pattern too well — it was the family's unspoken liturgy.

The screen door creaked open.

Shelia stepped out, her silhouette framed in the soft kitchen light behind her. A glass of sweet tea in one hand, a cigarette in the other. The porch light caught the faint gold in her hair, the silver of her earrings, the thin thread of smoke curling up like prayer. She let the door ease shut behind her and crossed the porch boards slow, lowering herself into the old wicker chair beside him.

"Well," she said finally, exhaling smoke through her nose, "that went about as smooth as a wagon on square wheels."

Van huffed out a quiet laugh that wavered between humor and defeat. "Guess I shouldn't have expected much else."

"Maybe not," she said. "But honesty never does come cheap. You pay for it one way or another."

She took another drag, flicked the ash into the tin tray perched on the railing. "Still worth every penny, though."

He nodded, eyes fixed on the yard. The frost had started to silver the grass again, the moonlight spreading over it like milk. The night held that soft quiet of a world caught between winter and spring — tired of being cold but not ready to thaw.

After a while, his voice broke the stillness, soft and unsure.

"I've been thinkin' a lot lately. About Grandma."

Shelia's gaze softened. "She's been gone a long time, but she'd like that. What about her?"

Van rubbed his palms together for warmth. "She used to talk about God like He was somebody you could sit down with at the table. Said He liked the smell of biscuits and garden dirt better than incense. Said He was in the quiet places more than the loud ones."

Shelia smiled around the edge of her cigarette. "Your grandma was right more often than she knew."

He stared at the yard a while longer before speaking again, his voice lower now. "I keep thinkin' about that — about the talks we used to have. I told her things I didn't tell anyone else. Guess I thought… maybe she'd still be listenin'."

Shelia tipped her head, eyes on him. "She is," she said softly. "And so is He."

The words landed like a hand on his shoulder.

He drew in a breath, and somewhere deep inside, memory stirred.

He was nine again — sitting on that same porch, but the boards were brighter then, the paint newer. The summer light was honey-thick, the air full of cut grass and cicadas. Grandma Shelton sat in her rocking chair, a shelling bowl in her lap and her apron dusted with flour. A radio played something soft through static from the kitchen — Patsy Cline, maybe, or Loretta.

"Hand me that bag, sugar," she'd said, nodding toward the paper sack beside him.

Van passed it over, the brown paper damp where it rested against the sweating glass of sweet tea. He remembered her hands — strong, freckled, a few small scars from years of cooking and church socials. She worked the beans slow, dropping them one by one into the metal bowl. The rhythm of it filled the silence between them, steady as a clock.

"You been quiet all mornin'," she'd said. "That usually means you're thinkin' too hard."

He'd shrugged, bare feet swinging off the step. "They were talkin' about hell in Sunday school again," he'd murmured. "Said if you don't fit in, you might end up there."

She'd looked at him long — not unkindly, but with that sharp sort of knowing that made hiding impossible. "Well, baby," she'd said, "folks talk about hell 'cause they don't know how to make sense of grace. But the Lord I know don't throw away what He made. Not even the parts people misunderstand."

Van had frowned. "You sure?"

She'd smiled, slow and certain. "I'm old enough to be. And if you ever get lost tryin' to find Him, you just talk to Him like He's sittin' right here —" she tapped the space between them on the porch rail, "— 'cause He is."

She'd leaned back in her chair then, the wood creaking beneath her. "Remember, Donovan Shelton — God ain't scared of truth. It's people that are."

The sound of a lighter snapped him back to the present. The porch around him was older now, worn the way memories always are.

Shelia's new cigarette flared, the smoke tracing its soft gray path toward the light.

Van's voice trembled when he spoke. "I've been talkin' to Him a lot lately. Tellin' Him things I probably shouldn't."

He hesitated. "That I really like Jeremiah. More than I ever meant to. But I don't know what to do with it. I'm scared of what'll happen when the rest of the church finds out."

The night held still around them. The crickets even seemed to pause, like they knew better than to interrupt confession.

Shelia took her time before answering. She lit her cigarette again, the tip glowing faintly.

"Honey," she said at last, "I reckon most of 'em already have. That sermon this mornin'? That wasn't about stray souls and wayward paths. That was a man with a pulpit tryin' to build a fence around his own fears."

Van turned toward her, searching her face. "You think Pastor Rich knows?"

"I think he suspects," she said, voice calm. "And I think the whole town's buzzin' like a hornet's nest because of it."

She looked at him — not pitying, just steady. "But that ain't your burden to carry, sugar. People talk when they're scared. Fear's a louder preacher than love most days."

Van swallowed hard. "If he knows — if everybody does — what happens now? To Jeremiah? To me?"

Shelia sighed, smoke curling through the air like a slow prayer. "Then you walk through it together. And if the ground shakes, that's just proof it's real. Love's supposed to rattle somethin'. Always has."

He dropped his face into his hands, whispering, "You make it sound simple."

"It ain't simple," she said gently. "But it's honest. And you can build a life on honest, even if it starts small."

She reached over, brushed a hand across the back of his head — mother-soft. "You got his heart, and you got yours. That's already more than most men figure out in a lifetime."

He let out a shaky laugh that broke halfway into a sob. "I wish I was brave like you."

Shelia smiled, flicking the last bit of ash. "You're braver than me, Van. You told the truth before you had gray hair to hide behind."

They sat like that for a long while — two silhouettes wrapped in porchlight and cigarette smoke. The night breathed around them. Somewhere far off, a dog barked, and then the long, low sound of a train horn rolled through the fields like thunder remembering itself.

Shelia stubbed her cigarette against the tray, glass clinking softly as she reached for her tea. "You keep talkin' to God, you hear? But make sure it's the one Grandma knew — not the one folks like Pastor Rich keep in a box."

Van smiled faintly, his voice no louder than the hum of the porch light. "Yeah. I think I'm startin' to tell the difference."

The silence that followed wasn't empty — it was full of crickets, cooling air, and something unspoken but safe.

Then, from the road beyond the trees, came the low rumble of an old Ford. The headlights cut through the pines, sweeping across the front yard and the porch rail. Jeremiah's truck — he knew that sound before he even saw it. The engine passed slow, deliberate, as if carrying the weight of something unsaid.

Van's breath caught. He watched the taillights fade through the trees, red against the gray air, until all that was left was the hum of night.

Shelia noticed. She didn't speak — just took a slow sip from her glass and murmured, "Looks like the Lord's still listenin'."

Van smiled — small, quiet, but real.

The porch felt warmer somehow.

Like peace had finally gathered enough courage to sit down beside him.

"Some ground has to break before it can grow anything worth keeping."

QUIET HALLWAYS

Piedmont Valley High — Monday Morning, March 2002
The world felt quieter that morning — not the kind of quiet that soothes, but the kind that hums beneath the skin, waiting. The weekend had passed in slow motion. Sunday had slipped through the house in whispers — his parents pretending calm, his sister keeping her head down over her cereal, his mother humming hymns without words.

Now it was Monday.

And the air outside smelled like thawed earth and diesel, the faint sting of chalk dust that clung to everything in March.

Van parked his car along the edge of the student lot, where the cracked asphalt gave way to patches of half-dead grass. The school loomed ahead — red brick, too proud for its age, with banners from past championships fading on the walls. A cheerleader poster curled at the edges beside the front doors, its slogan — *SPRING INTO SUCCESS!* — half peeled by the damp.

He sat there a moment with the engine ticking down, watching students filter through the double doors in small, buzzing groups. Laughter here, shouting there. The same morning ritual — the same people, same rhythm. And yet the air around him felt charged, like someone had whispered his name just out of earshot.

He turned off the ignition, grabbed his backpack, and stepped out. The gravel crunched under his shoes, the cold air brushing his face like a warning. He could feel eyes — not all at once, but in glances. A few too-long looks. A conversation that stopped just before he passed.

Inside, the fluorescent lights were already too bright.

The sound of lockers opening and shutting echoed through the hall — a metallic heartbeat. The whiteboards in classrooms gleamed clean for the week, each one carrying faint ghost-marks of what had been written before, sentences half-erased but still there if you looked close enough.

He walked toward his first class, blending into the tide. Some-one's Walkman leaked a tinny hum of *Matchbox Twenty*. A janitor pushed a mop down the far hall, radio clipped to his belt whis-pering weather updates. Everything looked the same — but it wasn't.

Van's locker creaked open with a sigh. A small photo fluttered from the door — the one of him, Jeremiah, Dana, and Avery at the diner a few months back. Grease-stained napkins on the table, syrup bottles, and Avery's peace sign caught mid-motion. He smiled faintly at it, then shut the locker before anyone else could see.

"Van!"

Lisa Cartwright's voice broke through the noise. She walked toward him, clutching her binder like it might anchor her to the floor. She was all neat edges — ponytail pulled tight, cardigan buttoned, a cross pendant glinting against the neckline. Her smile was practiced but not unkind.

"Hey," he said, softer than he meant to.

"You ready for the presentation prep?" she asked, her tone bright but tentative. "Mr. Pope said we'd have the library this week. I brought my outline."

"Yeah," he said, adjusting the strap on his bag. "I've got my notes. Just… haven't had much time to polish."

She nodded, a little too quickly. "That's okay. We've got a few days."

Her voice dipped, uncertain. "You okay? You seemed… quiet yesterday. At church."

Van's pulse jumped, a heat rising to his neck. "Yeah," he said, forcing a small laugh. "Just tired."

Lisa studied him, her brow pinching slightly. "You know, Pastor Rich's message really hit me. About truth, and… temptation. It's wild how he always says what people need to hear."

Her words landed soft, but they stung anyway — a reminder dressed as conversation.

Van swallowed. "Yeah," he said finally, "he's got a way of findin' words, all right."

She smiled, oblivious to the edge under his tone. "You want to meet at lunch to work on the thesis statement? I was thinking something about moral responsibility in modern culture."

"That's fine," he said, his voice flat before he could catch it.

"Cool." She hesitated, then added, "It's good we're doing this one together. You've always got a clear head for this kind of topic."

He almost laughed at that — *clear head*. If only she knew how noisy it was in there.

They parted at the corner. She turned down the hall toward English, and he stood there a moment, staring at the pale reflection of himself in the glass trophy case — distorted between old plaques and gold figurines of running backs from a decade ago.

"Hell of a Monday, huh?"

The voice came from behind.

Avery Reid — slouched against the lockers, one strap of his backpack hanging loose, a smirk tugging at his mouth.

He leaned there like he owned the hallway — one foot crossed over the other, denim jacket collar popped just enough to look accidental. His blond hair was styled with that calculated mess every guy pretended *wasn't* styled, the tips faintly frosted so they caught the fluorescent light. A silver thumb ring flashed as he spun his keys, and his layered Abercrombie tees — gray over white — fit in a way that made teachers sigh and parents whisper. Boot-cut jeans, lived-in Converse, and the faint, citrus-sharp trace of Clinique Happy cologne completed him. Avery didn't strut; he *glided*, like he was always walking toward the next good line in his own script.

"Didn't see you at all last week. Not the diner, or church, barely even at school," Van said.

"Got grounded," Avery replied, flipping his keychain around his finger. "Apparently skipping Wednesday youth group to watch *Queer as Folk* isn't God's plan for my life."

He grinned. "News to me."

Van cracked a small smile despite himself. "You never do make it easy for 'em."

"That's the fun part," Avery said, leaning closer, voice dropping low. "People around here only think they're polite. You start bein' honest, and suddenly everyone's got the Holy Spirit on speed dial."

Van huffed out a quiet laugh, glancing around. "You shouldn't—"

"Shouldn't what?" Avery said. "Say it out loud?" He shrugged. "Somebody's gotta."

He straightened up, eyes catching Van's. "You okay, though? You look like somebody unplugged your light."

Van hesitated, searching for words that wouldn't give too much away. "Just a long weekend."

Avery's expression softened — not pity, just knowing. "Yeah," he said. "Heard about Pastor Rich's little performance Sunday. Real subtle."

Van's chest tightened. "You heard?"

"Van," Avery said, voice gentler now, "it's Briar Hollow. You whisper in one end of town, and it echoes out the other before lunch period."

Van sighed. "Guess I shouldn't be surprised."

"Don't let it eat you," Avery said. "They only talk 'cause they can't imagine livin' without somethin' to point at."

He grinned again, the edge returning to his voice. "Besides, I kinda like bein' their sermon illustration. Gives 'em somethin' to do."

The bell rang overhead — long and metallic, swallowing the end of his sentence. Students began filing toward class. Avery gave Van a mock salute before disappearing into the crowd, his confidence trailing behind like the smell of cheap cologne and rebellion.

Van stood there a second longer, his backpack heavy on his shoulder. The world felt louder again — not in sound, but in pressure. The hum of lights. The scrape of shoes. The faint, ever-present sense of being seen but not known.

He made it through the morning on autopilot — Mr. Pope's voice droning over outlines, the scent of dry-erase markers, the rhythmic squeak of the whiteboard as he wrote *FACTS OVER FEELINGS* in neat, blue letters. The words stared back at him, too clean, too certain.

By lunch, Van had barely touched his tray. The cafeteria smelled of ketchup and fryer oil. Lisa waved him over, papers spread out on the table. Her notes were color-coded — yellow for quotes, pink for "personal reflection." She talked through her points with quiet conviction, quoting Proverbs like punctuation. Van nodded in the right places, but his thoughts drifted elsewhere — to Jeremiah's empty seat across the room.

Jeremiah sat two tables over, half-turned toward his friends on the basketball team. He was laughing at something, head thrown back, the sunlight from the window cutting across his profile. But there was a restraint in it — a politeness, like he was performing an emotion instead of feeling it.

Their eyes met for half a second. Then Jeremiah looked away.

Van's stomach twisted, the kind of ache that comes when you know better than to hope.

Lisa said something — he missed it.

"Sorry," he muttered. "What?"

"I said," she repeated gently, "I think Pastor Rich would be proud of this topic. It's what families need to hear."

Her words hit harder this time. They were innocent — painfully so — but they cracked something open in him.

Van leaned back in his chair, the cafeteria hum dimming around him.

"You ever think maybe," he said slowly, "that what people *need* to hear and what they're *ready* to hear ain't the same thing?"

Lisa blinked. "What do you mean?"

He searched for a way to soften it but couldn't find one. "Just seems like the people always preachin' about truth don't like it much when they finally see it."

Her expression tightened. "That's not fair."

"Maybe not," he said quietly. "But it's honest."

The silence that followed was brief but sharp. She looked down, gathering her papers. "I'll… finish the citations tonight," she said, her voice thinner now. "We can meet after school to put it together."

He nodded, though he wasn't sure she saw. She left before the warning bell for third period. Leaving Van alone in the sea of conversations and and waves of his name crashing from every corner.

THE REST of the day blurred.

History class. Notes. The smell of chalk. The squeak of sneakers in the hall. Jeremiah's laugh down the corridor — the kind that made Van's chest both ache and settle.

By the final bell, the sky had dimmed. The air outside was soft with the smell of coming rain. Students poured out in small groups, their chatter fading toward the parking lot.

Van walked alone.

He reached his car, dropped his bag in the passenger seat, and sat there with his hands on the wheel, the keys dangling from the ignition. The air smelled faintly of peaches and notebook paper. A song on the radio started mid-verse — Train's *"Drops of Jupiter"* — but he didn't turn it up. He just let it play quiet in the background, that familiar melody cutting through the stillness.

He stared out the windshield at the empty lot, the pale glow of the school windows, the reflection of himself in the glass — older somehow, or maybe just tired.

The hum of the engine joined the hum of his thoughts.

Out there, somewhere beyond the tree line, Jeremiah's truck would be on the road again. Van pictured it — headlights carving through dusk, the radio low, the steering wheel worn smooth from all the miles they'd already put between who they were and who they were allowed to be.

He breathed in, slow.

The silence inside the car felt heavier than the night before — but not empty.

It was the kind that meant something was about to shift.

And for the first time in days, he didn't feel like running from it.

Mercy don't need permission.

Mercy is the part of truth that sounds like love when everything else sounds like law.

UNEVEN GROUND

February settled over Briar Hollow like a sigh.

The sky never seemed to pick a color—just a long stretch of washed-out gray that made the world feel half-asleep. The trees along Main Street were still bare, their branches drawn like the veins of a hand pressed against heaven. It was cold, but not sharp anymore. Winter was loosening its grip; you could smell the dirt underneath.

Piedmont Valley High's parking lot gleamed with last night's rain. Puddles mirrored the flagpole and the low, sagging clouds. Van parked and sat for a minute, radio low, watching students cross the lot in little clumps of chatter and laughter. Somewhere behind the noise, his thoughts moved like slow water.

He didn't dread school anymore. He didn't look forward to it, either. It was just a place to be between everything else.

Lisa Cartwright waved when he entered English 11, her notebook already open, color-coded tabs lining the edge like a picket fence. She had that kind of cheerful discipline that made teachers love her. She smiled at him in a way that wasn't forced, and somehow that made him like her more.

"Morning, partner," she said.

"Hey." He slid into the chair beside her, shaking the rain from his jacket sleeve.

She tapped her pencil against the header on the page. "Okay, I've been thinking—what if we take the family-values idea and make it about how belief systems shape morality instead? Like how people use faith to define right and wrong."

Van blinked. "That's… pretty heavy."

Lisa laughed softly. "You're telling me. But Mr. Pope said he wants depth."

He looked down at her notes. She'd already drawn lines between ideas—*religion, culture, tradition, individual truth.* Seeing the words laid out like that made his stomach twist.

"You sure you wanna open that box?" he asked.

She shrugged. "If we can't talk about it in a classroom, then where?"

He nodded slowly. "Fair."

Mr. Pope strolled in right as the bell rang, coffee in hand, tie a little crooked as always. "Alright, scholars," he said, voice echoing above the chatter. "By next Friday, I need your outlines. Remember, research means facts—opinions don't pass for evidence, no matter how loud they are."

Someone groaned. Mr. Pope grinned. "That sound means I'm doing my job."

Van half-smiled. He liked the man's honesty. It was rare around here.

THEY MET in the library after school, the long windows tinted by a thin film of dust. The room smelled like paper, floor polish, and rain leaking faintly from somewhere near the back wall. Lisa spread her folders across the table. Van's notebook sat mostly blank beside them.

"So," she said, "what do you actually think?"

"About what?"

"Morality," she said, twirling her pencil. "Where it comes from."

Van thought about it longer than he meant to. "I think people like to believe it comes from rules," he said slowly, "but maybe it comes from mercy instead."

Lisa looked up. "Mercy?"

"Yeah," he said. "Like how you treat people when nobody tells you how to. Rules just give you excuses."

She studied him. "That's… actually really good. You write that down."

He smiled, embarrassed. "Nah, it's just talk."

"Talk's where the best writing starts," she said. "My daddy always says truth sounds better before it's been rehearsed."

They worked another hour, the kind of silence between them that wasn't awkward—just full. Outside, the rain eased to mist. Every so often, Van glanced at the doorway, half expecting Jeremiah to walk in. He never did.

By Thursday, word had spread about the topics everyone picked. It was the kind of thing Piedmont Valley fed on—idle talk between classes, whispered in the cafeteria line, traded like currency for a better seat at lunch. Dana caught up with him outside the vending machines.

"So, morality and family, huh?" she said, eyebrows up. "You sure you wanna let this school grade your soul?"

"Not my soul," Van said. "Just my essay."

She grinned. "Same thing around here."

Avery appeared beside her, dramatic as always. "Oh Lord, the preacher's son and the choir boy. They're gonna think you're takin' notes straight from the Book of Revelations."

"Let 'em," Van said. "At least I'll have the citations."

They laughed, living in a world of just them and no one else. It felt good—real laughter, not the nervous kind. Dana looped her arm through his. "Come on. Jeremiah's in the gym. Let's see if we can ruin his concentration."

THE GYM SMELLED like rubber and sweat and pine oil. The sound of basketballs echoed off the rafters. Jeremiah stood near the free-throw line, shooting slow, deliberate arcs. Colby rebounded for him in silence. When Van walked in, the sound changed—laughter dimmed, voices dipped. The ball hit the rim and rolled away.

Jeremiah wiped his forehead with his sleeve, eyes flicking up just long enough to catch Van's. A flicker of something passed there—gratitude, maybe, or guilt—but he didn't smile.

Colby tossed the ball back to him. "Game's private, Shelton."

Dana crossed her arms. "What, y'all startin' to charge admission now?"

Colby's mouth tightened. "Just keepin' practice clean."

Avery leaned against the bleachers. "Bless your heart, Colby. If gossip burned calories, you'd be state champion."

Van stepped forward, voice even. "It's fine, y'all. We were just leaving."

Jeremiah hesitated, the ball hanging loose at his side. "See you later?" he asked quietly.

Van nodded once. "Yeah. Library."

That small word—*later*—was enough to carry him through the rest of the day.

. . .

FRIDAY EVENING BROUGHT A RARE STILLNESS. Van sat at his desk, lamplight falling across open books and half-written notes. Lisa's neat handwriting filled the margins of their shared outline: *How belief defines morality.* Beneath it, she'd scribbled, *Van—find that mercy quote.*

He smirked. She'd remembered.

He flipped to a clean page and started to write.

Mercy don't need permission.

Mercy is the part of truth that sounds like love when everything else sounds like law.

He stopped there, staring at the line until it blurred. Then he wrote more—about hypocrisy, about sermons that smelled like fear, about the quiet kind of holiness that lived in kindness instead of pews. The words came fast, messy, but they came.

By the time he stopped, three pages were filled. He hadn't meant to write a confession, but that's what it looked like.

SATURDAY MORNING AT THE DINER, Marlene poured coffee into his cup without asking. "You look like you wrestled a ghost," she said.

Van smiled. "Homework."

"Lord," she said, shaking her head. "Ain't no ghost tougher than that."

Frank leaned out from the kitchen window. "Kid's turnin' into a philosopher," he said. "Long as he don't start quotin' Plato while flippin' pancakes, we'll keep him."

Van grinned. "I'll try to keep my existentialism in check."

The line cooks laughed. The easy noise of the place filled him —clatter, voices, the hiss of bacon. It was the first time in weeks he'd felt normal.

When the lunch rush slowed, Marlene leaned on the counter. "How's your friend Jeremiah?"

He hesitated. "He's… figuring things out."

"Mm," she said. "Ain't we all. Tell him he's welcome here, same as you. Lord knows this town needs more boys who listen better than they talk."

Van nodded, gratitude tight in his chest.

SUNDAY, Aunt Shelia came by the house unannounced, as usual. She carried a pie and a pack of smokes in the same hand. "Sweetness for the mouth, bitterness for the lungs," she said. "Keeps me balanced."

They sat on the porch while the wind fussed through the trees. The air smelled like woodsmoke and rain-damp dirt.

"How's school?" she asked.

"Fine."

"That a lie or a half-truth?"

"Half-truth," he said, smiling.

"That's progress," she said, lighting a cigarette. "You and Jeremiah still talking or did the pastor's sermon slap a dapper on that?"

"Some," he said. "It's just… everything feels watched."

She blew smoke into the cold air. "That's small towns for you. They stare till they see what they're afraid of."

He looked out at the road. "You think it'll ever stop?"

"No," she said plainly. "But you'll stop carin'. That's the trick."

Aunt Sheila finished her cigarette, catching herself from flinging the spent filter in the front yard, resolving to use the ashtray on the banister instead. Knowing Van's father would have something to say about it if she didn't. Resolved in the silence, Aunt Sheila leaned in a kissed Van's temple. Lingering just a moment to whisper, "Don't stay out here trying to answer the what if's because the world doesn't wait for you to figure it out. No don't be catching your death out here trying to move heaven and earth with your thoughts." The faint smoke smell still leaving a familiar tone to her advice.

"Yes ma'am, I won't." Van says, standing only to realize how cold he really was. He thought how funny it was how somethings aren't even a thought until someone points it out. And then that's all you can think about. Somehow that didn't seem fair but he resolved with his deep thoughts and chose to join the others for a piece of pie.

MONDAY CAME with sunlight so bright it looked like forgiveness. The halls of Piedmont Valley felt different—students buzzing with project nerves, teachers clutching coffee like survival. Van handed in the outline to Mr. Pope, who read the first few lines and raised an eyebrow.

"You write this part about mercy?"

"Yes, sir."

Mr. Pope nodded slowly. "Keep that voice. The world's already got enough echoes."

Van smiled faintly. "I'll try."

AT LUNCH, Dana slapped her tray down beside him. "Rumor says the prom theme's been decided."

"Oh?" Van asked. "What now—Heaven and Hell?"

"Worse," Avery said, appearing behind her with theatrical despair. "*A Night Under the Stars.* Because apparently we've run out of metaphors."

Dana rolled her eyes. "If they hang one more string of Christmas lights and call it décor, I swear I'll lose it."

Van laughed. "At least stars are free."

"Not if you're buying the tickets," Avery said. "Heard they're doin' couples discounts."

Van's laughter faded. The implication landed between them. Dana noticed.

"Hey," she said, softer now. "One thing at a time."

He nodded. But the thought stuck—the image of standing under a paper sky, Jeremiah beside him, flash of a camera, proof that they'd existed like everyone else for one night. The idea felt dangerous and holy all at once.

THAT EVENING, he drove the back roads home, sun bleeding gold through the tree line. The windows were down, cold air biting but alive. The radio hummed an old country song his mother loved—something about finding grace between the verses. He sang along without meaning to.

By the time he reached the driveway, the world had softened. His mother's car was gone; only his father's truck sat near the shed. He parked beside it, engine ticking as it cooled.

Inside, the house smelled of pot roast and lemon cleaner. The table was set for three. His father looked up from the paper. "You're late."

"Library," Van said.

His father nodded once. "Good. Keep your head in your books. Lord knows it's safer than people."

Van wanted to say *some people are worth the risk*, but he didn't. He just sat, spooned potatoes onto his plate, and let the silence stretch.

LATER, lying in bed, the dark pressed close and gentle. Somewhere outside, a dog barked once, then stopped as quickly as it started. He thought about Lisa's outline, Dana's loyalty, Aunt Shelia's fierce laughter, Jeremiah's quiet eyes. The world was still full of noise and fear, but inside all that, a thin thread of peace had started to hum. He didn't know what came next—only that he'd face it awake.

The clock on the dresser ticked toward midnight, each second soft as breath.

Van closed his eyes and let it count him forward.

THE SPARK BENEATH THE STARS

March came to Briar Hollow like a guest who didn't know when to leave.

The mornings were still cold enough to sting, but the afternoons carried a softness that smelled faintly of cut grass and diesel. Puddles shrank into the cracked asphalt of the Piedmont Valley High lot. Students traded flannel for T-shirts, boots for sneakers. The world was thawing, even if the people weren't.

Inside, the hum of the intercom broke through the morning shuffle of lockers.

"Good morning, Piedmont Valley High. This year's Junior Prom theme has been chosen: *A Night Under the Stars!* Tickets go on sale Monday in the front office — couples' discounts available!"

A wave of chatter swept the hallway. Dana groaned so loud it echoed.

"Lord, they've done it again. Somebody tell these people metaphors don't count as decorations."

Avery struck a dramatic pose against his locker. "Picture it — glitter everywhere, cardboard moons, one deflated balloon by nine o'clock. Romance in its purest form."

Van laughed, balancing his books. "You two sound traumatized."

"We are traumatized," Dana said. "Last year the theme was *An Evening in Paris*. They bought one fake Eiffel Tower and called it immersive."

"Maybe they'll hang fairy lights this time," Van offered.

"Maybe they'll hang us," Avery said. "Prom — where joy goes to die under budget constraints."

Lisa Cartwright passed by just then, smiling politely. "At least it's not Rustic Romance. My cousin's school did that. Hay bales and splinters everywhere."

Dana shuddered. "I take back my complaints. Hay belongs under cows, not corsages."

Lisa laughed softly — that quiet, steady kind of laugh that didn't demand attention but warmed the air around it.

"Still," she added, "a night under the stars sounds like hope if you let it."

Van caught that line and tucked it away. Hope always sounded better when Lisa said it.

The bell rang, cutting their laughter short. But for a moment — a rare, beautiful moment — it felt like being young again, before everything had to mean something.

Jeremiah found him between classes later that day.

He looked tired but softer, the way people do when they've stopped pretending for just a second. "You hear about prom?" he asked, leaning against the locker beside Van's.

Van grinned. "You mean *A Night Under the Stars*? I'm already pickin' out which constellation to fake-enjoy."

Jeremiah chuckled, low and warm. "You goin'?"

"Hadn't thought that far. You?"

He shrugged. "Coach says we're supposed to show up. School spirit or whatever."

Van hesitated. "We could go together. I mean—if you want."

The pause that followed wasn't long, but it stretched wide.

Jeremiah's jaw flexed, like he was chewing on words too heavy to swallow. "You sure about that?"

Van's chest tightened. "Not really," he said. "But I'm sure about you."

Something flickered in Jeremiah's eyes—hope, maybe fear, maybe both. "Then yeah," he said softly. "Let's go."

THE FOLLOWING MONDAY, the school buzzed with prom fever. Flyers taped crookedly to every wall, girls comparing dress sketches, boys pretending not to care while asking prices under their breath. Dana had already started a countdown in homeroom.

"You better be goin', Van," she said, pen tapping against her desk. "I'm not dancing alone while Avery pretends to be emotionally available."

Avery gasped. "Pretends? Girl, I'm the picture of availability—just highly curated."

Lisa laughed from the next row, soft but genuine. "You two should emcee."

Van smiled. "Nah. Jeremiah and I are goin'."

The words slipped out before he realized how easily they'd come. It felt good — like saying something that should've been said long ago.

Dana blinked. "Wait—together?"

"Yeah," Van said. "We're gettin' the tickets this afternoon."

Avery clutched his chest. "Scandal in Heritage! Somebody alert the prayer chain."

Lisa, to her credit, just smiled. "Good for you," she said quietly.

Van caught her eye and mouthed *thank you.* She nodded once.

No drama, no whispers — just kindness. It almost made him forget where he lived."

THE FRONT OFFICE was bright with fluorescent lights and the faint smell of lemon cleaner. Mrs. Henderson sat behind the counter, glasses low on her nose, a stack of ticket envelopes fanned out like cards in front of her. She was one of those women who could spot trouble before it made eye contact.

Van stepped up first. "Hi. Two tickets for prom."

She reached for the order sheet. "Names?"

"Van Shelton and Jeremiah Davis," he said.

The pause was brief — but devastating.

Her pen froze midair. She looked up over her glasses, her expression polite, practiced, and cold. "You mean one ticket each?"

"No," Van said carefully. "We're going as a couple."

Her smile didn't move, but her eyes hardened. "The couples' discount is for boy-girl pairs, sweetheart."

Jeremiah's posture stiffened beside him. "We'll still pay full price."

"That's not the issue," she said. "It's… school policy."

Van felt heat climb up his neck. "Where's that written?"

"Principal's orders," she said, tone final. "You can each buy an individual ticket. I'll put your names separately."

Jeremiah's voice came low. "Forget it."

"Jeremiah—" Van started.

But Jeremiah was already turning, jaw tight, fists clenched at his sides. The office door hit the frame harder than he meant. Every head in the hallway turned.

Van stood frozen for a moment, the fluorescent hum loud as thunder. Mrs. Henderson sighed and straightened the papers. "You boys take care now."

He nodded once, throat burning, and left.

BY LUNCH, the story had legs.

Rumor spread faster than truth in Briar Hollow, and this one was running laps.

Dana cornered him at their table. "Tell me it's not true."

"It's true."

Avery blinked. "They really said no?"

Van nodded. "Said it's 'policy.'"

Dana's mouth fell open. "Policy? What are y'all, a national threat?"

Lisa sat beside them, quiet but fuming. "That's not even legal," she said softly.

Then, almost to herself, "People forget kindness has rules too."

Avery leaned forward, whispering like a conspirator. "Honey, Piedmont Valley High runs on Jesus and denial. Legality is just decoration."

Van gave a humorless laugh. "I knew it'd be a problem. Didn't think it'd be so… small."

Jeremiah sat alone two tables away, staring at his untouched food. A few teammates laughed too loudly nearby. Van didn't have to hear the words to know.

Dana followed his gaze. "You want me to start a riot?"

"No," Van said quietly. "Not yet."

"Then when?"

"When it counts."

THAT NIGHT, he worked the late shift at the diner. Marlene watched him clean the counter for the third time in a row.

"You're gonna scrub the shine right off that," she said. "What's eatin' you?"

He hesitated. "Prom tickets."

Her brows lifted. "Lord, you sound like my niece."

"They wouldn't sell us couple tickets," he said. "Said it's against policy."

Marlene set down her mug, face softening. "Baby, I wish I could say I'm surprised."

"It's stupid," Van said. "It's just tickets."

"It's never just tickets," she said gently. "It's what they represent. People get scared when they can't control the picture."

He leaned on the counter. "Then maybe it's time we stopped letting 'em draw it."

Marlene smiled, proud. "Now that's the spirit. But pick your moment, sugar. Even truth needs good timing."

THE NEXT DAY, the hallway felt different. Heads turned, whispers curled through lockers like smoke. Some faces showed quiet support—nods, smiles. Others didn't bother to hide their judgment. Jeremiah met him by the vending machines, eyes shadowed.

"You shouldn't have pushed," he said.

"I didn't push," Van replied. "I asked for what everyone else gets."

Jeremiah rubbed the back of his neck. "It's not that simple."

"It's exactly that simple," Van said. "You scared?"

Jeremiah's jaw worked. "You don't get it. My dad—he's already on edge. If he hears about this—"

"Then he'll hear," Van said. "I'm done livin' like my happiness needs an apology."

Jeremiah looked at him a long moment, torn between admiration and fear. "You make it sound easy."

"It's not," Van said. "But it's right."

They stood there in silence, vending machine humming

between them, two boys on uneven ground but facing the same direction.

By Friday, the whispers had turned into something bigger. Lisa handed him a folded note in class — *Meet me after school.*

When the bell rang, he found her, Dana, and Avery gathered near the lockers, faces lit with the kind of mischief that usually meant trouble.

"What are y'all up to?" Van asked.

Dana grinned. "Organized rebellion."

Lisa held up a flyer. "Avery got into the principal's printer."

Avery bowed. "Don't ask how."

The flyer read:

Equality Under the Stars

If love's invited, all love belongs.

— Friday, March 21, Piedmont Valley High Prom Night

Van stared. "You're kidding."

Dana shrugged. "They want a scene? Let's give 'em one worth rememberin'."

Lisa didn't grin like the others — she just met Van's eyes, her voice steady.

"People are already talking," she said. "You've got more quiet supporters than loud ones. But the quiet ones last longer."

Van's throat tightened. "Y'all didn't have to do this."

Avery smirked. "Oh, we did. Somebody's gotta hold the match."

That weekend, Van lay awake in bed, the flyer taped to his mirror catching the faint glow of the streetlight. Outside, the wind moved through the trees like a tide. He thought of Jeremiah, of the empty seat at lunch, of the way fear kept good people quiet.

He whispered into the dark, not quite a prayer, not quite a promise.

"Let them see. Just once, let them see."

And in the stillness that followed, the word *stars* didn't sound like decoration anymore.

It sounded like hope — distant, unreachable, but burning all the same.

"It takes more courage to stay with your truth than to run from your fear."

THE ENVELOPE

*M*onday came quiet and gray, the kind of morning that didn't know what season it wanted to be.

A thin drizzle freckled the parking lot of Piedmont Valley, and the sky hung low, heavy with that pale Carolina light that made everything look like it was waiting to happen.

Van sat in his car a minute longer than usual, the wipers clicking slow arcs across the glass. His coffee had gone luke-warm, but he kept holding it like it anchored him. The radio hummed faint static between country and gospel. Every song sounded like waiting.

He'd worked the early shift at the diner, Marlene insisting he go home early with that knowing look she got when she could tell something was about to break open.

"Big week ahead, sugar," she'd said. "Walk in tall."

He'd smiled, but now — parked in front of the school, watching students cross the wet asphalt — tall felt like a word meant for somebody else. He didn't feel tall. He felt raw.

When he finally stepped out, the air bit his cheeks, and the familiar chorus of hallway sounds greeted him — lockers slamming, sneakers squeaking, laughter cutting sharp through the echo. Everything ordinary. Everything pretending to be the same.

But it wasn't.

Not since the flyers.

THE WEEK before had turned Piedmont Valley into something between a revival and a protest. Avery's *Equality Under the Stars* posters had multiplied overnight like wildflowers — taped to lockers, bathroom mirrors, even the vending machines. Someone had printed them on neon paper — hot pink, lime green, and one version scrawled in permanent marker on the back of a cafeteria tray.

The administration tried to tear them down by lunchtime, but that only made more appear. By Wednesday, even the janitor had one taped to his cart.

Some teachers smiled quietly when they saw them, their eyes saying more than their mouths ever could. Others frowned and muttered about "distractions."

But the students — they buzzed. Whispers in homerooms, folded notes in lockers, sideways glances that carried both curiosity and courage.

For once, Van didn't shrink from it. He walked taller than he had in months, shoulders square, every step saying *I'm still here.*

Jeremiah hadn't said much since the ticket incident. They'd talked once, behind the gym after practice. His voice had trembled more than the air.

"You shouldn't've pushed," he'd said.

"I didn't push," Van answered. "I just asked for what everyone else gets."

But that was days ago, and now they passed in the hallway like two pages in the same book read at different times. Their eyes found each other in the crowd, though — a thread stretched but unbroken.

. . .

By third period, the intercom crackled, rough and sudden.

"Van Shelton, please report to the principal's office."

The room stilled. Even the hum of the fluorescent lights seemed to falter.

Dana twisted in her seat. "What'd you do this time?"

"Probably existed," Avery murmured, still writing in the margins of his notebook.

Mr. Pope raised an eyebrow. "Take your things, Van."

Van stood, feeling every gaze follow him. His throat tightened, palms slick. As he gathered his papers, Lisa caught his arm, her voice low enough that only he heard.

"Whatever they say in there," she murmured, "remember — it doesn't change who you already are."

He managed a small, grateful smile. "Thanks, Lisa."

Then he stepped into the hall, the sound of the door closing behind him too final for comfort.

The walk to the office stretched longer than it ever had.

He passed bulletin boards plastered with motivational slogans — *Work Hard, Dream Big, Be Kind* — and wondered if anyone still believed those words or if they'd just become wallpaper.

Students glanced up from lockers as he passed, curiosity flickering in their eyes. Some smiled — small, nervous, the kind of smile that said *we're with you* even if they didn't have the words.

Others didn't look at all.

When he reached the office door, he paused, looking at his reflection in the small glass panel. He looked tired — older somehow. There was no anger, just the steady ache of someone learning how to stand without apology.

He stepped inside.

Mrs. Henderson was at her desk, glasses low on her nose, typing something that didn't seem to require much effort. The smell of coffee and lemon cleaner filled the room. She looked up briefly.

"Principal Moore will see you," she said, nodding toward the closed door.

Her voice carried that careful neutrality small towns reserve for uncomfortable situations — polite enough to pass for decency, distant enough to stay safe.

Van nodded, wiped his palms on his jeans, and knocked.

"Come in," a voice called.

PRINCIPAL MOORE'S office looked the same as it had since the first day of freshman year — dark wood furniture, framed photos of football teams and ribbon cuttings, a faded quote in cursive above the door: *Integrity is what you do when no one is watching.*

The irony wasn't lost on him.

Moore sat behind his wide oak desk, posture immaculate. Beside him, the assistant principal, Mrs. Carter, sat with a legal pad resting on her knee, though nothing had been written.

"Have a seat, Van," Moore said.

Van did, his chair squeaking as he shifted.

"Do you know why you're here?"

Van's heart beat hard enough to count. "I assume it's about prom."

Moore folded his hands. "You've caused quite a stir."

"I didn't mean to cause anything," Van said. "I just wanted the same thing everyone else gets."

Mrs. Carter leaned forward slightly. Her eyes weren't unkind, just tired.

"You and Jeremiah… asked to purchase couple's tickets?"

"Yes, ma'am."

"And you were told no?"

"Yes."

Moore sighed, the kind of sigh that came from years of believing progress was something best left for other people.

"You must understand, this is a small town. Piedmont Valley follows certain… traditions."

Van met his gaze evenly. "Tradition's not a rule, sir. It's just a habit people stopped questioning."

The silence that followed was long enough for him to hear the rain against the window. Mrs. Carter's pen stopped moving.

Moore exhaled slowly. "Son, I admire your conviction. But these things take time. You can't expect the world to change because of a dance."

Van's throat tightened. "No, sir. But I can expect to dance like everyone else."

Something flickered behind the principal's eyes — discomfort or something close to shame. He cleared his throat, reaching for a manila folder on the desk. He slid it toward Mrs. Carter without looking at Van.

"I think we're done here."

Mrs. Carter hesitated, then opened the folder, pulling out a white envelope. She turned it over once, thumb smoothing the crease. Then, quietly, she handed it to him.

His name was written across the front in pencil, faint and deliberate:

VAN SHELTON & JEREMIAH DAVIS

He blinked. "What's this?"

Moore's jaw shifted. "Consider it resolved. Tickets are approved."

Van stared. "Just like that?"

Mrs. Carter's mouth curved in a small, sad smile. "Sometimes the right thing needs the right nudge."

Van looked down at the envelope. His hands trembled slightly as he took it. The paper felt thin, but the weight of it filled the room.

Moore stood, signaling the end. "That's all, son. Try not to make a spectacle of it."

Van rose too, clutching the envelope. His pulse thudded in his ears. Something inside him steadied, like a compass finding north.

As he reached the door, Mrs. Carter spoke softly.

"Congratulations, Van."

He paused, met her eyes, and saw — just for a second — the quiet rebellion of a woman who'd fought smaller wars her whole life.

He nodded once. "Thank you."

THE HALLWAY OUTSIDE felt wider than before.

The fluorescent lights buzzed faintly, the linoleum reflecting thin lines of light that led straight toward the front doors. Every sound felt sharpened — lockers slamming, laughter echoing, rain whispering against the windows.

He walked slower than usual, the envelope pressed against his chest like something holy.

Halfway down the corridor, he stopped at the water fountain, leaning over to take a sip just to feel the cold metal against his hands. His reflection in the chrome looked different — older, steadier, freer.

He turned the corner, ready to head back toward class — and stopped.

Down the hall, just beyond the glass doors, he caught a flash of movement: his mother.

Her coat was buttoned tight, hair pinned neat, steps quick but composed. She didn't see him. Her head was bowed slightly, hands gripping her purse strap. She walked straight through the rain, not once looking back.

Van stood frozen.

It wasn't possible, not really — she should've been at work —

but something in his chest told him otherwise. He looked down at the envelope again, at the handwriting. Pencil, not pen. Hesitant but careful. *Familiar.*

He knew then. She'd been here.

Quietly. Softly. Fighting for him in the only way she could.

OUTSIDE, the drizzle had turned to a steady rain.

He stepped out into it, the cold drops flattening his hair, seeping through his collar. Across the courtyard, Avery and Dana huddled beneath one umbrella that had seen better days, arguing about something and laughing between gusts of wind.

Dana spotted him first. "Well? Are we organizing a protest or a parade?"

Van lifted the envelope.

Avery's mouth fell open. "They did it?"

He nodded, rainwater streaking his cheeks. "They did."

Dana threw her arms around him. "Lord, I love it when civil disobedience works before lunch!"

Avery fanned himself dramatically. "Piedmont Valley just experienced its first miracle. Somebody call Channel Five."

Van laughed, breathless. "Y'all started it."

"Please," Avery said, "we just printed the flyers. You're the one who made people listen."

Van looked out across the parking lot, where puddles reflected the gray sky like dull mirrors. "Maybe people were ready to."

"Maybe," Dana said. "But it takes someone to say it first."

JEREMIAH APPEARED THEN, hood up, backpack slung over one shoulder.

He stopped when he saw the envelope in Van's hand.

"You got them?" he asked quietly.

Van smiled, water glinting off his lashes. "*We* got them."

For a moment, Jeremiah just stared — and then something broke open in his face. Pure joy. Relief. Love, unguarded and too big to hide.

Before Van could say another word, Jeremiah crossed the distance between them, grabbing him up in a fierce embrace that lifted him clear off the ground. Van's startled laugh caught in his throat as Jeremiah spun him once, rain flying in wild arcs around them.

"Will you be my prom date, Donovan Shelton?" Jeremiah asked, his grin wide enough to split the gray sky.

Van's heart kicked hard. Laughter bubbled up through the shock. His cheeks flushed red, rain mixing with the tears he didn't try to stop.

"Yes," he said breathlessly, still lifted high in Jeremiah's arms. "Yes, I will."

Without a second thought, Jeremiah kissed him.

Right there in the middle of the courtyard — rain falling, students watching, the world paused between disbelief and awe. The kiss wasn't tentative. It was a declaration. The kind of truth too long silenced.

When they finally pulled apart, Jeremiah's forehead rested against Van's, breath trembling but steady.

"I'm so proud of you," he whispered. "Thank you for doing this — for us, for all the ones who couldn't find the voice. You're a hero, Van. And I love you."

It was the first time he'd said it.

And it felt like the whole world finally exhaled.

Dana stood frozen, eyes wide, hand over her mouth. Avery blinked twice, then whispered, "Well, damn."

A few students had stopped under the overhang, pretending to check their book bags but watching, the kind of hush that meant they knew they were seeing something sacred.

From across the lot, Colby stood near his truck, jaw tight, a storm flickering behind his eyes. Not anger — not exactly. Something quieter, heavier. Recognition, maybe. Loss.

Van didn't see him. He didn't see anyone.

For the first time in his life, he wasn't hiding.

The rain poured harder, but he didn't move. Neither of them did.

THAT NIGHT, Van placed the envelope on his dresser like it was a photograph. The lamplight turned the pencil gray into silver. Outside, thunder rolled softly over Briar Hollow, distant but constant — like a promise the sky wasn't finished keeping.

He sat on the edge of his bed, hands folded, eyes on the envelope.

"Thank you," he whispered into the quiet.

He didn't know if he meant God, his mother, Jeremiah, or the stubborn part of himself that refused to stay small.

Maybe all of them.

And somewhere beyond the window, beyond the rain and the thunder, he thought he could almost hear Aunt Shelia's voice —

steady, sure, and sweet as smoke —

"You keep your chin up, baby. God don't play favorites."

The thunder rolled again, soft and low, and Van smiled.

For the first time, it felt like the world was finally catching up to the truth.

ENCHANTED EVENING

The week before prom, the air in Briar Hollow turned warm and restless, like the town itself was holding its breath. Azaleas bloomed along every fence line, their pinks and whites spilling over like gossip too sweet to keep. School felt slower, hallways sticky with spring heat and anticipation, and everywhere Van went, someone was talking about dresses or tuxedos or who was going with whom.

At the dinner table one night, the conversation started like most things in their house did—harmless, then heavy. His father set his fork down, the sound a small punctuation in the quiet.

"So," he said, not looking up from his plate, "Proms coming. You got a date yet?"

Van glanced at his mother, hoping she might cut in, but she kept her eyes on the mashed potatoes she was stirring with quiet intensity. Aunt Shelia, perched at the far end of the table with her sweet tea, looking like she was waiting for the right moment to light a match.

"I do," Van said finally.

His father nodded once, still chewing. "That so? Anyone I know?"

Van's pulse thudded in his throat. "You might."

"From church?"

A small pause. "No, sir."

His father's eyes lifted, calm but sharp. "Boy or girl?"

The air thinned. The kitchen light hummed above them.

Van's mother whispered, "Jeff…" but his father didn't look away.

"Answer me."

"Jeremiah," Van said quietly.

A muscle worked in his father's jaw, once, twice. Then he leaned back in his chair. "You still think this is a joke? That this is just about who you take to a dance?"

"No, sir."

"Then what's it about?"

Van looked down at his plate. "It's about being honest."

His father gave a short, bitter laugh. "Honest don't mean flauntin' it. Folks already talk enough. I'd think you'd want less reason to give 'em somethin' new to whisper about."

Aunt Shelia set her glass down with a clink. "Lord, Jeff, you ever get tired of soundin' like a bad sermon?"

He turned toward her, the look on his face hard as concrete. "This ain't your concern."

"Family's always my concern," she said. "And if you'd stop worryin' about how this town sees your boy, you might notice he's turnin' into the kind of man worth seein'."

His mother's voice broke through, tired but steady. "She's right, Jeff. Enough."

He blinked at her, like he didn't quite recognize the woman sitting beside him.

"Millie—"

"No," she said, her tone flat but final. "You don't get to sit there and act like loving your son is some kind of shame. You should be proud of him."

Silence settled in again, thicker this time. The sound of the ceiling fan filled the space their words had emptied.

Emmalee, chewing the last of her roll, spoke up softly. "I think it's sweet."

Her father turned toward her. "You don't know what you're talkin' about."

"Yes, I do," she said, folding her arms. "Van loves Jeremiah. And Jeremiah makes him laugh. That's good, ain't it?"

Van's mother smiled faintly through the tension. "It is, baby."

Aunt Shelia raised her tea glass like a toast. "Out of the mouths of babes, y'all. Maybe she ought to start preachin' on Sundays."

Van couldn't help but laugh, even if it came out small. His father didn't respond. He just stared down at his plate like it had betrayed him.

After dinner, Aunt Shelia followed Van to the porch, a place that has become their connection spot. A place that allows Van to exhale and allow the weight on his shoulders to disappear. A place that with each push of the old wooden porch swing, created solutions for all of the worlds problems.

The evening air smelled like honeysuckle and rain with a haze of pollen showing the world flourishing to be born again.

"He'll come around," she said quietly. "Might take a while, but he will. Your mama already has."

Van leaned against the railing. "She the one who talked to the school."

Aunt Shelia smiled just before pulling a drag from her Virginia Slim cigarette. Creating a orange glow over her face. "I figured as much. She's got more spine than she lets on."

He nodded. "I just wish he saw it that way."

"He will," she said again. "But you can't live waitin' on someone else's permission to be yourself."

Van looked at her, at the way the porch light caught the subtle silver strands in her blonde hair. "You ever get tired of bein' right?"

"Every day," she said, reaching to drop the ashes from her cigarette in the ash tray. "But it's the cross I bear." Laughing together, Aunt Shelia went back inside the house while Van looked out over the railing to the world closing it's eyes to the day. Allowing night to reset the world for the adventures of tomorrow. But for now, even with the tension that lives in the unexpected moments of new questions and new experiences, he was being true. True to himself and true to what he believed.

PROM NIGHT CAME warm and golden. The sun sank behind the pines like a slow exhale, and the sky turned the color of rose-water and smoke.

Inside the Shelton house, chaos bloomed in waves—Aunt Shelia fussing with Van's boutonniere, Emmalee running around with a disposable camera, snapping every moment like she was the press.

Van stood in front of the mirror, adjusting his tie for the fifth time. The tux was simple—black with a faint satin stripe, fitted but not flashy. The boutonniere pinned to his lapel was white lilac and soft greenery, tied with a narrow gold ribbon.

"You look like a movie star," Aunt Shelia said, stepping back to admire him. "Only taller."

Van smiled. "You think so?"

"I know so. And if that boy of yours don't faint when he sees you, I'm marchin' down to that church and askin' God what He's doin' wrong."

Emmalee burst in, holding a hairbrush like a microphone. "Speech! Speech!"

Van laughed. "What kind of speech?"

"About prom!"

He thought for a moment. "Well, I guess I'm just glad to be goin' with someone who makes me feel like myself."

Emmalee nodded solemnly. "That's a good answer. I'm tellin' Grandma in my prayers tonight."

Aunt Shelia nearly dropped her sweet tea. "Lord, don't. Let that woman rest in peace for once."

From the living room came the sound of his mother's voice. "Van! Pictures before you leave!"

They gathered in front of the old piano, the same one that had survived two floods and a move across county lines. His mother stood beside him, smiling softly. His father hovered on the edge of the frame, his expression forced but present.

Emmalee took charge with the camera. "Okay, say cheese! No, wait—say love!"

"Love," Aunt Shelia echoed, throwing her arm around Van's shoulders.

The flash popped, bright and quick.

For a second, everything felt almost normal.

DANA'S HOUSE glowed like a lantern against the dusk. Cars lined the curb, laughter spilling from the porch. Someone had strung fairy lights across the yard, and music drifted from an open window.

Van stepped out of the car, nerves prickling his skin. He didn't have to look far to see Jeremiah—standing by the steps in a dark navy tux with a pale gold tie that matched Van's ribbon exactly.

When their eyes met, Jeremiah smiled, slow and shy, and Van forgot how to breathe.

"Hey," Jeremiah said.

"Hey yourself," Van answered.

"You look…" Jeremiah stopped, shaking his head. "Damn."

Aunt Shelia, standing by the car, fanned herself. "Alright now, I'm goin' home before y'all set the air on fire."

She didn't, of course. She stayed, camera in hand, taking photos like she'd been waiting her whole life for this night.

The group gathered on the lawn—Dana in a deep green gown, Avery in a suit with a bowtie that looked one shade too bright, Lisa in a flowing blue dress. Dana's parents hovered nearby, offering directions no one followed.

"Hold hands!" someone called. "Now look this way! Jeremiah, stand a little closer!"

Van's mother's car pulled up just as they were lining up for a group shot. Aunt Shelia waved her over like her presence was an act of defiance. "Didn't think you'd miss this."

His mother smiled, eyes glassy but proud. "Wouldn't dare."

When it came time for couple photos, Van hesitated for only a heartbeat before Jeremiah took his hand. Gasps fluttered from a few parents, but the flash went off anyway, capturing the moment in silver and light.

They stood there, hand in hand, not hiding, not explaining—just being.

THE RIDE to the prom was quiet at first. Jeremiah's truck smelled faintly of cologne and Armor All. The windows were down, the warm night air rushing in, whipping Van's hair against his forehead.

Jeremiah reached across the seat, finding Van's hand. Their fingers laced easily, naturally, like they'd been doing it forever.

"Feels normal," Jeremiah said after a while.

"It is," Van said.

Jeremiah smiled at the road. "Guess I just forgot what normal felt like."

They drove in easy silence, headlights sweeping across the long stretch of highway. Somewhere in the distance, lightning flickered behind the clouds, harmless and far away.

When they reached the hotel, the parking lot glittered with

sequins and taillights. The ballroom inside was transformed—paper lanterns hanging from the ceiling, strings of lights draped like constellations. A banner above the stage read: *A Night Under the Stars.*

It looked cheap and magical all at once.

Dana met them at the door, practically glowing. "Y'all made it!"

Avery followed, grinning. "About time. We were about to start slow dancing without supervision."

Jeremiah offered Van his arm with a little bow. "May I?"

Van laughed, looping his arm through. "You may."

As they stepped onto the dance floor, the chatter around them dimmed. Some faces turned. Some didn't. But no one stopped them.

The first song was something slow and old—strings and piano, a melody meant for small-town love stories. Jeremiah's hand rested on Van's waist, warm and steady.

"You okay?" Jeremiah whispered.

Van nodded. "More than okay."

They danced. Not perfectly, not gracefully, but with a kind of sincerity that made everything else blur.

Across the room, Dana twirled dramatically while Avery tried to remember which foot was left. Lisa laughed from the sidelines, clapping to the beat.

When the song ended, Jeremiah leaned close. "You know this is the best night of my life, right?"

Van smiled. "Mine too."

They stepped aside for the next song, catching their breath. That's when the photographer called out, "Couples! Photo booth's open!"

Jeremiah looked at Van. "You ready?"

"Always."

They walked together, hand in hand, to the backdrop—a wall of silver fringe and star-shaped balloons. The photographer adjusted the camera while Van and Jeremiah checked to make sure they looked their absolute best for this big moment.

"Closer," she said.

Jeremiah slid his arm around Van's waist, pulling him close. The flash went off once, twice, freezing them in that small, brilliant moment.

When the last photo clicked, Jeremiah turned to him, eyes soft. "Thank you," he said.

"For what?"

"For this. For us. For makin' it real."

Van swallowed hard. "You did that too."

Jeremiah hesitated, then smiled. "Then I guess we both did."

And before Van could say another word, Jeremiah kissed him.

It wasn't shy or hidden—it was full, certain, the kind of kiss that silenced the room. A few gasps, a few cheers, a few camera flashes that didn't belong to the photographer.

When they finally pulled apart, Jeremiah rested his forehead against Van's. "I'm proud of you," he whispered. "I love you."

The words hit Van like warmth breaking through a long winter.

He smiled, voice barely steady. "I love you too."

LATER, back at Dana's house, laughter echoed through the yard. Shoes were off, jackets undone, hair coming loose. The night had softened into something easy and tired.

Avery and Dana argued over who'd won the "Best Dressed" superlative while Lisa collected the scattered corsages from the porch railing.

Van leaned against Jeremiah's truck, hands still faintly sticky from the punch they'd spilled earlier. Jeremiah leaned beside him, tie undone, smile lazy and content.

"You think it'll always feel this good?" Van asked.

Jeremiah looked up at the sky, where the real stars had finally outshone the paper ones. "Maybe not always," he said. "But I'll take tonight."

They stood there for a while, the crickets loud, the world quiet.

From inside the house came Avery's laugh, bright and familiar, mixing with the others.

Jeremiah's hand found Van's again. "You ready to go?"

Van nodded. "Yeah."

They climbed into the truck. The engine hummed to life, headlights cutting across the dark road ahead.

As they pulled away, Dana's porch light grew smaller behind them, a warm glow fading into the night.

Van looked out the window, watching the trees blur by, Jeremiah's hand still linked with his.

For the first time in a long time, he didn't feel like he was chasing the light.

He was part of it.

And somewhere deep inside, beneath the hum of the engine and the rhythm of the road, he knew this was only the beginning.

THE RECKONING OF QUIET THINGS

(COMPLETE MANUSCRIPT — PARTS I & II)

The days after prom arrived quiet, as if the whole town had exhaled.

The music, the glitter, the laughter that had filled the Piedmont Valley ballroom all settled into memory—soft and shining. The gossip died slower than the echoes, but it, too, began to thin. By mid-May, exam week had the hallways hushed, and the air outside smelled like wet pavement and honeysuckle. Summer leaned close enough to touch.

Van felt it everywhere—the stretch of possibility in the light, the way the evenings lingered longer now, gold turning to lavender over the pines. Prom hadn't fixed anything, but it had changed something; there was no pretending the world was the same once you'd danced inside it without shame.

He worked extra shifts at the diner. The regulars still called him "son" and asked about school, as if nothing monumental had happened. Maybe for them, nothing had. But every time he wiped a counter or refilled a glass, he caught himself smiling at how much lighter his own body felt, how much easier it was to stand straight.

Jeremiah stopped by sometimes after practice, sitting in the corner booth with a chocolate shake, his hair still damp from the locker room. They didn't talk much about school or about what came next. They just sat there—two boys in the lull between what had been and what might still become.

THE LUNCH RUSH had come and gone, leaving the diner in that soft in-between quiet where the air smelled of lemon cleaner, bacon fat, and coffee going lukewarm. The ceiling fans turned lazily overhead, stirring the sunlight into faint ribbons across the counter. Van was wiping down the last booth when the bell over the door gave its soft chime.

His mother stepped in, Emmalee in tow, her hand still sticky from what looked like a half-eaten popsicle. They looked slightly out of place against the chrome and vinyl—Sunday clothes on a Thursday afternoon. She hesitated at the entrance, like she was unsure whether to come farther, before Marlene's voice cut through the hush.

"Well, look who wandered in from the good side of town," she said with a grin, already reaching for two clean mugs. "Take a seat, honey. You look like you could use somethin' sweet."

Van's mother smiled, polite and weary. "Tea, if you don't mind. Just plain."

"Plain is a myth," Marlene said, turning to fill the kettle. "But I'll do my best."

They sat at the counter. Emmalee spun lazily on the red stool, her shoes kicking against the chrome footrest. Van hesitated before walking over, drying his hands on his apron. His heart pinched at the sight—his mother sitting in the same spot she had years ago when she'd bring him lunch during double shifts. But back then she'd smiled without restraint. Now her face held that quiet, polite expression reserved for public places and delicate subjects.

Marlene poured the tea with ceremony, adding the smallest

squeeze of lemon before sliding the cup forward. "On the house. You look like you've been thinkin' too much."

Van's mother laughed softly. "Is that so obvious?"

"Only to folks who've been guilty of the same," Marlene said, winking as she drifted back toward the register.

Van leaned on the counter, pretending to check the sugar jar. "Didn't expect to see y'all here."

His mother stirred her tea, watching the spoon trace circles in the amber liquid. "We were drivin' past and Emmalee said she wanted pie. Thought maybe I could get a word with you, too."

Van's chest tightened. "I'm not in trouble again, am I?"

She shook her head, smiling faintly. "No, baby. Not trouble. Just… talkin'."

Emmalee piped up, "Can I get chocolate pie?"

"You can get manners," Van teased, ruffling her hair.

"Chocolate, please," she corrected, grinning.

He went to plate a slice, giving his mother a moment to gather whatever it was she'd come to say. When he returned, she was tracing the rim of her cup, her eyes following Marlene as if weighing whether to speak in front of her.

"Your daddy's still rough around the edges," she said finally, voice low but steady. "But he sees you tryin'. He just don't know how to meet you there yet."

Van looked down, the simple honesty of her words cutting deeper than any lecture. "He don't have to," he said quietly. "I'll keep walkin'."

His mother's eyes softened. "You sound like your Aunt Shelia when you say things like that. Makes me proud, and scared, all at once."

He smiled faintly. "That's probably how Shelia feels most days too."

Emmalee, mouth full of pie, mumbled, "Daddy says Shelia don't think before she talks."

His mother sighed. "Well, maybe the rest of us should think less and feel more."

From behind the counter, Marlene pretended not to eavesdrop, polishing the same section of chrome that had been spotless ten minutes ago. She turned just enough for her voice to reach them. "That's all any of us do, sugar—walk till the light catches up."

Van's mother smiled at that—one of those small, tired smiles that carried more grace than she realized. "Marlene, you oughta write that down."

"I don't need to," Marlene said, topping off her cup. "It's stitched somewhere deep in the fabric. I just repeat it when the night gets too long."

For a moment, none of them spoke. The only sound was the hum of the refrigerator and the faint buzz of a fly trapped between the window and the world outside. Van watched the steam curl from his mother's tea, thinking how strange it was that peace could find its way into the simplest corners—an empty diner, a plate of pie, a mother's half-apology wrapped in love she couldn't quite say out loud.

When she rose to leave, she slipped a few crumpled dollars under the saucer despite Marlene's protests. "You keep it," Marlene said. "Put it toward forgiveness. Costs more than tea these days."

His mother laughed quietly, tucking a strand of hair behind her ear. "Then maybe I should've ordered a pot."

Van walked them to the door. Outside, the light had shifted, spilling through the clouds like mercy. Emmalee reached for his hand. "Next time you come home, can we make pancakes again?"

"Yeah," he said, crouching to meet her eyes. "You bring the chocolate chips."

She giggled and ran ahead to the car. His mother lingered, one hand on the doorframe. "You're doin' fine, Van. Even when it don't feel like it."

He swallowed, nodding. "Love you, Mom."

"Love you too," she said, voice barely above a whisper. Then she was gone, the bell over the door chiming once more, leaving the air trembling in her absence.

Marlene leaned on the counter, watching him watch the empty doorway. "That right there?" she said softly. "That's the sound of a heart rememberin' how to stay open."

Friday night brought fried chicken and thunder-less tension.

Van's father sat at the head of the table, hands folded on either side of his Bible, its leather cover worn shiny. His mother moved between the stove and table, her movements quiet but sharp, each gesture a small prayer for calm.

Emmalee swung her legs under the table, humming the jingle from a toothpaste commercial. Aunt Shelia sat at the counter with her glass of sweet tea, already half-finished.

"So," his father said at last, "you done with exams?"

"Yes, sir."

"And you think you did all right?"

"I think I did fine."

"Fine don't get you scholarships."

Aunt Shelia snorted. "Fine gets you peace of mind. Maybe he could use a little of that."

Van's father shot her a look. "Some of us still think ahead."

"Some of us think with love," she said smoothly.

"Shelia…" Van's mother warned, but it was too late. The air had already sharpened.

Van's father set down his fork. "I'm only sayin' the boy needs to keep his head. Folks are still talkin' about that dance."

"What folks?" Aunt Shelia asked. "The ones who whisper about everybody else just to hear their own voices?"

Van's father ignored her. "You can't go round drawin' attention, Van. Life ain't kind to boys who don't blend in."

Van met his gaze. "I'm done blending."

His mother's hand stilled halfway to the butter dish. Aunt Shelia's smile turned proud.

Van's father's jaw worked. "You think you know everything at seventeen?"

"I know enough not to lie about who I am."

The room went quiet, heavy with what wouldn't be said.

His mother finally spoke. "Jeff, maybe the Lord's trying to teach us something, not punish us."

His father blinked. "Millie—"

"No," she said, voice rising. "You've been angry long enough. You don't have to like it, but you don't get to make him small because you're scared."

Aunt Shelia lifted her glass in salute. "Now that's a sermon worth hearin'."

Van's mother gave her sister a look somewhere between gratitude and exhaustion. "We're not fightin' tonight. We're eatin'."

Van smiled faintly. "That's fine by me."

Van's father sighed, rubbing the bridge of his nose. "Just... be careful, son. The world's watchin'."

Van nodded. "Then I'll give it something worth seein'."

For once, Van's father didn't argue. He just stared at his plate, as though maybe the mashed potatoes might hold an easier truth.

Emmalee broke the silence with her small, bright voice. "Can somebody pass the rolls?"

Everyone laughed—quietly, but together—and for the first time in months, dinner ended without slamming doors.

THE NEXT DAYS unfolded in that slow, stretched way only late May can.

The air was heavy with the smell of honeysuckle and cut grass, every afternoon shimmering like the world couldn't decide whether to hold on to spring or let summer through the door.

Piedmont Valley High felt softer now, its edges dulled by the nearness of freedom. Teachers stopped yelling about tardies. Hallway chatter hummed with plans for lakes and road trips and long naps that stretched into August.

Yearbooks arrived in thick stacks, corners already bending, pages filling with looping signatures and half-meant promises. *Never change. Stay cool. Don't forget me.*

Van's had a dozen ink hearts and doodled stars by the end of the first day.

Jeremiah's had fewer words but more meaning—handshakes from teammates who didn't quite know what to say anymore, awkward scribbles that tried to apologize without using the word *sorry.*

After school, Van worked at the diner till closing, the rhythm of clattering plates and the smell of coffee grounding him. Marlene hummed hymns under her breath while Frank cursed softly at the fryer. It was the kind of ordinary that saved him— quiet, unspoken grace.

He'd drive home afterward with the windows down, the night pressing cool against his face, the sound of cicadas swelling like applause.

Jeremiah, meanwhile, spent his evenings helping Coach Thomas break down the field—rolling up nets, stacking cones, locking the shed behind the bleachers. He'd shower in the locker room long after the other boys had gone, the echo of water against tile a small comfort in its solitude. When he texted Van after, it was never much—just *still up?* or *you eat yet?*—but it was enough.

They'd built a language between them made of small things.

By Thursday, the last of the exam schedules were pinned to classroom doors, and the air buzzed with the half-wild energy that comes from the edge of change.

That evening, Jeremiah swung by the diner near closing,

leaning against the hood of his truck as Van locked the front door.

"You look half-dead," Jeremiah said, grinning.

Van tossed him the rag from his back pocket. "And you look like you wrestled the sun."

"Coach made us clean out the shed. Found a football from 1998 and a raccoon that's probably been dead since then."

"Sounds like a trophy."

They grabbed milkshakes from the gas station across the road —chocolate for Jeremiah, strawberry for Van—and drove to the back of the ball field. The lights over the bleachers were still on, painting the grass in pale gold. The air smelled faintly of dirt and diesel, the kind of scent that meant endings and beginnings all tangled up.

They climbed into the bed of the truck, backs against the cab, legs stretched out. The sun had dipped low, orange melting into violet, the horizon a long, quiet bruise of color. A single bat circled above the outfield lights, dipping and darting like it knew something the world had forgotten.

Van took a slow sip of his milkshake, straw rattling against the bottom of the cup.

"Feels like we survived somethin'," he said finally.

Jeremiah chuckled, low and easy. "Prom? Or junior year?"

"Both," Van said. "Maybe the whole damn year."

"Yeah," Jeremiah said softly. "Both."

The silence that followed wasn't awkward—it was familiar. The hum of cicadas, the distant bark of a dog, the soft thump of Jeremiah's fingers drumming against the metal—all of it folded into something peaceful. For the first time in months, there wasn't anything to hide or explain. Just breath and warmth and the simple miracle of still being there.

Jeremiah leaned back on his elbows, eyes tracing the last sliver of sunlight. "You think people'll ever stop talkin'?"

"Probably not," Van said, smiling faintly. "But maybe they'll run outta breath first."

Jeremiah laughed, quiet and genuine, the sound catching in his throat. "You really think we can just live like this? Out loud?"

Van looked at him—really looked. The orange light caught in Jeremiah's eyes, making them look almost gold. There was so much there: the exhaustion, the stubborn hope, the fear that never quite left.

"We already are," Van said.

Jeremiah's lips parted, like he might argue, but no words came. Instead, he reached over and laced their fingers together. His hand was warm, calloused from years of basketball, still faintly smelling of the pine tar Coach Thomas used on the bats. Van squeezed back, and the world felt smaller—manageable in that moment.

"You ever think about leavin'?" Jeremiah asked after a while. "This town, I mean."

"Sometimes," Van said. "Then I think about who I'd be if I did."

Jeremiah tilted his head. "Who's that?"

Van smiled. "Probably still me. Just less tired of explainin' it."

Jeremiah grinned, but there was sadness under it. "I don't know if I could leave. My folks'd see it as quittin'."

"Maybe stayin's the harder thing," Van said. "Living honest when everyone's waitin' for you to hide."

Jeremiah let out a slow breath. "You ever get scared?"

"Every day."

"And you still do it anyway?"

Van shrugged. "Guess fear's just proof you're awake."

Jeremiah looked down at their joined hands, thumb tracing the edge of Van's wrist. "You make it sound easy."

"It's not," Van said. "But it's right."

They fell quiet again. The sky above them deepened, stars beginning to blink through like shy witnesses. The field lights hummed softly, their glow turning the air to honey. Jeremiah leaned closer, shoulder brushing Van's. The simple touch sent a pulse through both of them, something unspoken but certain.

A car passed on the distant road, headlights sweeping across the grass, catching them for a brief instant like a photograph. Two boys in a truck bed, milkshake cups between them, fingers intertwined beneath the fading light.

Jeremiah broke the silence first, voice barely above a whisper.

"You know, when I was little, my dad used to bring me out here. He said the field was holy ground. Said every game was a lesson in discipline and faith."

Van turned to him. "You believe that?"

Jeremiah smiled sadly. "Maybe not the way he meant it. But… yeah, I think it's holy. Just not for the reasons he thinks."

"What reasons then?"

Jeremiah gestured toward the open sky. "Because it's the only place I ever felt like I could breathe. No sermons. No rules. Just sky."

Van nodded. "Then maybe that's faith too."

Jeremiah looked at him for a long moment. "You think God's mad at us?"

Van thought about it—the way the stars didn't dim for anyone, the way the wind kept moving even when hearts broke beneath it. "No," he said finally. "I think He's proud."

Jeremiah laughed softly. "You sure?"

Van smiled. "Pretty sure. You don't give people this kind of love just to punish 'em for it."

The words hung there between them, fragile and beautiful. Jeremiah blinked hard, eyes glinting under the stadium light. Then he leaned his head against Van's shoulder, letting the world go quiet again.

Time slipped sideways. The sounds of the town faded until all that was left was the chirring of crickets and the rhythmic sound of their breathing. Somewhere far off, a train whistle moaned across the valley, the sound echoing like a memory too stubborn to die.

Van felt Jeremiah's weight against him—solid, real, unashamed. The milkshake cups had long since emptied, the straws gone soft. He turned his head slightly, catching the faint scent of Jeremiah's shampoo, a mix of cedar and cheap cologne.

"Hey," Van murmured.

"Yeah?"

"If this is what out loud feels like," Van said, "I don't ever wanna whisper again."

Jeremiah lifted his head, eyes bright with something too wide to name. "Then don't."

Van met his gaze, the last of the light spilling across their faces, and for a moment it didn't matter where they were or who might see. They were just two souls caught in the same gravity, daring the world to look away first.

The night deepened around them. Stars thickened overhead, and the air cooled enough for goosebumps to rise on Van's arms. Jeremiah noticed, shrugging off his jacket and draping it over Van's shoulders without a word.

"Thanks," Van said quietly.

Jeremiah smiled. "Guess I'm still tryin' to be a gentleman."

Van laughed softly. "You're doin' a damn good job."

They stayed there until the field lights clicked off with a metallic hum, plunging everything into darkness. Fireflies took their place, blinking slow and steady.

Van lay back against the ridged metal of the truck bed, staring at the stars. "You ever notice how it's never completely dark?" he asked.

Jeremiah followed his gaze. "Guess even night's got cracks in it."

"Maybe that's where grace gets in," Van said.

Jeremiah smiled at that, small and sad and full of hope all at once. "You sound like my mom."

"Yeah, but I don't quote Corinthians."

Jeremiah laughed—a deep, unguarded sound—and Van felt it vibrate through the metal beneath them. When the laughter faded, Jeremiah turned toward him again. "You ever think about next year?"

"All the time," Van said. "And try not to."

"Same."

"What do you see when you do?"

Jeremiah hesitated, then said softly, "You."

Van's breath caught. "You mean that?"

"Every word."

The moment hung there, quiet and infinite. Then Jeremiah reached out, his fingers tracing the back of Van's hand, slow and sure, as if memorizing it.

The world had shrunk to the space between their breaths.

And as a distant church bell rang out the hour, neither of them moved.

Because right then—beneath that bruised and beautiful sky—they weren't surviving anymore.

They were living.

SATURDAY BLOOMED WARM AND CLOUDLESS, the kind of Carolina day that made you forget winter ever happened. The group planned to meet at the park by the river—Dana bringing sandwiches, Avery promising music.

Jeremiah pulled up in his truck just after four, radio low, windows down. Van slid in beside him, the seatbelt squeaking.

"You sure we're not late?" Van asked.

"Nah," Jeremiah said, glancing at the clock. "I just need to swing by the house first, grab a clean shirt."

They turned off the main road, gravel spitting under the tires.

The Davis house sat neat and symmetrical behind a row of crepe myrtles, the white paint blinding in the sunlight. A wind chime tinkled on the porch, soft and deceptively gentle.

Jeremiah parked, hesitating. "Won't take long."

"I'll come in," Van said.

Jeremiah looked like he might protest, then just nodded.

Inside, the air smelled of lemon polish and Sunday perfume. A cross hung above the entryway, the words *As for me and my house, we will serve the Lord* stenciled in cursive beneath it.

Jeremiah's footsteps slowed as they passed the den. His parents were there—Pastor Rich in his armchair, newspaper folded across his knee, Ms. Denise at the table sorting mail into neat little piles.

"Hey," Jeremiah said, voice tentative. "We're headin' out with some friends."

His father looked up. "Friends?" His eyes flicked to Van. "I see."

Ms. Denise smiled thinly. "Y'all have a nice time."

Jeremiah turned toward the stairs, but before he could move, his father unfolded from the chair, one envelope still in hand.

"Jeremiah," Pastor Rich said. "You know anything about this?"

Jeremiah froze. The envelope bore the school's return address. The flap was already torn.

"I was about to open it," his father said, but he already had. He slid the photograph free and turned it toward them.

It was the prom photo—Van in his black tux, Jeremiah beside him, hands clasped between them, both smiling wide beneath the shimmer of the backdrop stars. The silver lettering at the bottom read *Piedmont Valley Junior Prom—A Night Under the Stars.*

For a second, the room stayed utterly still. Then the mask slipped.

"You explain this," Pastor Rich said, voice trembling with fury. "You tell me why my son thought this was acceptable."

Jeremiah's mouth opened, but no sound came.

Ms. Denise rose from her chair, face pale. "You told us it was just friends going together. You let us sit in that church, praising your goodness, while you—"

"While I what?" Jeremiah said quietly. "While I loved someone?"

"Don't you dare use that word!" his father barked. "Love is righteous! Love is holy! This—" he waved the photo—"is sin dressed up in glitter!"

Van took a step forward. "Sir—"

"Don't speak to me." The words cracked like thunder. "You've already done enough."

Ms. Denise's voice quivered but didn't break. "How long has this been going on?"

Jeremiah swallowed hard. "A while."

Her hand flew to her chest. "My God."

"Your God," Jeremiah said, eyes shining now, "is the same one who made me."

"Watch your tone," Pastor Rich warned.

"I am," Jeremiah said, voice low but steady. "For once, I'm watchin' it real close."

"You will not talk to me that way," his father snapped. "You will not stand in this house and mock the Word."

"I'm not mocking it," Jeremiah said. "I'm living it. Love thy neighbor, right? Even when they scare you."

Pastor Rich's face turned red. "Get out."

"Dad—"

"Out!"

Jeremiah flinched but didn't move. "Where am I supposed to go?"

His father's voice dropped to a deadly calm. "You made your choice, Jeremiah. Go live with it."

For a heartbeat, no one breathed. Ms. Denise's lip trembled, but she said nothing. The silence was worse than the shouting.

Van stepped closer, heart hammering. "We'll go," he said softly.

Pastor Rich's glare found him again. "You'll stay away from my son."

Van held his ground. "That's not your call anymore."

The pastor's hand twitched, like he might strike something, but Jeremiah stepped between them. "Don't."

"Jeremiah—" Ms. Denise's voice broke for the first time. "Please."

He turned to her, his own face collapsing at the edges. "I didn't want it to be like this."

"Then why make it?" she cried. "Why choose this path?"

Jeremiah's voice cracked. "Because it's mine."

He grabbed Van's hand, pulling him toward the door. Behind them, Pastor Rich shouted something about repentance, about forgiveness, but the words blurred into noise.

The screen door slammed open, sunlight pouring in like absolution. Outside, the air was thick with the hum of cicadas. The world didn't stop. Birds still sang. Somewhere down the street, a lawnmower droned on.

Jeremiah stood on the porch, chest heaving, tears glinting but unshed. Van reached for his shoulder.

"You okay?" he asked quietly.

Jeremiah gave a broken laugh. "Not even close."

Van squeezed his hand. "You don't have to be."

They walked to the truck in silence, gravel crunching beneath their feet. When the engine started, Jeremiah didn't drive right away. He just sat there, staring at the steering wheel, the photo still clutched in his fist.

Finally, he whispered, "Guess the park's out."

Van looked out the window, the sunlight flickering through the trees. "We'll find another place."

Jeremiah nodded slowly, voice thick. "Yeah. Maybe Aunt Shelia's got room for one more."

Van smiled through the ache. "She always does."

The truck pulled away from the curb, dust rising behind them, the Davis house growing smaller in the mirror. Inside, the curtains shifted as Ms. Denise watched from the window, one hand pressed to the glass.

Neither of them saw her cry.

"You didn't lose your faith tonight, sugar. You just lost someone else's version of it.

INHERITANCE OF THE UNBURDENED

The truck rolled down the narrow country road, the last of the daylight breaking itself against the windshield. The air outside still smelled like cut grass and rain, but inside, it was heavy—thick with the kind of silence that meant something sacred had cracked.

Jeremiah kept both hands on the wheel, white-knuckled, jaw tight. The radio was off. The world was off. The only sound came from the tires grinding over loose gravel and the faint click of the cooling engine when he finally slowed down at a stop sign no one obeyed.

Van could still hear the shouting—Ms. Denise's voice snapping like a hymn gone sour, Pastor Rich's words sharp and sure and shaking all at once. He could still see the envelope on the table, torn open, the prom photograph half-crumpled in Jeremiah's father's hand like proof of sin.

He could see Jeremiah's mother trembling behind him, her wedding band glinting in the kitchen light. *"You let us sit in church with them knowin',"* she'd said.

And Jeremiah—quiet, steady, still trying to breathe—had answered, *"I didn't think you'd care."*

That was when the shouting had really begun.

Now, the echo of it hung between them like a second heartbeat.

Jeremiah finally spoke, voice low and scraped thin. "He said he doesn't have a son anymore."

Van didn't look at him, just kept his eyes on the road ahead. "He's wrong."

A bitter sound escaped Jeremiah's throat—half laugh, half sob. "He told me to get out before I cursed the house."

Van turned his head slowly, the passing fields reflected in his eyes. "You didn't curse anything, Jer. You just told the truth. That house was already sick from lies."

Jeremiah blinked fast, his hands trembling where they gripped the wheel. "I don't know where to go."

"Yeah, you do," Van said softly. "Aunt Shelia's."

Jeremiah shook his head. "She doesn't even know me."

"She don't have to," Van said. "She'll know enough."

The truck fell quiet again. The road narrowed into a corridor of trees, their shadows long and soft in the dying light. When Jeremiah finally turned down the gravel drive toward Aunt Shelia's house, the porch light was already glowing—a soft, amber halo against the dark.

Aunt Shelia stood waiting in the doorway, framed in the light like she'd seen this coming. Apron still tied, hair wrapped in a scarf patterned with sunflowers, a cigarette balanced between her fingers.

"Well," she said, stepping onto the porch. "If it isn't heartbreak and trouble showin' up uninvited."

Van climbed out first, voice small but steady. "Hey, Aunt Shelia."

She looked him over, her sharp eyes softening when they found Jeremiah. "And you must be the boy half of Briar Hollow's whisperin' about. Lord, you look like sin on Sunday and sorrow on Monday. Get inside before the skeeters find your blood type."

Inside, the house smelled like butter, lemon oil, and comfort. Family photos lined the walls—generations of stubborn eyes and crooked smiles. A record played low in the other room, something old and bluesy.

"Sit," Aunt Shelia said, waving toward the kitchen table. "Cry, curse, or both. Just don't bleed on my rug."

Jeremiah hesitated, still by the doorway. "I don't wanna cause—"

"You already did," she said. "Now sit down so I can feed you before you apologize yourself to death."

She disappeared into the kitchen and came back with three plates—fried chicken, collard greens, cornbread glistening with honey butter. She poured sweet tea into tall glasses, the kind with the fogged sides from ice cubes melting too fast.

Jeremiah stared at the plate. His hands shook when he picked up the fork.

Aunt Shelia leaned on the counter, eyes sharp. "You're gonna tell me what happened before I march over to that man's porch and deliver a sermon he won't forget."

Van glanced at Jeremiah, who kept his head down. "They saw the prom photo," Van said quietly. "Didn't take it well."

Aunt Shelia snorted. "These folks still think love's a moral hazard. I swear, if heaven's got a dress code, they're gonna show up overdressed and under-graced."

Jeremiah's voice broke when he tried to speak. "He said I was an abomination. Said I made God ashamed."

Aunt Shelia set her tea down hard enough for it to slosh. Then she walked around the table and crouched beside him. "Baby," she said, her voice soft but certain, "the only thing God's ashamed of is the way people use His name to hide their fear."

Jeremiah's breath hitched. He pressed his palms to his eyes, shoulders shaking.

Aunt Shelia reached up and touched his cheek, thumb

brushing a tear away. "You didn't lose your faith tonight, sugar. You just lost someone else's version of it. That's grief, not sin."

The kitchen went quiet except for the ticking of the wall clock.

When Jeremiah finally looked up, his eyes were red, but clearer. "I don't know how to thank you."

"You don't," she said. "Just eat. You can't rebuild a life on an empty stomach."

Van smiled faintly. "She says that about everything."

"'Cause it's true," she said, straightening. "Now, Van, be useful and grab the cobbler out the oven. Second shelf."

The cobbler steamed as Van set it on the counter, the smell of cinnamon and peaches filling the air.

Aunt Shelia lit another cigarette and leaned against the doorway. "You boys can stay here as long as you need. I got room, and the neighbors mind their own damn business. Mostly."

Jeremiah looked up sharply. "You mean it?"

Aunt Shelia gave him a long, even look. "Baby, if I didn't mean it, I wouldn't have said it. I know what broken hearts look like. This house is built for repair."

After dinner, Van helped wash dishes. The warm water fogged the window, and the night outside hummed with crickets.

"She's somethin'," Jeremiah murmured from the table, watching Aunt Shelia hum to herself as she dried the plates.

"Yeah," Van said softly. "She's what faith looks like when it survives people."

Later, after the dishes were put away, Aunt Shelia handed Jeremiah a folded quilt. "Spare room's through there," she said. "Bathroom's down the hall. Water's hot if you treat it gentle."

"Thank you," he whispered again.

She brushed his shoulder. "Quit thankin' me. You're family now. Family don't come with receipts."

By the time Van followed him out to the porch, the air had

cooled. The sky stretched wide, full of stars sharp enough to cut. Fireflies blinked near the fence line.

Jeremiah sat on the steps, elbows on his knees, face hidden in his hands. Van joined him quietly, setting two glasses of sweet tea down beside them.

For a long while, neither said anything.

Then Jeremiah spoke, voice barely above a whisper. "I thought maybe love would be enough."

"It is," Van said. "Just not theirs."

Jeremiah turned his head, eyes catching the porch light. "How do you do it? Keep believin'?"

Van thought about it. "I don't believe the way they told me to. I believe in what's left after all that burns away."

"What's left?"

"You," Van said simply. "Us. Aunt Shelia. The good that survives the noise."

Jeremiah's throat moved like he was swallowing something heavy. "I love you," he said suddenly, voice breaking on the words.

Van blinked, then smiled—small, trembling. "Say it again."

Jeremiah leaned closer, forehead brushing his. "I love you."

The sound of it felt like light coming back.

From inside, Aunt Shelia's voice floated through the open window—soft humming, a hymn too old to name, slow and tender. The kind sung over babies and graves alike.

Van leaned back against the railing, hand finding Jeremiah's. "You think they'll ever understand?"

Jeremiah stared out over the fields. "Maybe not. But maybe one day they'll see we didn't fall—we rose."

Van smiled faintly. "You sound like her now."

"Guess that's what inheritance is," Jeremiah said.

They sat there until the stars blurred into the first suggestion of morning haze.

When Van finally drifted to sleep in the small guest room, the smell of lemon oil and fried okra still clung to the air. Through the thin wall, he could hear Jeremiah tossing, murmuring in his sleep. Then—soft footsteps. Aunt Shelia's voice, low and steady, whispering comfort only a woman who'd raised half the town could manage.

"It's alright, baby," she murmured. "You're safe. Nobody's takin' you from love tonight."

The next morning dawned pale and clean. Coffee percolated on the stove, bacon sizzled in the pan. Aunt Shelia stood in her robe, cigarette in one hand, spatula in the other, gospel radio humming low.

Jeremiah wandered in first, eyes puffy but calmer. Van followed, barefoot, hair mussed.

"Y'all look like resurrection morning," Aunt Shelia said. "Eat before the Lord changes His mind."

They laughed softly and sat. The table was set for three—biscuits, eggs, peaches slick with syrup.

Jeremiah hesitated with his fork. "I don't know how to start again," he said.

Aunt Shelia smiled without looking up from the stove. "You don't start again, baby. You just keep goin'. That's the trick nobody preaches."

Van reached across the table and took Jeremiah's hand. "Then we'll keep goin'," he said quietly.

Aunt Shelia turned, spatula raised like a benediction. "That's what I like to hear. Now pass me that jam, and don't you boys forget—family's what you choose, and love's what you keep."

The morning light spilled across the table, catching on the glass jar between them, turning the whole kitchen gold.

For the first time in a long while, Van believed it might just stay that way.

THE SUMMER TABLE

June came slow to Briar Hollow, like someone turning down the volume after a storm. The mornings were soft again, washed in gold, the air thick with honeysuckle and cut grass. The world smelled like things learning how to grow back.

At Aunt Shelia's, life had found a rhythm—small, ordinary, holy.

Van woke each day to gospel radio crackling from the kitchen, bacon sizzling, and Aunt Shelia's voice calling, "Coffee's on, lazybones. Don't let the Lord drink it all."

Jeremiah was always up first, mowing the yard or fixing the old porch rail. Van followed with breakfast duty—eggs, biscuits, sometimes peach jam if the mood struck.

By week's end, Aunt Shelia's place looked more like a home than a refuge. Marigolds lined the front fence, laundry swayed on the clothesline, and the scent of lemon oil drifted from open windows. Even grief, it seemed, had learned its manners.

They worked. They rested. They laughed.

But every night, when the porch light flickered on, Van still felt that quiet ache—home wasn't supposed to have been rebuilt from ashes.

ONE AFTERNOON, Aunt Shelia sat on the porch shelling peas while Van fixed the loose step.

"You ever gonna call your folks, baby?" she asked without looking up.

"I wrote 'em," Van said. "Told them I was okay."

"That's not what I asked."

Van tightened a screw. "If I call, Dad'll just talk himself in circles. I don't have the strength for circles."

Shelia chuckled. "No one does. But sometimes you gotta walk through a storm again just to show it didn't drown you."

He smiled faintly. "You're sayin' I should go see them."

"I'm sayin' if you don't, the silence'll start sayin' things you don't mean."

BY SUNDAY, Van knew she was right.

He borrowed her car that evening—Jeremiah insisted on coming, but Van said no. "I need to do this myself."

He changed into a pressed shirt and the good jeans his mother had ironed last Christmas. On the way, the sky blushed purple with dusk, the smell of honeysuckle thick on the air.

The porch light at his parents' house was already on. His mother stood watering the petunias by the steps, her movements careful and small. She looked up when he pulled in, her face softening before she even smiled.

"Van."

"Hey, Mom."

She set the watering can aside and wiped her hands on her apron. "You look healthy."

"I am."

"You eatin' enough?"

"Aunt Shelia makes sure of it."

His mother smiled faintly, sadness flickering behind her eyes. "Of course she does."

Van hesitated. "Is Dad home?"

"In the kitchen. You want me to—?"

"I'll talk to him."

Inside, the air felt cooler—cleaner, quieter. His father sat at the table, the same table where a hundred small wars had been fought in whispers. He didn't look up right away.

"Evenin'," Van said.

His father folded the paper. "You've been scarce."

"I know."

His father studied him a moment, then nodded toward the chair. "Sit."

Van sat. The air between them hummed with unsaid things.

"I came to tell y'all I'm stayin' with Aunt Shelia for a while," Van said. "Jeremiah too. We're helpin' her with the place."

His father's jaw tightened. "You mean that boy's livin' there with you?"

"Yes, sir."

"And she's just fine with that?"

"She's more than fine. She's proud of us."

His father leaned back, exhaling through his nose. "You think that's somethin' to be proud of?"

"I think being kind is."

The quiet stretched until it felt like another presence in the room.

"You don't understand the damage this brings," his father said finally. "People talk. They judge."

"They always have," Van said evenly. "But I'm done helpin' them do it."

His father's voice hardened. "You think you can just start over like none of this matters?"

Van met his eyes. "No, sir. I just don't think shame's the foundation I want my life built on."

For a moment, he thought his father might stand, might shout—but instead he just looked tired, the kind of tired that settles in the bones.

Van's mother appeared in the doorway then, drying her hands on a towel. "Jeff," she said softly, "let him be."

"This isn't right, Millie."

"No," she said, voice trembling but sure. "What's not right is you makin' him believe love's a sin. You keep sayin' you're protectin' him, but all I see is a man protectin' his pride."

Jeff stared at her, stunned. "You takin' her side now?"

"I'm takin' our son's," she said.

Van's heart broke open at that—quietly, but fully.

His father looked at the floor. "I don't know what to do with this."

Van rose, steady. "You don't have to do anything, Dad. I'm not askin' permission."

His mother wiped her eyes, then stepped forward and cupped his cheek. "You'll always have a home here, Van. But if peace is where she is—"

Van smiled through the ache. "It is."

"Then go have peace."

He hugged her tight, breathing in the smell of her shampoo and detergent, the familiar mix that once meant safety. When he pulled back, his father hadn't moved. The man's hands were clasped together, trembling just enough to be human again.

Van nodded once to him—small, respectful, final—then left.

THE DRIVE back to Aunt Shelia's felt different. Lighter somehow, though the air was thick with summer heat. When he parked, Jeremiah was sitting on the porch steps barefoot, guitar in his lap, fingers idly picking a tune that sounded like a hymn softened by memory.

Van walked up, heart still thudding from the weight of what had just passed.

"How'd it go?" Jeremiah asked quietly.

Van sat beside him. "Better than I thought. Worse than it should've been. But… my mom—she stood up for me."

Jeremiah smiled, small and warm. "Guess courage runs in the family."

Aunt Shelia pushed open the screen door, cigarette glowing in the dark. "It better," she said. "I put enough of it in y'all's sweet tea."

Jeremiah laughed, setting the guitar aside. Van leaned his head against his shoulder. The night hummed with crickets and the faint sound of the radio from the kitchen.

"Feels like a new start," Van whispered.

Aunt Shelia exhaled smoke toward the stars. "It ain't new, baby. It's just finally yours."

TWO DAYS LATER, the house filled again—this time with laughter, sunlight, and friends. Avery's convertible rolled up the drive in a cloud of dust, Dana in the passenger seat holding a pie like it was treasure. Lisa arrived moments later, basket of peaches in hand.

The kitchen filled with chatter and the clatter of dishes. Aunt Shelia's table groaned under the weight of food—fried chicken, collards, baked beans, cornbread, sweet tea, and the peach cobbler Van had made that morning.

They ate outside beneath the big oak tree, where string lights hung from the branches like captured fireflies. Fire crackled in the grill, and the air smelled of smoke and laughter.

Dana leaned back in her chair, sipping tea. "If this is what freedom tastes like, count me in."

Avery grinned. "I told you. Gay folks throw better dinners. It's statistically proven."

Lisa smirked. "You're not even invited to statistics class anymore."

Everyone laughed. Even Aunt Shelia, shaking her head, raised her glass. "To all of us—however the world calls us. May we keep provin' it wrong."

The glasses clinked. The air glowed.

Van looked around the table—Jeremiah laughing, Dana wiping her eyes from laughter, Avery telling some impossible story, Lisa listening with that half-smile that meant contentment. And Aunt Shelia at the head, pride and softness mingled in her gaze.

He thought about his mother's trembling words, his father's silence, the fear that had shadowed them all year. For the first time, he didn't feel burdened by it. He felt like he'd outgrown it.

Jeremiah reached under the table and laced their fingers together. Van squeezed back.

"This," he whispered, "this feels like home."

Jeremiah smiled. "That's 'cause it is."

The night deepened, stars pricking the sky in slow bloom. Fireflies drifted between the trees, and Aunt Shelia hummed a hymn so old it might've been written just for them.

And there, under the soft light of her backyard, Van realized the truth of it all —

Home wasn't a house or a name or the silence you learned to survive.

It was the table that waited for you when the world said you didn't belong.

The arms that pulled you close anyway.

The laughter that said you did.

AFTERWORD

Sunday came with sunlight too bright for comfort.

The air felt heavy, still—like the world was waiting for something it didn't want to see happen. Birds sang, but even that sounded nervous.

Aunt Shelia was in the kitchen, pressing dough for biscuits with one hand and holding her cigarette in the other. Van sat at the table, chin resting on his fist, half-listening to the low hum of the gospel station. Jeremiah was on the porch, tuning the old guitar they'd picked up at a yard sale.

"Y'all better eat good," Shelia said, flicking ash into the sink. "Somethin' tells me it's gonna be a long day."

She was right.

Just before noon, the gravel driveway stirred with the slow

crunch of tires. Through the window, Van saw a silver Buick pull in—a car that gleamed like judgment.

Jeremiah froze mid-strum. "That's my parents."

Shelia didn't flinch. She wiped her hands on her apron, set the cigarette in the ashtray, and squared her shoulders. "Then let's go greet the saints."

Pastor Rich stepped out first, Bible clutched like a badge. Ms. Denise followed, her face drawn tight, lips pressed to a line sharp enough to cut.

"Morning, Sister Shelia," Pastor Rich called. His voice had that honeyed calm preachers use right before they strike the match. "Mind if we come in a moment?"

Shelia crossed her arms, leaning against the porch post. "Well, that depends, Brother Rich. You bring casseroles or condemnation?"

Denise flinched. "We came to talk sense into our boy. This isn't a joke."

"Good," Shelia said. "'Cause I stopped laughin' at foolishness a long time ago."

Jeremiah's knuckles whitened at his sides. "Mama, please—"

"Don't you 'Mama' me right now," Denise snapped. "Do you have any idea what you've done to this family? To your father's reputation?"

Jeremiah took a breath that trembled all the way down. "I didn't do anything wrong."

Pastor Rich stepped forward, lowering his voice like it might make the words merciful. "Son, the Devil dresses up sin to look like love. You've been deceived. This isn't who God made you to be."

Van's jaw tightened. "And who'd you say God made him to be, sir? Afraid?"

Rich turned on him, eyes sharp. "Donovan, I would advise you to keep your tongue—"

"Then maybe you should keep your sermon," Aunt Shelia cut in. "'Cause it seems to me the only thing gettin' preached here is pride."

Denise looked scandalized. "You think you know more about the Word than a man of God?"

Shelia took a slow drag from her cigarette, blew the smoke toward the sunlight, and smiled without humor. "Honey, I've known God longer than you've known your reflection. And I know He don't need a man with a microphone to translate love."

The silence that followed was thick enough to choke on.

Rich's voice hardened. "You're encouragin' sin under your roof."

"I'm encouragin' life under my roof," Shelia said evenly. "And forgiveness. And honesty. Things you might remember if you stopped hidin' behind scripture like it's a shield."

Jeremiah's lip quivered. "Dad—"

Rich turned on him. "You will come home, Jeremiah. We'll get you the help you need."

Shelia stepped between them, eyes blazing. "You so sure he needs help? Maybe it's you that needs it—therapy for a man who can't tell the difference between love and control."

Denise gasped, clutching her pearls like they could protect her from the truth. "You are out of line."

"No, baby," Shelia said, voice low and steady, "I'm right on it."

She looked at Jeremiah's parents with the calm fury of a woman who'd seen too much and swallowed too little.

"You two been teachin' that boy that shame is holy. You sayin' his joy offends God? Then you best pray He's deaf, 'cause love's been shoutin' louder than your sermons."

Rich's hand tightened around his Bible. "You're mockin' His word."

"I'm livin' it," she said. "The part y'all skip over—the part about mercy, and justice, and the truth settin' folks free. Funny how y'all only quote that when it benefits your power."

Denise's eyes filled with tears. "You're destroyin' him. You're leadin' him straight to hell."

Shelia tilted her head, voice soft now, almost tender. "If love sends him there, then I guess I'll start packin'. 'Cause I ain't lettin' him walk it alone."

Van felt something break open inside him—a hush of awe. Jeremiah's breath hitched, and for the first time since that night, he stood tall.

Pastor Rich's jaw worked, but no words came. For a long moment, he looked at the woman in front of him—the sister of the quiet congregation he'd spent years leading—and realized he couldn't win this one.

He lowered his Bible. "You'll regret this."

Shelia smiled. "I've regretted less for worse reasons."

He turned, motioning to Denise. She followed, weeping quietly into her handkerchief. The Buick's tires spat gravel as they left, dust curling behind them like the last of their certainty.

Inside, no one spoke for a while. The air felt charged, holy in a way that had nothing to do with scripture. Aunt Shelia leaned against the counter, shaking slightly, though her smile never broke.

Jeremiah finally whispered, "You didn't have to do that."

She turned to him. "Yes, I did. Somebody's got to start doin' right by y'all before fear eats this town alive."

Van stepped closer, eyes glinting with tears. "You were incredible."

"Child, I wasn't incredible," she said softly. "I was tired. And tired people tell the truth."

She reached for Jeremiah's hand and squeezed. "You remember somethin', both of you. The church ain't the walls that shut you out. It's the table that still makes room for you. And if the only holy ground left is this kitchen floor, then by God, we'll set communion right here."

The light through the window caught her face, warm and unwavering. For a second, Van swore he could see it — the halo of something divine, not in myth, but in defiance.

He looked at Jeremiah, whose shoulders finally relaxed for the first time in days. Then back at Aunt Shelia, cigarette trembling just slightly in her fingers.

This was faith, he thought. Not the kind that demanded kneeling, but the kind that taught you how to stand.

Van raised his glass of tea. "To Aunt Shelia," he said softly. "For remindin' the good Lord what He actually meant."

She laughed, that deep, raspy laugh that could shake dust off a hymnbook. "Don't toast me, baby. Toast love. It's what's doin' the heavy liftin'."

Jeremiah nodded, eyes damp. "Then to love," he said.

They clinked their glasses. Somewhere outside, thunder rolled low—distant, tired, harmless.

And for the first time, Briar Hollow felt different. Like maybe holiness had finally changed addresses.

Just before the night settled in with the sun retreating behind the bloomed magnolias trees, the air still, thick with the smell of fried okra and ash. Van stepped outside, cordless phone in his hand, thumb hovering over the numbers long memorized for his parent's house.

He turned the phone on and dialed the number before he could talk himself out of it.

It rang once, twice. Then, "Van?" Her voice was soft, startled.

"Hey, Mom."

"Oh, baby. You okay?"

"I am," he said. "But there's somethin' I need to tell you."

A pause. "Alright."

"I'm stayin' here. With Aunt Shelia. For good, I think."

He could hear her breath catch. "Your father won't—"

"I know," Van said. "But this ain't about him anymore."

The silence on the other end was long. Then, quietly: "You found peace there?"

"I did. And I found family that don't require pretendin'."

His mother's voice wavered. "You've always had family."

"I know, Mom. But you can love people and still not be safe with 'em. I need to be safe right now."

There was another pause, softer this time, filled with breath instead of argument. "I understand," she said. "I don't like it, but I understand."

"Tell Dad I love him," Van whispered. "Even if he can't say it back yet."

"I will."

He swallowed hard. "And Mom?"

"Yes?"

"Thank you for standin' up for me that day. I saw it. I won't forget."

She sniffed quietly. "You get that strength honest, Van. Must run in the family."

"Guess so."

When he hung up, the crickets had taken over the night.

He looked out across the yard — Jeremiah's shadow moving near the porch light, Aunt Shelia smoking under the oak tree, her silhouette framed like some southern saint.

For the first time, Van felt the word *inheritance* take shape — not money, not blood, but courage. The kind that comes from women who refuse to let men rewrite God in their image.

He went back inside, light spilling across the kitchen table where Aunt Shelia was pouring three glasses of tea.

"Well?" she asked.

"She knows," Van said.

Shelia nodded. "And?"

"She didn't fight me."

"That's somethin'. Sometimes quiet's the loudest apology folks can manage."

Jeremiah smiled faintly, his eyes still red but clearer. "You think they'll ever forgive me?"

Shelia shook her head. "You don't need their forgiveness, baby. You just need to live well enough that they start askin' for yours."

Van laughed softly, and Jeremiah did too.

Shelia raised her glass. "To truth, to peace, and to the day when even the church remembers what love looks like."

They clinked their glasses.

Outside, thunder rolled far off in the distance, gentle and tired — not the kind that warns, but the kind that cleanses.

And as the rain began to fall soft against the roof, Van looked between Jeremiah and Aunt Shelia and knew:

They hadn't escaped the storm.

They'd simply learned how to outlast it.

Epilogue – *Inheritance*

July spread over Briar Hollow like warm honey.

The heat shimmered above the roads by noon, and the air carried that sweet mix of cut grass, dust, and magnolia that meant summer had officially settled in for a while. Days didn't rush anymore; they drifted.

The world had slowed itself to the rhythm of porch fans, lazy cicadas, and nights full of small lights flickering in the dark.

Van had learned to breathe again in the quiet.

Aunt Shelia's house sat at the edge of town, past the old pecan grove, surrounded by a yard that seemed to hum with life. Her porch was wide enough for a dozen chairs, and her kitchen big enough to feed half the county if she felt like it — which, most days, she did.

Van's mornings began with sunlight pooling across the floorboards and the smell of coffee already brewing. Jeremiah usually beat him to the kitchen, barefoot, hair tousled, standing over the stove like he'd been raised to do it. He'd hum sometimes — old gospel tunes, slow and steady — and Van would sit at the table, pretending to read the newspaper while mostly just watching him.

Aunt Shelia would notice but say nothing. She'd pour Van a cup of coffee, push the sugar bowl toward him, and mutter, "You'd best drink it while it's hot, baby. I'm too old to reheat love or caffeine."

The three of them had fallen into an easy rhythm. Shelia would tend to her garden in the mornings; Van would head into town to help at the diner or pick up shifts at the feed store; Jeremiah would practice guitar on the porch or help Coach Thomas with summer ball camps. Evenings brought everyone back together like clockwork.

It wasn't perfect, but it was peace — the kind that lived quiet and steady in the bones.

Friends came and went through that house like family.

Dana showed up most often, talking fast, hands full of projects and ideas for senior year. Avery would appear whenever he was "bored of civilization," which usually meant his internet went out. Lisa came, too — sometimes with books, sometimes with silence. She'd sit in the corner of the porch and write, her eyes soft but distant, like she was still piecing together everything they'd survived.

They talked about everything and nothing — about graduation, colleges, dreams that no longer felt impossible. Jeremiah would play sometimes, soft chords weaving under the conversation like a heartbeat.

One afternoon, Avery was sprawled across the porch swing, fanning himself dramatically with a church bulletin.

"Lord, this heat's disrespectful," he groaned. "Feels like walkin' through a sermon."

Dana tossed him a lemon wedge from her drink. "You're dramatic in every season. You'd complain if heaven didn't have air conditioning."

Aunt Shelia laughed from her chair. "He's right about one thing — it's too hot to argue."

Van leaned against the railing beside Jeremiah, who was sketching something in a notebook — chords or maybe lyrics. "You writin' something new?"

Jeremiah shrugged, smiling. "Maybe. It's about starting over, I think."

"Sounds familiar," Van said.

Jeremiah looked up at him, the smile deepening. "It should."

Their eyes held for a beat longer than usual — and for once, no one looked away. Avery saw it, of course, and fanned himself again with exaggerated flair. "If this were a movie, that'd be the scene where the credits roll."

"Then it'd be a long one," Shelia said, chuckling. "These boys still got a lot of livin' left before the music fades."

Later that month, the air thick with humidity and honeysuckle, a familiar car pulled into the gravel drive.

Van knew the sound of that engine — the uneven idle, the low hum of memory tied to it. His chest tightened, but he didn't move. Jeremiah looked at him from the porch steps, eyebrows raised.

"Want me to go inside?" he asked quietly.

Van shook his head. "No. I want them to see what peace looks like."

His parents stepped out, dressed for church even though it was Saturday. His mother carried a casserole dish; his father held a small cardboard box of Emmalee's old board games.

Shelia came out wiping her hands on her apron, voice warm but steady. "Well, look what the Lord drug in," she said. "You two found my house without callin' first? That must be a sign of the end times."

Van's mother smiled faintly, the tension in her shoulders softening. "Thought we'd stop by before the heat got worse."

The back door of the car opened, and Emmalee bounded out barefoot, curls wild, one of Shelia's old sunhats sliding down her face.

"Van!" she squealed. "Mama said I could stay if I don't let the chickens out again!"

Shelia hollered from the porch, "Don't make promises you can't keep, sugar!"

Everyone laughed — even Van's father, who bent down to fix the hat before Emmalee darted toward the fence, chasing butterflies and tripping over her own joy.

His mother shook her head, smiling. "That child's got more energy than the Lord intended."

Shelia grinned. "That's alright. We got room for all that joy around here."

They lingered on the porch, talking about nothing that mattered but everything that did.

Van's mother hugged him first, long and tight, like she was trying to make up for every time she'd let go too soon. "You look good," she whispered. "Peaceful."

He smiled. "Feels that way."

His father hovered near the steps, awkward but present. "Heard you're fixin' up the porch," he said.

"Yep," Van replied. "Jeremiah's been helpin'."

His father nodded once. "Looks good."

It wasn't forgiveness. It wasn't understanding. But it was *something*. And that *something* was enough.

Aunt Shelia came out carrying glasses of sweet tea, the condensation already pooling down her hands. "Y'all hungry?" she asked. "I made enough food to keep a small army from sinnin'."

Van's father laughed under his breath. "You always do."

"That's my ministry," she said. "Feed 'em till they quit fightin'."

Dinner was a slow, golden thing — laughter spilling over the table, the scent of fried chicken and biscuits mingling with the sweet sting of peach cobbler cooling on the counter.

Avery and Dana joined later, bringing noise and energy. Lisa came too, with her camera, capturing moments no one else thought to frame — Emmalee holding up a firefly jar, Jeremiah's arm brushing Van's as they carried dishes, Aunt Shelia mid-laugh.

At one point, Avery raised his glass. "To family," he said. "The ones that raised us, and the ones we chose after."

Dana added, "And to Aunt Shelia's biscuits, which could end any war."

Shelia swatted at her with a towel. "Girl, you flatter me one more time and I'll start charging for dinner."

Even Van's father smiled — a small, honest curve of the mouth that made Van's chest ache in the best way.

The night deepened. The porch light flickered against the sky. Jeremiah strummed his guitar softly while Emmalee hummed along. Fireflies blinked through the yard like sparks of memory.

Van leaned back in his chair, eyes tracing the familiar faces around him — his family, his friends, his peace. For the first time in a long while, the world didn't feel like it was waiting to take something away.

When the laughter quieted and the dishes were cleared, Van's father stepped out onto the porch. Van followed, the air thick with that end-of-summer hum.

His father stared out at the trees. "You always liked it out here," he said.

"Yeah," Van said quietly. "Feels honest."

His father nodded slowly. "Your mama told me you'll be stayin' here for senior year."

Van took a breath. "Yeah. Aunt Shelia offered — and Jeremiah, too. It feels right."

The silence that followed was long but not sharp. Just still.

Finally, his father sighed. "I don't understand it all. But I reckon understanding ain't the same as lovin'. And I do love you, son."

Van blinked, the words hitting harder than he expected. "I know," he said softly. "That's enough for now."

His father's hand found his shoulder — firm, brief, trembling a little. "Don't make your aunt work too hard. She's done enough savin' for one lifetime."

Van smiled. "She'd argue with that."

"I bet she would," his father said, and for a moment, they both laughed quietly — the sound more like relief than humor.

Later that night, long after the porch lights dimmed and the guests had gone, Van sat out beneath the big oak tree, Jeremiah beside him, both of them barefoot in the grass.

The air was thick with the smell of summer — honeysuckle, cut hay, and something sweeter neither of them could name.

"You think it'll always feel like this?" Jeremiah asked quietly.

Van looked over, smiling faintly. "Like what?"

"Like we made it through."

Van thought for a long time before answering. "Maybe that's what it means to inherit somethin'. Not money, not land — just… peace. The kind you work for and don't let go of."

Jeremiah leaned closer, their shoulders touching. "Then I'll take that inheritance."

Van laughed softly. "Good. 'Cause I'm not givin' it back."

They sat like that until the crickets outnumbered their words, until the stars blinked awake above them — patient, eternal, a sky full of forgiveness.

When dawn came, Aunt Shelia was already on the porch, coffee in hand, watching the world yawn itself awake.

Van joined her, hair messy, eyes still heavy with sleep. "You ever get tired of doin' all this?" he asked.

She smiled without looking at him. "Baby, this *is* rest. Watchin' y'all find your peace? That's all the Sabbath I'll ever need."

He nodded, quiet for a moment. "Thank you."

"For what?"

"For givin' us a home."

She turned then, eyes glistening. "You gave it back to me, honey. I just swept the porch."

The days stretched long after that, each one brighter than the last.

Dana got her first acceptance letter. Avery declared he was going to apply "anywhere with air conditioning and moral ambiguity." Lisa started talking about publishing.

Jeremiah and Van painted the porch, fixed the screen door, planted tomatoes that grew wild and sprawling. Every night they'd fall asleep to the sound of wind in the pecan trees, hearts steady, futures wide open.

Sometimes, when Van looked out at that yard — the light spilling through the branches, Emmalee chasing fireflies, his mother laughing with Shelia on the porch — he thought about everything they'd lost, and everything they'd found.

He thought about *inheritance.*

Not the kind written into wills or bound by blood, but the kind carried in the heart — mercy, love, and the courage to tell the truth no matter who's listening.

Because maybe that was what they'd all been chasing all along:

to live without apology,

to love without fear,

to be *unburdened.*

Jeremiah came up behind him one evening, slipping his arms

around Van's waist, chin resting on his shoulder. "You're thinkin' again," he murmured.

Van smiled. "Always am."

"What about?"

"Tomorrow," Van said. "Senior year. College. All of it."

Jeremiah kissed the side of his neck. "Whatever it is, we'll face it together."

Van leaned back into him, the fireflies rising like sparks around them. "Together sounds good."

And as the sky deepened into night — the stars blinking alive one by one — the world around them felt infinite again. Not because it had changed, but because they had.

They'd inherited a world that once told them to hide.

Now, it was theirs to live in the light.

Unburdened.

ABOUT THE AUTHOR

JR Gray-Heim is a North Carolina–based author whose work blends vivid story-telling with raw emotional depth, creating narratives that linger long after the last page. With a background as both a creative visionary and community builder, Gray-Heim writes with a voice that is as intimate as it is universal—capturing the weight of burden, resilience, and redemption in the human spirit.

Beyond writing, Gray-Heim is a salon owner, educator, and philanthropist, dedicated to elevating both art and community. When not immersed in his latest manuscript, he can be found designing intentional spaces, mentoring young artists, or championing local causes.

The Unburdened Series marks Gray-Heim's debut into the literary world—an exploration of the ties that bind us, the secrets that haunt us, and the strength it takes to break free.

ACKNOWLEDGMENTS

To my husband, Adam — your love has been the quiet light that led me home through every dark and uncertain chapter. Your patience, humor, and unwavering faith in me became the very rhythm of this story's heartbeat. You are still my compass, still my calm, and always the reminder that love is the truest form of courage. This book—this ending—exists because you never stopped believing that I could carry it to the light.

To our son, Caleb — watching you grow has taught me what inheritance truly means. Your kindness, your curiosity, your bravery—these are the stories I hope live long after my own. You remind me that legacy isn't what we leave behind, but how we love while we're here. You are my greatest unburdening.

To my mentors, teachers, and creative kin — thank you for reminding me that art and faith are not opposites, but reflections of the same reaching. You helped me find language for grace and form for chaos. Your wisdom has shaped far more than pages—it has shaped the person I became while writing them.

To the early believers—the readers who heard the first whispers of *Burdens Beneath the Hymns* and stayed through *The Weight of Witness*—thank you for holding space for these characters as they grew, fractured, and healed. You saw their truth before I could name it myself.

And to everyone who has ever carried the quiet ache of becoming—this final book is for you.

For the ones learning to forgive their past.

For the ones building homes out of honesty.

For the ones brave enough to unburden themselves and still reach for joy.

You are the proof that redemption is not a destination—it's a daily choice.

Thank you for walking all the way here with me.

— JR Gray-Heim